D0429524

# X MARKS
# THE SCOT

Books by Kaitlyn Dunnett

*Kilt Dead*

*Scone Cold Dead*

*A Wee Christmas Homicide*

*The Corpse Wore Tartan*

*Scotched*

*Bagpipes, Brides, and Homicides*

*Vampires, Bones, and Treacle Scones*

*Ho-Ho-Homicide*

*The Scottie Barked at Midnight*

*Kilt at the Highland Games*

*X Marks the Scot*

Published by Kensington Publishing Corporation

# X MARKS THE SCOT

## KAITLYN DUNNETT

KENSINGTON BOOKS
www.kensingtonbooks.com

KENSINGTON BOOKS are published by

Kensington Publishing Corp.
119 West 40th Street
New York, NY 10018

All Kensington titles, imprints and distributed lines are available at special quantity discounts for bulk purchases for sales promotion, premiums, fund-raising, educational or institutional use. Special book excerpts or customized printings can also be created to fit specific needs. For details, write or phone the office of the Kensington Special Sales Manager: Kensington Publishing Corp., 119 West 40th Street, New York, NY, 10018. Attn. Special Sales Department. Phone: 1-800-221-2647.

Kensington and the K logo Reg. U.S. Pat. & TM Off.

Library of Congress Card Catalogue Number: 2017951322

ISBN-13: 978-1-4967-1259-2
ISBN-10: 1-4967-1259-5
First Kensington Hardcover Edition: December 2017

eISBN-13: 978-1-4967-1261-5
eISBN-10: 1-4967-1261-7
Kensington Electronic Edition: December 2017

10  9  8  7  6  5  4  3  2  1

Printed in the United States of America

# X MARKS
THE SCOT

# Chapter One

"That is one ugly portrait," Sherri Campbell said.
"I know." Despite her agreement, Liss Ruskin raised
her paddle to signal that she'd start the bidding at twenty-
five dollars.

The auctioneer ramped up his patter, hoping to encourage others to bid. A dark-haired man standing at the back
signaled that he'd go to fifty dollars. Before Liss could get
her paddle in the air, someone else went to seventy-five.

She hesitated, despite being egged on from the platform
set up beneath a large awning in the open area behind the
Chadwick mansion. Surely the bidding wouldn't go much
higher. This wasn't the original, after all, only a very good
copy of a moderately famous depiction of a bagpiper. She
upped the bid to one hundred dollars.

The *Piper to the Laird of Grant* that belonged to the
National Museums of Scotland had been painted in 1714.
Its subject was a man named William Cumming, a member of a family of musicians who had already been in the
retinue of the leader of Clan Grant for some seven generations by the time he took his turn. Since Liss's own family,
the MacCrimmons, had also been famous for playing the
Highland bagpipe a few centuries back, it would be ap-

propriate to acquire the portrait and hang it in Moose-tookalook Scottish Emporium, the shop in which she sold Scottish imports and Scottish-themed gift items and clothing.

"Beautiful piece of art! Look at those legs."

The auctioneer, an out-of-stater brought in by the new owner of the Chadwick mansion to sell off the contents, probably thought he was being funny. A few people in a crowd of perhaps 150 encouraged him by laughing.

The legs in question were clad in hose knit in a different pattern than the kilt, and the kilt itself had been painted in a tartan no member of Clan Grant would recognize in the twenty-first century. At least the banner and the depiction of Castle Grant in the background appeared to be fairly accurate.

The dark-haired man bid one hundred and fifty dollars.

The other rival bidder, a sturdy specimen who was sixty if she was a day, waved her paddle in the air and called out that she'd jump to two hundred.

So much for twenty-five-dollar increments! Liss winced, but nodded when the auctioneer looked her way, the signal that she'd up the bid by another fifty. She'd already gone over the limit she'd had in mind when she started. That was the trouble with auctions—they brought out the competitive spirit in nearly everyone.

The woman bid again, followed by the man, bringing the high bid to three hundred and fifty dollars. Liss swallowed convulsively, but gave it one last shot. In for four hundred dollars, she surreptitiously crossed her fingers.

Neither of her competitors lifted a paddle.

"Sure you don't want to make another bid? Sir? Madam? It's a real bargain! No?" He shook his head, as if he took the disappointment personally. "I think you're making a big mistake! No? Sure? Well, then—going once!"

When he paused to give the other parties one last chance to reconsider, Liss held her breath, but the only person who moved was the photographer who'd been shooting pictures of the event.

"Going twice." The auctioneer made it sound like a question, but this time he hesitated only an instant before banging down his gavel. "Sold! Item goes to the little lady with paddle number twenty-two!"

Liss expelled a puff of pent-up air. She'd paid way too much, but she'd won. She was now the proud owner of an authentic copy of a truly ghastly portrait of an eighteenth-century bagpiper.

"Next up, a trunk full of books and papers. I've got no idea what's in here, folks. Could be stock certificates for all I know. You'll have to bid to find out if you've made your fortune."

Sherri gave a delicate snort. "Unless leprechauns hid a pot of gold in there since I last saw it, that's a trunk full of junk."

"Old books can be valuable," Liss reminded her.

"Don't tell me you're going to bid on it."

Liss shook her head. Aside from the fact that three people were already waving their paddles in the air, she didn't see the sense in wasting money on an old steamer trunk, no matter what it might contain.

"The books looked like ledgers to me," Sherri added. "Dull business stuff."

"I'll take your word for it."

Sherri, Liss remembered, had been stuck with the thankless task of comparing the contents of the house after a theft had been discovered with the inventory made when the town took possession of the property for back taxes. That had been the only way to determine which items were missing.

Liss placed her paddle on the grass beneath her folding chair, further reducing the chance that she'd give in to temptation a second time. When a light breeze stirred the warm air and dislodged a strand of her dark brown hair, she resisted the urge to reach up and tuck it behind her ear. At an auction, even an innocent movement like that could be taken as a bid.

She hadn't come with the intention of buying anything. Plain old curiosity had brought her back to the Chadwick mansion. Nearly eight years earlier, she had spent a good deal of time surrounded by the items that were now up for sale. She'd volunteered to turn the abandoned house, an example of high Victorian architecture built on the outskirts of her hometown of Moosetookalook, Maine, into a Halloween attraction. The project had not exactly gone as planned. Perhaps they should have known better than to think it would, given that the house had once been owned by a notorious gangster.

Sherri hadn't bothered to sign up to bid. She was in attendance because she was Moosetookalook's chief of police. Crowd and traffic control were her responsibility. She didn't expect any problems. People who came to country auctions were usually courteous to one another, but there were bound to be problems if everyone decided to leave at the same time. Cars, vans, and trucks filled the small parking area next to the mansion and extended in a single line all along a quarter mile of winding driveway and out onto the shoulder of the two-lane rural road beyond.

If Sherri hadn't been in uniform, she'd never have been taken for a cop. She was a petite, blue-eyed blonde. In her private life she was a wife and the mother of three. She was also a textbook example of how appearances could be deceiving. As Liss well knew, her friend was fully capable of taking down an angry drunk twice her size. She could have him in handcuffs before he knew what hit him.

A four-poster bed was the next item offered for sale. It looked a good deal better than the last time Liss had seen it. All those years ago, it had been covered with dust and cobwebs. Someone had taken the trouble to clean and polish all the furniture in the auction and had done what they could to spruce up other items, too.

"I'm amazed this stuff is in such good shape," she whispered to Sherri. "Did the last owner ever do anything with the place other than install better locks?"

"Not that I heard."

The Chadwick mansion had been sold twice since that fateful Halloween. The first time, the town had let the place and its contents go for a song, anxious to be rid of the burden of keeping trespassers off the property. Liss had never met that buyer. The next she'd heard of him, he had died and his heirs had unloaded the property. The new owner proposed to knock down the old house and build senior citizens' housing in its place.

Both before and after the portrait of the piper was auctioned off, a steady stream of household furnishings came up for bid. Many of the items seemed familiar to Liss, even after such a long time. She'd definitely remembered that standing wardrobe chest, and the hall tree that stood more than six feet tall, and the avocado green kitchen appliances that dated from the 1950s. There had been dozens of framed pictures in all sizes and shapes, and almost as many pedestals, tables, and curio cabinets.

"This auction offers nothing if not variety," she remarked when the auctioneer's helpers brought out a parlor organ that was at least a full century older than the stove and refrigerator.

Another bed followed the organ, this one elaborately carved. The same bidder bought it and the matching highboy that was offered next, paying what Liss considered an exorbitant amount of money. He was undoubtedly "from away."

"And now," the auctioneer announced, "what you've all been waiting for—the original owner's outstanding collection of the taxidermist's art."

First up was a stuffed pheasant that had seen better days. It appeared to be molting. The moth-eaten moose head that came next was just as repulsive, but people bid on both and seemed happy to win them.

"No accounting for taste," Sherri muttered.

Quickly losing interest in wildlife that had been dead longer than she'd been alive, Liss shifted her attention to Sherri. She watched her friend scan their surroundings with her professional cop's eyes. The crowd was beginning to thin out now that the best items had been sold and only more stuffed birds remained. A small traffic jam had developed at the rear of the covered area, where winning bidders went to pay for what they'd bought and collect their prizes. A few buyers were growing impatient, but so far no one had caused any problems.

Liss was in no hurry to leave. She'd bummed a ride to the auction with Sherri, which meant she'd be staying at the site until the bitter end. She was content to amuse herself by people-watching.

The dark-haired man who'd bid against her for the portrait had purchased at least a dozen framed pictures, making her wonder if he was after the ornate wooden frames rather than the artwork. She doubted the frame on the Grant piper was all that valuable, but perhaps he, too, had been caught up in the bidding frenzy. Either that, or he'd been miffed to discover he had competition and had driven up the price out of spite.

As Liss strolled closer to the line of people waiting to pay, she looked around for the second rival bidder. She didn't see the older woman in the crowd, but she did catch sight of the steamer trunk that had been sold right after the portrait. A woman small enough to fit inside it was attempting to haul it toward the parking area. She gave a mighty heave that moved the trunk a few inches but wasn't making much progress overall. If it was full of ledgers, as Sherri had said, it must weigh a ton. Liss increased her walking speed.

"Can I give you a hand with that?"

The woman gave a start and turned wide hazel eyes upward to meet Liss's gaze. At five-foot-nothing, she was a full nine inches shorter than Liss. Somewhere in her mid-twenties, she had curly light yellow hair. In the bright sunlight and displayed against equally pale skin, it almost looked white.

As if to emphasize her lack of color, the trunk's new owner had dressed in black slacks and a burgundy-colored tunic. It had loose, gauzy sleeves gathered at the wrists, but it struck Liss as being much too warm for a nice day like this one. The outfit stood out for another reason, too. Almost everyone else, Liss included, wore jeans and T-shirts. An estate auction in rural Maine was not an occasion to dress up, especially if you expected to cart off heavy pieces of furniture when it ended.

When the woman didn't say anything, giving the impression that the offer was unwelcome, Liss forced herself to smile and try again. "You look like you could use some help."

It was second nature for her to be friendly and helpful to strangers, especially those who were out of their element, but it belatedly occurred to her that a woman as tiny as this one might well have a streak of independence twice her size. She'd have trouble lifting a folding chair, let alone a steamer trunk full of books, and that must gall her.

A cute-as-a-button turned-up nose wrinkled and the blonde huffed out an exasperated breath. "I'd appreciate that. Thank you! I didn't think it would be so heavy."

She spoke in a high, little-girl voice that was a good match for the rest of her. A smile blossomed on her face, revealing dimples in both cheeks and sparking a memory Liss couldn't quite grasp.

"I'm Liss Ruskin," she said aloud.

"Benny Beamer."

Liss blinked at her.

"Yes. I know it's a silly name, but Benny is less of a mouthful than Benedicta. Don't you just love old family names? Is Liss a nickname too? Or did I misunderstand? Is it Lisa? I'm babbling. Sorry. It's been a long day." She put one hand to the small of her back. "I think I pulled something."

Liss couldn't help but sympathize. "It's Liss and it's short for Amaryllis. My mother is named Violet. She was going for a flower theme."

Working together, they maneuvered the heavy trunk another few feet, but it was obvious they weren't going to be able to move it much farther. Liss rested her fists on her hips and assessed the situation. "Maybe this would be easier if we unloaded it first."

"I don't have any boxes for the contents and I don't want to risk damaging anything."

"Are you a book dealer?"

"Oh, no. This is research for an article I'm writing on businesses in the nineteen twenties." Her grin broadened and her sausage curls bounced as her head bobbed. "I can hardly wait to dive in."

At Benny's words, Liss pictured her poised on the edge

of the open trunk as if it were a swimming pool. The image was quickly replaced by an iconic scene in black-and-white from a very old movie, and Liss suddenly realized why Benny's appearance had seemed so familiar. Benny Beamer had the look of a grown-up Shirley Temple, the moppet who had been a child star back in the 1930s. She wondered if Benny knew the words to "On the Good Ship Lollipop."

"We need a dolly," Benny said, cutting short Liss's imaginings.

"The auctioneer probably has one."

"He's still selling stuffed birds." Benny dimpled again. Liss didn't suppose she could help it.

"Tell you what," she said. "You stay here with the trunk and I'll go find some muscle. I have to pay for what I bought today anyway. The cashier should be able to flag down one of the auctioneer's helpers."

Liss left her new acquaintance sitting on top of the steamer trunk in the warm June sunshine. Odd what some people considered fascinating reading, she thought. When it came to running her own business, Liss's least favorite part of the job was the bookkeeping. There was no way she could see herself getting excited about a stranger's statements of profit and loss, especially when those records were nearly a century old.

She paid for the portrait she'd bought and collected it, but by the time she located a man with a dolly and turned to point him in the right direction, Benny had already been rescued. Her white knight was a muscular young man strong enough to hoist the trunk onto one shoulder as if it contained nothing heavier than feathers.

Amused, Liss watched them move away. Benny was self-reliant and had the brains to write articles on obscure subjects. She was also smart enough to know when it was to her advantage to fall back on her natural assets. Young women who were pretty, petite, and helpless-looking could get away with murder!

With a shrug, Liss half dragged and half carried her own purchase toward the far end of the driveway. Sherri had deliberately parked the cruiser there to make sure she didn't get blocked in, as she might have if she'd chosen a spot closer to the house. Liss took her time, passing scattered groups, some silent, some chatting and laughing, and being passed by other people less burdened with their purchases than she was. As she trudged along, the auctioneer's increasingly frantic attempts to raise the bid on a worse-for-wear stuffed owl grew fainter and fainter.

Liss didn't anticipate much of a wait when she finally reached the cruiser. A good many cars and trucks had already left the site and the number of vehicles parked on the shoulder of the narrow road rapidly decreased even as she watched. She caught sight of the steamer trunk again as Benny's hero loaded it into a white van. The dark-haired man who had bid against her for the Grant piper nodded to her as he stacked framed prints in the trunk of a dark blue hatchback.

At that moment, Sherri came up behind her. "Ready to go?"

"You're not staying till the bitter end?" A steady stream of departing auction-goers continued to pass by them.

Sherri shook her head. "They've mostly cleared out. There aren't enough people left to snarl traffic."

Opening the back door of the cruiser, she reached for one end of the portrait frame at the same time Liss tried to pick it up from the other side. Just as they started to lift, Liss lost her grip. As if it had a life of its own, the painting leaped out of her grasp to land with considerable force on one corner of its frame, striking the tarmac with an ominous cracking sound.

In slow motion, the portrait tumbled forward to land on its face. Liss stared down at it in dismay. The wooden backing had split open, leaving a gap through which she could see the reverse of the stretched canvas . . . and something else, something that did not belong there. She bent closer to work it free.

"Talk about a cliché," she murmured.

"What is it?" Sherri asked.

"You're going to think this is crazy," Liss said, "but I think I just found a treasure map."

It wasn't until that evening that Liss was able to share her day's adventure with the rest of the family. She and her husband, Dan, were joined for supper by her aunt, Margaret Boyd, as a thank-you for Margaret's having kept the store open while Liss attended the auction. Margaret was accompanied by her two Scottish terriers, Dandy and Dondi, which meant that any meaningful conversation had to be delayed until after the dogs were reeducated as to the proper pecking order by Liss's two cats.

The animals settled in more easily now than they had when Margaret first adopted the two Scotties. Liss suspected that was because Lumpkin, her overweight Maine coon cat, was getting on in years. He still enjoyed spurts of energy, including wrestling matches with his younger feline companion, Glenora, but he no longer lit into everything, be it feline, canine, or human, that invaded his territory. Liss wasn't sure how old Lumpkin was, but he was at least fifteen. He had been well past the kitten stage when she'd inherited him.

Glenora had been the first interloper into Lumpkin's kingdom. The little black ball of fluff had appeared out of nowhere, showing up one wintry day at Moosetookalook Scottish Emporium to worm her way into Liss's heart. Liss shook her head as she watched the four animals interact with one another. Sometimes it hardly seemed possible that nine years had passed since Glenora's arrival in her life, or that she and Dan were coming up on their eighth wedding anniversary.

A glance at her husband, who was also watching the byplay of cats vs. dogs, brought a smile to her lips. She'd known Dan Ruskin most of her life and could still remember what a scrawny, skinny kid he'd been in junior high school. Between then and now, he'd sprouted all the way to six foot two and filled out in the nicest possible ways. The years he'd spent working for his family's business, Ruskin Construction, had been responsible for most of those muscles. Now that he was self-employed as a custom woodworker, he still kept in shape. As for the rest of the package, in Liss's admittedly biased opinion it was hard to beat sandy brown hair, worn a little on the long side, and molasses-brown eyes.

She found it easy to read her husband's mood by studying his face and body language. Right now, he was relaxed, happy, and content, all feelings she shared. She was also excited, but she could wait to make her big announcement until she'd heard how Margaret's day had gone.

"Sales were slow but steady," Margaret reported when they were gathered around the kitchen table eating bowls of the stew Liss had started in the slow cooker before leaving for the auction. The freshly baked dinner rolls to go with it had come from Patsy's Coffee House.

That was about what Liss had expected to hear. Fortunately, her business did not depend on walk-in customers to turn a profit. Moosetookalook Scottish Emporium generated most of its sales through its Web site.

"Beth Hogencamp stopped by," Margaret said. "She wanted to know if you need any part-time help."

"What did you tell her?"

"That she'd have to talk to you, of course. I'm not the owner anymore and haven't been for years." She sent her niece an impish grin that had Liss rolling her eyes.

Until she'd sold the business to Liss, Margaret had spent a decade as sole proprietor. Before that, she had been co-owner with her brother, Liss's father, of a business that had been founded by their father way back in 1955.

Liss reached for another roll. "Now that Angie's Books has been rebuilt and is open for business, I'm surprised Beth's mother doesn't need her there full-time."

"Apparently, Angie wants Beth's little brother to get some work experience this summer. There isn't enough to keep three people busy."

"Much as I love Beth, I don't think I could keep her fully occupied either. I get a bit overwhelmed when one of the tour buses stops in the town square, but the rest of the time there isn't much to do but fill orders that come in by mail or online and keep the place clean."

"You should talk to Angie," Margaret said. "And Beth, of course."

"I'll do that. Did you have lunch at Patsy's? Any tidbits of local gossip to pass on?"

Around noon on most days, Liss hung out her BACK IN FIFTEEN MINUTES sign and walked across the town square to the combination coffee shop and café. That Patsy was a genius in the kitchen was reason enough to develop this habit, but Liss also went there to find out what was going on in town.

"Alex Permutter has new hearing aids, and since everyone knows it, he's had to stop pretending he can't hear when what he really wants is to avoid talking to people."

An explosion of barking from the living room interrupted before Margaret could say more about one of their more eccentric neighbors.

"What on earth?" Dan started to rise from his chair but stopped when Margaret held up a hand.

"Don't encourage them. They probably just heard a car pass by on the street out front. Or if Dandy was on the window seat, she may have spotted a squirrel."

"Do they bark at every strange sight and sound?" Liss reached for her glass and took a sip of ice-cold root beer.

"Not usually, no. In fact, that's what makes Scotties such good watchdogs. But Dandy's been getting more vocal lately, and if she barks, so does Dondi. They settle down faster if I ignore them. It's self-preservation," she added with a chuckle. "I'd be worn to a frazzle if I got up to look every time one or the other of them wanted my attention."

Margaret's comment had Liss taking a hard look at her aunt. In common with Lumpkin, who was currently lurking under the table in the hope that a bit of stew beef would fall into his mouth, Margaret had slowed down as she got older. Even the way she spoke had undergone a gradual change over the last few years. Liss could remember a time when her aunt always talked a mile a minute, hardly pausing to draw breath. Now her conversation was slower and more considered, as if she wished to conserve energy for more important things.

*She's nearly seventy,* Liss reminded herself. *It's amazing that she's stayed as active as she has.*

Margaret had only recently retired from a job as events coordinator at The Spruces, the hotel owned by Joe Ruskin, Dan's father. Within a month, she had taken on a half dozen new responsibilities, everything from volunteering at the food kitchen to serving on the board of the local historical society to joining a bowling league.

The barking had quieted, but now started up again at even greater volume. Margaret swung her head in that direction, a movement that set her silvery-gray hair in motion. To celebrate her retirement, she had driven all the way to Portland, patronized an outrageously expensive hairdresser, and come home with a short and sassy do that made her look at least five years younger.

"Dandy! Dondi!" she shouted. "Be quiet!"

Silence descended.

Smiling, Margaret shifted to a far less commanding tone of voice. "Dandy! Dondi! Come here, my darlings. Come to Mama."

Obediently, both Scotties trotted into the kitchen and plunked their compact little bodies down next to their mistress's chair. Liss had to smile. With their small, dark brown, almond-shaped eyes, they epitomized the expression "bright-eyed and bushy-tailed" . . . except that she could hardly call those erect stubs that passed for tails "bushy," not when compared to the magnificent plumes Lumpkin and Glenora sported. There was, however, one thing all four animals had in common—the hopeful look that said, clearer than words, "Look how cute I am, now feed me before I starve to death."

Margaret appropriated Dan's empty stew bowl and, along with her own, placed it on the floor in front of the dogs. Fur bristling in outrage, Lumpkin shot out from beneath the table. *Dogs* were cleaning supper dishes? That was his prerogative! A low growl issued from his throat, but Dandy and Dondi ignored him.

Before her cat could launch an attack, Liss hurriedly

scooped out the last chunks of beef and vegetables in her bowl and offered it to Lumpkin. He deigned to sniff the contents. Having established that he was doing her a favor by cleaning up the liberal coating of broth, he dove in. His enthusiasm surpassed even Dandy's.

"Well, that was exciting." Dan got up to take a Boston cream pie out of the refrigerator.

Glenora was curled up on top of the appliance but showed no interest in hopping down. In fact, as far as Liss could tell, she was sound asleep and completely uninterested in begging for food. If they'd had fish for supper, it would have been a different story.

"Getting back to Beth Hogencamp," Dan said when he'd served up dessert and resumed his seat at the table. "If you can't use her, Maud could probably do with some help."

"I'll mention it to Angie when I talk to her," Liss promised.

Maud Dennison was the only full-time employee at Carrabassett County Wood Crafts, the retail outlet where Dan and other local craftspeople sold what they made. She was a retired teacher about to celebrate her eightieth birthday, which meant they were all on call to help out when she needed some heavy lifting done. Although Dan spent long hours in his workshop behind the house, worked the occasional shift at The Spruces, usually when one of his father's employees called in sick at the last minute, and pitched in when needed at Ruskin Construction, the company now run by his brother, he stopped in at least once a week to give Maud a break.

"So how was the auction?" he asked, giving Liss the opening she'd been waiting for.

"I ended up buying a painting—that copy of the Grant piper that used to hang in the dining room at the Chadwick house—and I got a bonus along with it."

"Another purchase?" Margaret asked.

Liss shook her head. "Something extra tucked into the backing. You'll never in a million years guess what it is."

"Treasure map?" Dan suggested.

Liss's face fell.

"No, really?" Margaret started to laugh, then caught sight of Liss's face. "You're serious."

"Well, it's a map. What it leads to isn't clear, but there *is* a big old X marking the spot."

Liss had taken the precaution of slipping her find, which measured slightly smaller than eight inches by ten, into a clear page protector and storing it out of sight in the drawer of one of the end tables in the living room. While she left the kitchen to fetch it, Dan cleared away the dishes, including those prewashed by the pets.

Returning to the table, Liss placed the map so that both Margaret and Dan could see it. They studied it with identical expressions of bemusement on their faces.

"What is this a map *of*?" Margaret asked. "Or should I say *where* is this a map of? There doesn't seem to be any indication of location, or anything to say which way is north or south."

"Or any scale of miles," Dan added.

"But it has been carefully drawn," Liss pointed out. "Trees, outcroppings of rock, even a river."

"But no towns." Dan spread his hands apart in a gesture of futility. "No houses. No names. No distances. Shouldn't there at least be something along the lines of 'Walk ten paces east from the oak tree, then twenty paces south to the stone wall'?"

"Old as that map seems to be," Margaret said, "the trees shown on it have probably been cut down by now."

Their comments and general lack of enthusiasm had Liss

frowning. She already knew that locating X was a long shot. She doubted she'd ever be able to discover why the map had been hidden behind the portrait. Still, she had hoped for a little encouragement. If they all put their minds to it, surely they could discover *something* about her find.

She picked up the page, meaning to store it somewhere safe.

"What's that on the back?" Dan asked.

Liss turned the map over, squinting at a faint series of markings she hadn't noticed before. "I can't make it out."

Dan and Margaret each took a turn but had no better luck deciphering the squiggles.

"It's probably not important," Dan concluded. "Unless it's like the directions in the first Indiana Jones movie."

Liss punched him in the shoulder. He pretended it hurt.

"You know," Margaret said, "there were a lot of stories about the Chadwicks, back when there *were* still Chadwicks."

"I know about Blackie O'Hare," Liss said.

The notorious hit man for the Boston mob had married the Chadwick heiress and inherited the mansion after his wife's death. There had been rumors that he buried his ill-gotten gains somewhere on the property, but if any such cache had ever been found, the person who discovered it had kept it quiet.

Liss had a theory about that, not that she ever intended to pursue it, but whatever the fate of Blackie's loot, it could have no connection to this map. She was no expert on the age of paper, but to her it looked old. *Really* old.

"I bet this dates from well before Blackie married Alison Chadwick," she said aloud.

"I think you're right," Margaret agreed. "And if those

stories I mentioned are to be believed, Alison's parents and grandparents weren't exactly law-abiding citizens."

"The rumor I heard is that the Chadwicks made their fortune smuggling liquor into Maine from Canada during Prohibition," Liss said. "Is there more to it than that?"

"Isn't that enough? Of course, that was well before my time, so I have no firsthand knowledge of what went on, but I'm sure we could find out more about the family's history. Maybe there's a clue there to tell us what the landmarks on this map represent."

From Dan's place at the sink, where he'd started to wash the supper dishes, he was smiling to himself. "Well, there you go," he said over his shoulder. "Locate where X marks the spot and dig deep enough and you know what you'll find?"

Liss accepted the teasing with good grace. When she stopped and thought about it, the whole idea of a quest for buried treasure *was* pretty silly. "Go ahead. Tell us."

"A lost shipment of bootleg whiskey, of course. Could be worth quite a pretty penny by now. After all, it will be really nicely aged."

# Chapter Two

Three days later, on a gloomy, overcast Tuesday, Liss sat behind the sales counter at Moosetookalook Scottish Emporium staring fixedly at the painting of the Grant piper. She had hung it in a place of honor on the wall directly across from her perch. She did not look away when her aunt came in through the back door and entered the shop from the stockroom. A few minutes earlier, Liss had heard Margaret make her usual morning pilgrimage down the outside stairs from her apartment above the shop to let Dandy and Dondi into the fenced-in backyard.

"Wishing he could talk?" Margaret asked.

Liss responded with a rueful half smile. "The portrait intrigues me. Or rather, the mystery surrounding the map hidden behind it keeps nagging at me. I can't help but think that there has to be some way to find out what place it shows."

"Maybe there is."

Narrowing her eyes, Liss gave Margaret her full attention. "What do you mean?"

"I've been doing some thinking too. About the Chadwicks. Old as that map looks, it must have been one of the family who hid it." Margaret looked a trifle smug, as if she was hugging some delicious secret to herself.

"Go on," Liss said. Whatever her aunt was up to, she wanted to hear it, especially if it led to a speedy solution to the mystery of the map.

"Family tree."

Liss's hopes plummeted. She had zero interest in genealogy, one of Margaret's new, post-retirement passions. Who cared what the MacCrimmons had been up to hundreds of years ago?

"That's the only way to go." Margaret's eyes were bright with enthusiasm. "In fact, I've already started."

She proceeded to sketch out the steps she'd taken so far to track down Chadwick ancestors. At first, Liss listened with only half an ear, but there were no customers in the shop to distract her and before long the gist of what Margaret was saying began to sink in. It made sense that the clue to whatever place was shown on the map would be found in the family that had owned the portrait.

"You know," Margaret said as an aside, "if you'd paid this much attention at Christmas, when I was telling you about the history of our family, you'd already have thought of doing this sort of research yourself."

"Hey, I listened!" Liss grinned at her. "I heard every word, right up until you said it was probably impossible to tell which one of about fifteen Archibald MacCrimmonses was our ancestor. Besides, you're the one with access to that genealogy Web site."

"The library has a subscription."

"The library is only open twenty hours a week, most of them when I'm working."

"Point taken. So it's a good thing I have my own account." Coming around to Liss's side of the counter, Margaret appropriated the computer that doubled as a cash register to call up the family tree she'd created for the Chadwicks. "There's nothing in the rules that says it has to be your own family you chart. Now, here is the last of the Moosetookalook branch."

With a few deft key strokes, she took Liss back four generations and clicked on the lozenge for Jeremiah Chadwick, born in 1799. Liss read the information in the pop-up, surprised to see that he had been born in Chadwick, Nova Scotia.

"He had a town named after him?"

Margaret shook her head. "His family founded it two generations earlier. There may or may not still be Chadwicks living there, but here's the thing: what if the chunk of land shown in your map is someplace in that area? In Canada."

"That's a stretch."

Liss reached under the counter for her feather duster. Keeping hundreds of small items and the surfaces upon which they were displayed clean was a never-ending task in a shop that sold just about every Scottish-themed knick-knack available. She started her chore with the figurines on the shelves to the right of the counter.

"Is it? I wonder. . . ." As her voice trailed off, Margaret's eyes took on an unfocused look, as if her thoughts were miles away. "The library," she said after a short silence.

Not so far away, after all, Liss thought. Moosetookalook Public Library was on the second floor of the municipal building right across the town square from the Emporium. "What about it?"

"As librarian, Dolores keeps files of clippings of local interest. Surely she has one on the Chadwick family."

Moving from pewter pipers to ceramic Highland dancers, Liss had to admit that her interest was piqued. Margaret's enthusiasm was contagious. "She does. I borrowed it back when I was working on turning the Chadwick mansion into a haunted house for Halloween, but I never got around to reading much of what was in it. Do you suppose she still has it?"

Margaret chuckled at that. "Dolores never throws anything away if she can help it." She glanced at the clock on the wall behind the sales counter. "She'll be coming in soon. I'll go over there and check it out as soon as I see the light go on. In the meantime, we should think about what we're going to do when we get to Nova Scotia."

"When we *what*?" Without dusting it, Liss abruptly replaced the ceramic Loch Ness Monster she'd just picked up. She stared at her aunt. "I can't just go haring off to Canada at the drop of a hat."

"Why not? You've been saying for months that you need to find some new items for the shop. Scottish-themed gifts made in the Canadian Maritimes will sell almost as well as those imported direct from Scotland. Besides, what better opportunity to find a new kilt maker?"

"Margaret—"

"We can combine hunting for answers about the Chadwicks with a buying trip, and as an added bonus we can take in the highland games at Antigonish."

Liss had fond memories of trips to Antigonish in the days when she'd competed in Highland dancing. Later she'd turned professional, touring for several years with a dance company in a show called *Strathspey*. "Think *Riverdance*, only Scottish," she'd always told people when they asked about it.

"Confess. You want to go. A buying trip is long overdue and a side trip to Chadwick will satisfy our curiosity."

"I'm tempted," Liss admitted.

She'd been without a reliable kilt maker since the previous year. She didn't get all that many orders, but she'd sold quite a few ready-made kilts and the rack was half-empty. There were only three left in Royal Stewart, the most popular tartan.

Tossing the feather duster back beneath the counter, she brought up her online calendar. At first glance, leaving seemed impossible and she felt a stab of disappointment.

"If we're going to hunt up new suppliers as well as attend the games, that will put us in Canada over Fourth of July weekend. That's a bad time for the Emporium to be closed."

"There's no need to close up shop," Margaret said. "Remember what I told you about Beth Hogencamp? She's eager to work for you and she's the perfect temporary employee. It's a match made in Heaven."

"I haven't talked to Angie yet."

"Do it today. Heck, do it now. I'll mind the store."

"Even if Beth is available, there will barely be time to train her before we have to leave. And what about accommodations? Every hotel and motel and B&B near Antigonish is probably booked by now."

"I'm working on it," Margaret assured her. "Trust me. We won't have to sleep in the car."

"What about Dan?"

Margaret's eyebrows shot up. "What about him? He can take care of himself for a week. He did just fine on his own before you two got married." She wagged a finger at her niece. "And don't tell me he'll want to come along, not to Nova Scotia, and especially not to Antigonish. You know he can't stand the sound of bagpipes."

Liss literally threw her hands in the air to signal that she surrendered. "Okay. Okay. I give up. Dan can stay here and take care of the dogs and the cats. If her mother agrees, I'll spend the next few days training Beth so she can run things here in the Emporium. Happy now?"

"Delirious," Margaret said with just a touch of sarcasm. "Go talk to Angie."

Six months after reopening, the bookstore still smelled of new wood and fresh paint. And of books—one of the most delightful scents on the planet. A little less than two years earlier, Angie's building had been completely destroyed by fire. Then there had been delays getting started on the rebuilding. She'd had insurance, but in cases of arson insurance companies tend to drag their feet before coughing up a payment.

Ruskin Construction had begun work the moment the money came through. They did good work, but getting everything just right took time. In this case, they had to duplicate the architecture of the original two-story clapboard house so that it would match its neighbors around Moosetookalook's historic town square. They'd succeeded admirably, and the icing on the cake was that they had modernized and improved both the retail space on the first floor and the apartment on the second.

Liss looked around her with a sense of great pleasure, taking in the brightly painted open bookshelves and the sparkling glass surface of a display case that held first editions. She didn't see Angie at first, but she could hear the faint murmur of voices from a far corner of the shop. Following the sound, she rounded the end of a six-foot-high bookcase and found herself in the local history section.

"Oh, hi, Liss," Angie said, momentarily looking up from her customer.

"Hey, Angie. Hello, Benny," Liss added, recognizing the other woman's distinctive height and bouncy yellow curls.

Most of Benny's slight form was hidden behind Angie. The bookseller was only a few pounds over her ideal weight and wasn't all that big to begin with, but her disproportionately small customer made her look like the Hulk. Liss had to fight the urge to stoop when she asked Benny how her back was doing.

"It's fine. Why do you ask?" A puzzled frown made Benny's pale eyebrows knit together. Her voice was as annoyingly high-pitched as Liss remembered.

"Last time I saw you, you said you thought you'd pulled something trying to move that heavy trunk."

At once Benny's expression cleared. "Oh, that! It was just a twinge. I slapped on some liniment and by the next day I'd forgotten all about it."

"Lucky you," Angie said. "After all the packing and unpacking and lugging boxes of books around before we reopened, I ached in every muscle for a month."

"Well, you're old," Liss teased her friend. They'd known each other long enough that she could get away with the remark. Since Angie was only in her late forties, she wasn't all that much older than Liss.

The much younger Benny didn't seem certain how to take their easy banter. Apparently deciding to ignore it, she settled herself on the floor to better examine the books on a bottom shelf.

"Finding what you need?" Angie asked.

"I'm all set," Benny said.

"Then I'll leave you to it."

"You've done a great job here, Angie," Liss said as the two women made their way to the front of the store. "The place looks wonderful." She'd said so several times before, but it bore repeating.

"Thanks. We've finally got the apartment whipped into

shape too." She held up crossed fingers. "This summer, I think I can actually relax and enjoy the good weather and the tourists."

"Business coming back okay?"

Angie waggled her hand back and forth. "Slowly. Thank goodness I started to sell online while the building was going on. That gives me a second customer base to augment the brick and mortar store." Gazing out at the street through a display window with a colorful arrangement of new hardcover titles, she smiled. "All in all, I can't complain."

"Margaret tells me Beth is looking for a part-time job."

Angie chuckled. "She'd like to get out from under Mom's eagle eye."

"Because you're such a tyrant?" Liss knew better!

"She's eighteen. Her first year at college gave her a taste for freedom."

"I'm surprised she didn't look for a job at the coast for the summer."

"Moosetookalook still has its attractions. The biggest one is your cousin."

"Boxer?"

"Please! Now that he's almost twenty, he's dropped the nickname, or so Beth tells me."

"So . . . Teddy?" That was what his mother had always called him.

Angie shook her head. "Ed."

"Not Edward?"

"Have you read the *Twilight* series? No boy his age wants to be accused of *sparkling*!"

"Huh." Obviously, it had been too long since she'd last seen her much-younger cousin. Liss wondered if Margaret knew about the name change. She probably did. She was his grandmother, after all.

"So, about Beth working for you," Angie said. "Do you really have enough to keep her busy? If it's just make-work, I can come up with that here."

"I can't say for certain about the rest of the summer, but I do need someone full-time next week. Margaret and I want to take a trip to the Maritimes." Standing beside Angie, Liss had a good view across the town square of the front of Moosetookalook Scottish Emporium. She saw a couple stop to study the display in the window, then enter the shop, and her heart did a little flip of joy at the thought that they might be paying customers.

"Buying trip?" Angie asked.

"Mostly."

Angie's eyebrows rose in a question.

Liss shrugged. "There are Highland Games at Anti-gonish."

But Angie knew her too well and could tell there was more to Liss's plans than she'd said. "And?"

Liss saw no reason *not* to tell her. "We plan to visit a little town in Nova Scotia called Chadwick."

"Same name as the family that built our haunted mansion?"

"Exactly the same. We've been trying to solve a little mystery. Margaret thinks stopping there might provide a clue."

"Okay. Be that way."

"What way?"

"You're wearing that cat-that-ate-the-canary look." Angie wagged a finger at her in mock disapproval. "I expect to hear the full story sooner rather than later."

Liss laughed. "Send Beth over to start training with me tomorrow morning and I'll think about spilling the beans."

With a wave, she headed back to the Emporium. She'd

tell Beth all about the portrait and the map and let her, as a good, dutiful daughter, pass the story on to her mother. They'd both get a kick out of Liss's treasure hunt, just as they'd both think her chance of success was right up there with spotting a unicorn or winning the next Megabucks drawing.

On the first Sunday in July, Liss and Margaret drove as far as the border between New Brunswick and Nova Scotia. The next day, they set out early in the morning and reached the small community of Chadwick by quarter to nine. In common with many places in the Canadian Maritimes, it had started life as a fishing village, growing and shrinking with fluctuations in the economy and the occasional change in government.

"I imagine the original settlers in this area were French," Margaret remarked.

Liss made a noncommittal sound, concentrating on maneuvering her car along a narrow, twisty, treelined street. She kept an eye out for street signs, slowing to a crawl so she wouldn't miss their turn.

"The Acadians were thrown out by the British," Margaret continued, spouting knowledge she'd gained from her recent reading. "The English-speaking population was then bolstered by Scots who came in droves because troubles at home made staying in the old country unbearable, and later they were joined by American Loyalists, who suddenly found themselves very unpopular in the brand-new country to the south. Some of them fled to Canada even before the end of the Revolutionary War."

Liss spotted the sign she'd been looking for and signaled a left turn. She wasn't much interested in history. Besides, the map wasn't *that* old. If it had been made in the eighteenth century, surely it would be about to crumble away from sheer age.

No matter what era it came from, Liss hadn't wanted to damage it with careless handling or, worse, spill coffee on it. The map, still protected by its clear plastic sleeve, was inside a file folder, the folder was inside a padded envelope, and the whole thing was tucked into a pocket in her sturdy tote bag, the one with the zipper to keep the contents from spilling out.

Catching sight of the number she sought on a nondescript white two-story clapboard building with green shutters, Liss made another left into a miniscule parking lot. Only after she'd shut off the engine did she locate the small sign identifying the place as the Chadwick Historical and Genealogical Society.

"Remind me again who it is we're meeting," Liss said as she freed herself from her seat belt.

"He's the town historian," Margaret said. "An archivist by the name of Orson Bailey. I made the appointment last week. He was very encouraging in the e-mails we exchanged. He said there were quite a few things available on the Canadian branch of the Chadwicks and that he'd make copies of them for me. He also said he has a nineteenth-century atlas that will show us the exact location of the original Chadwick property."

"But there are no actual Chadwicks left in Chadwick?"

"That's what he said in his first reply. Apparently, it was a fairly small family to begin with and, as with the American branch, it dwindled down to nothing." Margaret got out of the car, shading her eyes against the bright morning sunlight. "The only Chadwick not accounted for is a younger son who left here back in the nineteen thirties and was never heard from again."

Together they walked toward the building's entrance, a

door that was also painted green. The society's hours were posted next to it. Ordinarily the place was closed on Mondays, but Margaret had made special arrangements to consult with the town historian on the premises.

"His instructions were to just come on in and give a holler," Margaret said. "His office is at the rear of the building."

But when Liss tried the door, she found it locked. She rapped on the glass. "Maybe he's not here yet. I don't see any other cars."

"Why don't I stay put," Margaret suggested, "while you take a quick look around. Maybe there's another entrance."

Liss followed a flagstone-lined path and discovered a second, even smaller parking lot at the back of the building. One vehicle was already there and a second was just pulling in. A redhead wearing tailored slacks and three-inch heels emerged from the driver's side of a nondescript four-door car and reached into the back seat to retrieve a stack of papers. She gave a start when Liss called out a greeting.

"Sorry. I didn't mean to scare you. My aunt and I were supposed to meet Mr. Bailey here, but he's not answering the door."

"He probably forgot to unlock it," the redhead said, shaking her head. "The man's brilliant but he fits right into that old cliché of the absent-minded professor. I'm Cindy Fitzgibbons, by the way, executive secretary of the Chadwick Historical and Genealogical Society. Wait just a second and I'll let you in."

Although there was a back door, Cindy escorted Liss around to the front, where Margaret was waiting. Liss introduced herself and her aunt as Cindy inserted her key in the lock.

"Nice to meet you both."

Once the door was open, Cindy indicated that they should follow her past the receptionist's desk. Its surface was bare except for a stack of fliers about the society. Liss snagged one to study later and tucked it into an outside pocket of her tote.

To their left they passed an old-fashioned, book-lined reading room filled with library tables and wooden chairs. On their right, a short corridor branched off from the main hallway that ran front to back. Cindy stopped at the intersection.

"Keep going. He should be in his office. It's the last room on your left. If he's not there, sit tight and I'll be along in a minute to help you track him down."

Juggling her armload of papers, she unlocked the first door along the short corridor and disappeared inside. As instructed, Margaret continued on with Liss trailing behind her.

"Mr. Bailey?" Margaret called out. "We're here."

Silence greeted this overture.

"Maybe he can't hear you," Liss said, thinking of the ever-increasing number of older people she knew who were slowly going deaf.

Together, they peered into the office that belonged to Orson Bailey. The lights were off and no one was there. Turning back, Liss tried the other doors off the hallway, one after the other. The first two were locked. Offices, she supposed. Or archives that were off-limits to the general public. The third door opened to reveal a break room, nicely furnished with a half dozen chairs arranged around a cloth-draped table. A stove, a counter with a sink at one end and a coffeemaker at the other, and a full-size refrigerator were ranged along one wall, with brightly painted kitchen cabinets above them.

Liss was about to pull her head back out and continue their search for Orson Bailey when she caught sight of a shoe.

It was a man's black dress shoe, lying on its side.

Only an inch or so was visible, sticking out from beneath the floor-length tablecloth.

Margaret saw it a moment after Liss did. "Oh, no," she whispered.

After swallowing convulsively, Liss crept inside. She braced herself for an unpleasant discovery. Where there was a shoe, there was likely to be a foot, one with a body attached. Since this one was hidden under a table, the odds were good that it had not gotten there by accident. Using only her fingertips, she slowly lifted the cloth.

It was still raised, revealing a very dead body, when Cindy joined them. At the sight, she shrieked Orson Bailey's name and burst into tears.

It was left to Liss to phone the police.

# Chapter Three

Liss was, sadly, all too familiar with police procedure when it came to investigating a homicide. She willed herself to be patient when the local authorities arrived, separated her from Margaret and Cindy, and isolated her in one of the previously locked rooms at the Chadwick Historical and Genealogical Society.

There was one significant difference this time around. When the first officer on the scene had asked for identification and she'd shown him her Maine driver's license, he'd also asked to see her passport. Then he'd confiscated it.

That was one way, she supposed, to make sure she didn't leave town. Without her passport, she wouldn't be allowed back across the border.

Since she wasn't wearing a watch and her cell phone and iPad were in the car, Liss had no accurate idea of how long she'd been left to twiddle her thumbs. The small room where she was sequestered was apparently used to make repairs on old books. After a while, in spite of the climate-controlled air that circulated through the entire building—no doubt a necessity to prevent damage to the many documents housed there—the decidedly musty smell coming off some of the volumes in for repair began to bother her. She tried to open the window but with no success. At some point in the building's history, it had been painted shut. She had just given up the struggle and returned to her seat at the worktable when the door opened and a sergeant in the Royal Canadian Mounted Police walked in.

Sergeant Childs fit Liss's image of a Mountie to at T . . . except for the fact that he was not wearing a bright red uniform. She kept this observation to herself. She doubted he'd be flattered if he knew she was comparing him to Dudley Do-Right, as portrayed in an over-the-top comedic performance by Brendan Fraser in a movie she'd seen years ago. Childs was, however, tall, muscular, square-jawed, and stone-faced.

It occurred to Liss, as he took a moment to review notes he'd already made, that he probably had a lot in common with a certain Maine State Police detective named Gordon Tandy, someone with whom she'd had far too many professional encounters in the course of the past decade. As was the case with Gordon, she could not read Sergeant Childs's expression. Until he spoke, she had no idea if he considered her a witness or a suspect.

"It's unfortunate you had to walk into such an unpleasant situation on your visit to Nova Scotia, Ms. Ruskin," Childs said. "I have a few questions for you, but I will try to delay you for as short a time as possible. I understand you had an appointment with the deceased."

Liss let out a breath she hadn't realized she'd been holding. It didn't sound as if he considered her a suspect, despite the fact that she'd been the one to find the body.

"My aunt and I were supposed to meet with Mr. Bailey at nine o'clock this morning." When he gave her an encouraging nod, she went on. "Aunt Margaret corresponded with him by e-mail about some research we're doing into the Chadwick family and he agreed to search the society's collections for us. He was going to make copies of everything he found and give them to us today."

"Was there a specific reason why you needed to meet with him in person?"

"Could he have mailed the copies or e-mailed them as attachments, do you mean? Yes, he could have, but my aunt and I were coming to Nova Scotia anyway. . . ."

With a shrug, she let her words trail off. She'd be a fool to mention the map unless she had to. She could imagine what he'd think—crazy American tourist! The assessment might not be far wrong, at that. Other than in books and movies, when did X *ever* mark the spot where treasure was buried?

Fortunately, the sergeant had other things on his mind. "Where were you before arriving in Chadwick?"

Liss provided the name of the motel where they'd stayed the previous night. "I have the receipt," she added, reaching for her tote. It didn't appear that she and Margaret needed an alibi, but it didn't hurt that the credit card slip had the time and date on it or that the motel in question was at least an hour's drive away from Chadwick.

"That's not necessary," Childs assured her. "Were you planning to stay here in Chadwick tonight?"

Liss shook her head. "We have another appointment in Truro this afternoon. Then we're headed for Cape Breton and we'll spend the weekend at Antigonish." That, at least, needed no explanation. Everyone in Nova Scotia was aware of the annual Highland Games.

Apparently satisfied that he could find her if he needed to, Sergeant Childs took Liss through the details of her arrival at the headquarters of the Chadwick Historical and

Genealogical Society leading up to the discovery of the body. He took careful notes.

"Did you touch anything in the room or move the body?"

"I lifted the tablecloth to see if there was anything I could do for him. One glimpse of his face was enough to tell me he was beyond help." She repressed a shudder at the memory. Bailey's eyes had been wide open but empty of life.

"Mrs. Boyd was there with you?"

"Yes. Right behind me. And then Ms. Fitzgibbons came in and saw the body and recognized him as Mr. Bailey."

"Did she touch anything?"

"I don't think so. I backed out of the room and closed the door. Mr. Bailey's office was the closest one that was unlocked, so the three of us went there to phone the police."

He frowned. "Is that where you waited?"

Liss shook her head. "Once help was on the way, we went out to the parking lot at the front of the building to wait."

Childs made a note, then tapped the eraser end of his pencil on his pad. "Did you see anyone else or hear anything when you first entered the building?"

He'd already asked her that question, phrased in a slightly different way. Liss had a feeling that he would repeat all of his questions before he was through. Gordon always did, looking for discrepancies in a witness's account and making sure no seemingly insignificant detail was accidentally left out.

When Sergeant Childs finally put his notebook away, Liss asked a question of her own. "How did he die? I didn't see any blood."

She supposed it was too much to hope for that Bailey's

death would be ruled something other than a homicide. It seemed unlikely. People who died from natural causes didn't usually crawl under tables to breathe their last. It was equally difficult to suffer a fatal accident in such a location. Someone had to have hidden Bailey's body there *after* he died.

"It's too early to say." The enigmatic mask was back in place. All cop, Childs rose and gestured for her to precede him into the hallway. "If you'll come with me?"

Liss sighed. "You probably wouldn't tell me anyway." She sent a rueful smile in his direction and was surprised when he returned it.

"True enough," he admitted.

He escorted her into the area at the front of the building that she'd earlier identified as a reading room and settled her in at a table. Then he asked, very politely, that she wait there until he told her she could leave. Canadian to the core, he once again apologized for delaying her departure.

"You haven't talked to my aunt yet, have you?"

"That's next on my list." He disappeared into the back of the building . . . without returning her passport.

Liss folded her arms on the tabletop and bent forward to rest her forehead against them. As the full force of her grisly discovery belatedly hit home, she wanted nothing so much as to cover her eyes with her hands and make the rest of the world go away.

Less than ten minutes later, Liss was up and pacing. All she'd managed to do by closing her eyes was bring a vivid image of Orson Bailey's dead face into her mind. She stared out the window at her car, wishing Childs would finish with her aunt so they could be on their way. She couldn't wait to put Chadwick in her rearview mirror.

Forgetting what had happened here would be harder. As it should be, she supposed. Death should never be trivialized and murder was the most heinous of crimes. That Liss had encountered homicides before did nothing to make this experience less harrowing.

She turned at a faint sound from the doorway and was hit full force by the tantalizing aroma of freshly brewed coffee. Cindy Fitzgibbons entered the reading room carrying a tray that held two steaming mugs, a sugar bowl, and a small pitcher of cream.

"You look like you could use a pick-me-up," she said, placing it on one of the tables and waving Liss back into her chair. As soon as she was seated, Cindy joined her.

"You, on the other hand, look like you could use a drink of something stronger than coffee," Liss said.

It was not a tactful observation, but it was nothing less than the truth. Cindy's light green eyes were red-rimmed from crying and her face was unnaturally pale, even for a redhead.

"You're right about that, but all I have in my office is a small coffeemaker and the basic supplies to go with it. I keep them there for those times when I don't want conversation with my morning break."

Liss doctored her coffee with cream and sugar and took a tentative sip, then another when she was sure she wouldn't burn her tongue. She'd had a difficult morning, but it had been a hundred times worse for Cindy.

"Did you work with Mr. Bailey for a long time?"

Cindy's lower lip trembled before she got it under control. "Five years. As president of the society and town historian, Orson was trying to get the organization's records into some sort of order. He was a trained archivist, you know. We were lucky to have him." She swiped at the fresh tears with her fingers, then fumbled in the pocket of her slacks for a tissue.

"I'm so sorry for your loss."

"The society isn't even open today," Cindy said as she dabbed at her eyes. "Orson only came in because he wanted to help you and your aunt find information on your family. He was always willing to give a hand to amateur genealogists."

Liss didn't bother to correct the impression that she and Margaret were descended from the Chadwicks. She did wonder what had become of the copies Bailey had planned to make for her aunt, but this wasn't the time to ask. Cindy had enough on her plate.

"Did he often come in when the building was closed?" she asked instead.

"He was selfless. Dedicated."

Liss let her eulogize, all the while trying to decide if Cindy knew that her idol had been paid handsomely for the time he'd spent researching the Chadwicks. True, Bailey *had* volunteered to go over what he'd found with them in person without additional charge, but that didn't qualify him for sainthood.

"He was the one who suggested using the society's headquarters as a meeting place," she ventured.

"Oh, yes. I'm sure he was planning to be here anyway, on his own except for me. He liked being able to work without interruptions."

"He was going to leave the front door unlocked for us."

Cindy frowned. "Yes. I was surprised when I had to use my key to get in."

She didn't think it unusual that he was unconcerned about strangers walking in on him, and yet she'd just said that he liked to work without fear of interruption. Cindy's statements were contradictory, but Liss made allowances. She was upset by her colleague's murder. Who wouldn't be?

*Stop imagining skullduggery,* Liss cautioned herself. People *were* inconsistent in their habits. And it certainly wasn't un-common to leave a door unlocked in a small town in broad daylight. This neighborhood seemed safe enough, made up mainly of private homes and older houses broken up into apartments. There was a small mom-and-pop restaurant just down the block and an art supply store next door to the society's headquarters, but it wasn't a high-traffic area, nor was it high-risk.

"It's strange," Cindy murmured, holding her cup in both hands, as if she needed its warmth. "He knew you were coming. No matter when he got here, he should have let himself in and left the door unlocked for you."

"You mean he might have come in quite a bit earlier?"

"Oh, yes." In spite of her sorrow and distress, Cindy managed a fond smile. "Orson just loved doing research. Often he arrived here at the crack of dawn to work on some project or other. You aren't the only American to write to us about finding her roots, you know. Why, I'll bet we get a half dozen letters and e-mails every week from people wanting to know something or other about the past. Orson just ate that stuff up. Bread and butter, he'd say."

A drop of moisture appeared at the corner of one of Cindy's eyes and rolled slowly down an already tear-stained cheek to plop into her coffee. She sniffled again, fished a tis-sue out of a pocket, and noisily blew her nose. "Sorry."

"Don't you dare apologize." Liss reached out to pat the other woman's arm.

At a guess, they were about the same age, but Cindy had an innocence about her that made Liss think she had not had much prior experience dealing with the death of some-one she'd known and liked. Maybe it was even more than liked, given that they'd worked closely together for such a long time. The glimpse she'd had of Orson Bailey had shown him to be an older man, closer to Margaret's age than her own, but perhaps he'd been a father figure to the younger woman. It didn't really matter. What did was that Cindy was grieving and Liss's heart went out to her.

"He often came in early," Cindy reiterated. " 'The early bird gets the worm,' that was one of his favorite sayings."

Only in this case, Liss thought, the worm might have turned.

They didn't say much else to each other during the remaining time they had to wait for Sergeant Childs to reappear. Liss found it comforting to have company and suspected Cindy felt the same.

As soon as Margaret and the sergeant entered the reading room, Liss scrambled to her feet. "Are we done here?"

"You are free to continue your trip," Childs said, and returned her passport. He also gave her a card with his name and contact information printed on it. "If you think of anything else between now and when you leave the country next Monday, please let me know as soon as possible."

Liss assured him that she would.

Once outside, she drew in a deep breath of fresh Canadian air. "I feel like I've just been let out of jail," she confided as she and Margaret walked toward the car.

"Well," Margaret said, philosophically, "there is a certain cachet in being able to say we were interrogated by the Mounties. That's the kind of story you can dine out on for months to come."

Liss wished she could match her aunt's upbeat attitude. As in any investigation of a homicide, witnesses ended up doing a great deal of sitting around and waiting. She'd had entirely too much time to think about grim topics like sudden death, crime, and violence. Add to that the fact that she'd been asked a lot of questions, the kind that made even an innocent person start to feel nervous, and she was more than ready for a change of topic.

Unfortunately, Margaret was still fixated on the crime. "How long do you think Mr. Bailey had been dead?" she asked when they were in the car with seat belts fastened. "You got a better look at him than I did."

"I have no idea, but if they thought he was killed *after* we arrived in Chadwick, I'm pretty sure they'd still be grilling us." Liss knew she sounded sour, but it took too much effort to sweeten her tone. She turned the key in the ignition with rather more force than necessary.

She kept hoping she'd never have to be involved in another murder investigation again, and here she was, smack-dab in the middle of a new one. Worse, even though they were apparently off the hook as suspects, she couldn't stop feeling a connection to the crime. Cindy had implied that Bailey might have been there, door unlocked, even if he hadn't been expecting them, but how could she not feel partially responsible? Except for turning over the research he'd done at Margaret's request, he'd had no specific reason to be at the society's headquarters on this particular day.

She shook her head to clear it. Time to hit the road. They had an appointment with a kilt maker in Truro at three in the afternoon. She steered the car out of the parking lot and away from the scene of the crime. Somewhere between here and there, they'd have to find a place to have lunch, but right now all Liss wanted was to put Chadwick far behind her.

*Focus on business,* she told herself.

Good intentions were not enough. As she drove, her thoughts kept returning to the events of the morning. Like it or not, she was involved in this homicide, and since she was, she wanted to know who had killed Orson Bailey and why and, most of all, when.

Determining the time of death was tricky unless the victim's watch happened to get broken at the exact moment he was killed. There would probably be a window of several hours. Still, it was a good thing she and Margaret had an alibi. Since they'd spent the night a good hour's drive away from Chadwick, they were probably completely in the clear, although it wouldn't surprise Liss if she got back home and found out the RCMP had been checking up on her.

Margaret's thoughts were apparently running along the same lines as those of her niece. "Do you suppose Sergeant Childs will contact the Maine State Police?"

"I don't know." She thought for a moment. "Probably. If he's good at his job, he'll check up on everyone connected to Orson Bailey."

"Well, it isn't as if we have anything to worry about. Neither one of us has a criminal record." Margaret sounded uncharacteristically prim.

"If Sergeant Childs talks to one particular state trooper, he'll get an earful."

Margaret chuckled. "Maybe he'll skip Gordon and contact the Moosetookalook chief of police. Sherri will vouch for our sterling characters."

Liss bit back a groan and felt her hands tighten on the steering wheel. "I think I'd rather he talk to Gordon. If he calls Sherri, Dan is sure to find out that I've found another body."

"You'll tell him, surely."

"Yes. We don't keep secrets from each other. But I'm hoping to put off true confessions until I can talk to him face-to-face."

Call him at the first opportunity? Or hope that he wouldn't find out from someone else? She couldn't decide.

"Why does this sort of thing keep happening to me?"

"Karma?" Margaret suggested.

Liss made an incoherent sound and a concerted effort to focus on the road signs up ahead.

"I am not, repeat *not*, going to fall into the temptation of trying to solve the mystery of Orson Bailey's murder, not even as an intellectual exercise. Canada's finest does not need the help of Liss MacCrimmon, girl detective. I'm nearly forty years old. It's time I concentrated on being Liss Ruskin, sole proprietor of Moosetookalook Scottish Emporium, all grown up and fully capable of minding my own business."

Margaret was smiling by the time Liss wound down. "Of course, dear. After all, the sergeant seems quite capable. And of course, he was very polite, even when I asked him why he wasn't dressed in his fancy red uniform, the one you see Mounties wearing when they ride in parades. I expect he gets asked that a lot."

This observation, coming as it did from out of left field, made Liss chuckle. "Well, don't keep me in suspense— what was his answer?"

"He said those fancy duds are the ceremonial uniform. They don't wear them for every day. Do you know why?" She waited a beat, aware that timing was everything when delivering the punch line of an old joke: "The spurs get caught in the carpeting!"

Liss groaned, but as she continued driving toward Truro, she was in a much better frame of mind.

Later that afternoon, Liss and Margaret entered the shop of Duncan MacTaggart, Custom Kilt Maker. On display were finished kilts and all the paraphernalia that went with them, from sporrans and kilt hose to clan crest kilt pins and other jewelry. The lone salesclerk was busy with a customer, trying to explain to him the difference between plaid, pronounced "plad" and plaid pronounced "played."

"The first is a pattern. It is applied to what should properly be called tartan. The second refers to an item of Scottish dress." She selected an example from a nearby rack. "It's worn draped around the upper body."

"That's a shawl," the customer said in a drawl that pinpointed his origins as somewhere south of the Mason-Dixon line. "Or maybe a cape."

Liss exchanged a been-there-done-that look with her aunt and set about exploring the shop until the clerk was free. They were a bit early for their appointment with the proprietor and she welcomed the opportunity to get a feel for what kind of business she'd might be dealing with. Inspecting the merchandise he carried was a good way to start.

While Margaret browsed in a display of ladies' skirts made in various clan tartans, Liss headed straight for the rack of kilts. She remembered fondly the time that Margaret, who had made a kilt or two in her time, had tried to teach her niece how to sew one. The effort had not been a notable success, but it had left Liss with a firm knowledge of the basics. She could appreciate the finicky, time-consuming work that went into producing each garment. It was well worth the cost to let others deal with making all those pleats, but only if they did it well.

She was not impressed by what she saw of MacTaggart's offerings. When she ran her fingers over the fabric of a kilt in the Royal Stewart tartan, she thought it had an odd feel to it. A peek at the tag told her why. She was frowning when Margaret came up beside her.

"I'm willing to cut MacTaggart some slack, since he

hasn't been in business long," she whispered, "but a kilt made of viscose and acetate?"

"It's lightweight," Margaret whispered back. "And it's machine washable. No need to fuss with dry cleaning."

The sign above the rack advertised CASUAL STARTER KILTS and Liss supposed that might appeal to those who weren't sure they wanted to invest a lot of money in an outfit they'll only wear once or twice a year. The synthetic fiber would be cheaper for outfitting pipe bands, too. The kilt she was looking at was priced at 199 dollars Canadian. Imported to the States and translated into U.S. dollars, that would still be a bargain price.

"The kilts sold in Moosetookalook Scottish Emporium have always been made of wool."

"Neither of us are purists when it comes to Scottish traditions," Margaret reminded her.

"Not usually, no. But there's just something about mixing acetate with the ancient tartans that strikes me as wrong."

Margaret's tone of voice was soothing. "Since we're here, let's see what Mr. MacTaggart has to say."

MacTaggart turned out to be a fast-talking little man with a patter that wouldn't quit. He extolled the virtues of his in-house shop, but did not offer them a tour. Instead, he pulled out kilt after kilt, all in the same twenty-four-inch length. Without exception, they were made of lightweight synthetic fabrics, which he seemed to think was a plus, and he was inordinately proud of being able to offer both "fashion kilts" and "camouflage kilts."

"Just send us the measurement and we'll fix you right up. Not the pant size. Measure at the waist, at the level of the belly button."

"We'll think it over." Liss had to struggle to remain diplomatic. MacTaggert pushed all the wrong buttons.

"Can I interest you in children's kilties? They come in the Royal Stewart, Black Watch, Cape Breton, Nova Scotia, and Maple Leaf tartans, although for Maple Leaf they have to be special ordered. Retail, they're forty-two ninety-five, but for you—"

"No. Thank you." Liss began to edge toward the door. Margaret followed.

"You won't find better prices anywhere," MacTaggart called after them.

Over her shoulder, Liss managed a credible smile, but it took an effort. "That's very likely true. Will you be at Antigonish this weekend?"

MacTaggart's friendly demeanor never slipped, but his eyes hardened. "We're much too busy here."

"We'll let you know," she promised, "but we do plan to speak with the vendors there, and before that we'll be visiting several other kilt-making establishments, including MacIsaac on Cape Breton."

"Overpriced," MacTaggart grumbled. "And too heavy. Lightweight polyviscose, that's the wave of the future."

Liss exited the shop so quickly that she almost ran head-on into a dark-haired gentleman just passing by the storefront. Head down, he sidestepped and kept going. She stared after him, beset by the odd sensation that she had seen him somewhere before.

"Is something the matter? You look confused." Margaret had been right behind her niece, but Liss's body had blocked her view of the man she'd nearly bowled over.

Liss shook her head. "Nothing's wrong. For a minute, that guy reminded me of someone, although I can't think who."

That bothered her. As they walked to the car, parked just down the block, she kept glancing in the direction the stranger had gone.

"I hate it when that happens." Margaret slid into the passenger seat. "Half the time it turns out that the person I was thinking of wasn't anyone I actually knew. The sense of familiarity was because he or she bore a passing resemblance to some movie or TV star. It would be nice if he were a celebrity. I mean, who wouldn't mind bumping into George Clooney or Hugh Jackman?"

Liss rolled her eyes and started the engine. "This wasn't either of them. For one thing, his hair was too dark—oh!"

"You've remembered? Was it someone you know?"

"I . . . I'm not sure, but at least I've figured out who it is he reminded me of. It was the man who bid against me for the painting of the Grant piper at the auction." Liss checked her rearview and side mirrors before pulling away from the curb. "The bidder was a stranger. I never talked to him and I never got a very good look at him, either— hardly more than the glimpse I just had of that man in front of the shop. I suppose that's why I thought there was a resemblance."

She put the incident out of her mind. After all, it would be a heck of a coincidence if she'd run into the same person in both Moosetookalook, Maine, and Truro, Nova Scotia.

# Chapter Four

The next couple of days went smoothly. On Thursday, Liss and her aunt visited the Gaelic College in St. Ann's, a Cape Breton institution where traditional music, dance, language, and crafts, including kilt making, were taught.

"I could happily spend a week here," Liss said as they left the weaving studio and turned their steps toward the Outdoor Performance Centre.

At the moment, they were enjoying spectacular summer weather, but she felt certain that their surroundings would be just as impressive in winter. The campus overlooked St. Ann's Bay and boasted panoramic views of the Cape Breton Highlands. The whisper of a summer breeze provided counterpoint to the murmur of voices and the distant skirl of bagpipes.

"My parents would love this place," she added. "I wonder if they've ever been here."

When Margaret didn't immediately reply, Liss turned her head to look at her. Her aunt's face wore a peculiar expression, one she could not interpret, and Margaret's thoughts seemed to be a million miles away. Whatever she was pondering, it was not a pleasant subject.

"What's the matter?" Liss asked. "Aren't you feeling well?"

"Let's sit down for a moment." Margaret indicated the bench seating on the hillside. At this hour of the afternoon, it was deserted.

Something about Margaret's demeanor warned Liss that whatever was troubling her, it was serious. Unsettling explanations weren't hard to find. They came thick and fast for the remainder of the short walk. Liss's first thought was that Margaret was having more eye trouble. She'd undergone surgery for a vision issue a couple of years earlier. Or was it something new? Something worse? Was Margaret having chest pains? Anyone could have a heart attack, especially after they hit their sixties. Her aunt didn't seem to be in any physical distress, but she was clearly hesitant concerning what she was about to confide in her niece. What if she had been diagnosed with cancer? That situation was all too common, and the symptoms weren't always obvious.

As soon as they were seated, Liss demanded answers.

Margaret took a deep breath. "I've been putting off telling you this. I didn't know how you'd take it, but I can't wait any longer."

A giant fist squeezed Liss's heart at Margaret's words. Tension tightened every muscle in her body. Braced for terrible news but determined to think of Margaret first, not her own growing sense of despair, she burst into speech. "Whatever it is, we'll work it out. Anything you need, you know Dan and I—"

She broke off at Margaret's shocked expression.

"It's not about me!"

At a loss, Liss just stared at her. "Then what . . . ?"

"Oh, dear. This is going to be harder than I anticipated. All right, here goes. Now don't panic, but it's your parents."

Liss felt the color leave her face. All the concerns she'd

had about Margaret returned, but with Don and Vi Mac-Crimmon taking her place. Liss's always abundant imagination supplied a vivid slideshow. Pictures of her parents seriously injured in a car accident were followed by a series of scenes of them in a hospital ICU, stuck full of tubes and hooked up to frantically beeping machines. She swallowed convulsively.

"What about my parents?"

"They're moving back to Moosetookalook." Although Margaret kept her voice calm and soothing, her words had the same effect as a spray of shrapnel.

Liss spoke without thinking. "Oh, God! It's worse than I thought!"

At once, she clapped both hands over her mouth, horrified by what had come out of it.

Margaret burst out laughing. Before she could regain her self-control, she had to fumble in her bag for a tissue to wipe away her tears.

Liss fidgeted, embarrassed by her thoughtless words. Thank goodness Margaret understood the whole tangled history of Liss's relationship with her mother.

"Why?" she asked when Margaret had regained her composure. "Why are they coming back home? It makes no sense for them to relocate in Maine at this stage of their lives. They've spent the last twenty years in Arizona. They've been happy there, or so they've always told me."

They'd moved to the Southwest shortly after Liss graduated from high school with the hope that the weather would ease her father's arthritis. Thanks to wise investments, he'd been able to leave the family business in his sister's capable hands and abandon the cold Northeast. As far as Liss knew, he had never looked back. As for her mother, a history teacher, she'd found a new job and been able to continue molding young minds until she'd put in a full thirty-five years in the classroom.

Margaret patted Liss's hand. "I don't know all the details, but I'll try to answer your questions as best I can."

"Has something happened? Is one of them ill?"

"They aren't as young as they used to be." Margaret shrugged. "None of us are."

"But what about Dad's arthritis? That hot, dry climate was good for him. How is he going to manage here?"

"He's actually doing better after his hip surgery, and he had his knees replaced a few years ago. His hands are the biggest problem."

"And Mom? Is she okay?" Liss's imagination was working overtime. The onset of a terminal illness would certainly explain her sudden desire to return to her childhood home.

"As far as I know, she's fine, although she does have a few medical issues."

"I wouldn't know." Liss couldn't quite keep the bitterness out of her voice. "Despite the fact that I talk to my parents on the phone almost every Sunday afternoon, Mother repeatedly fails to share information about her health. It was months after the fact before I found out that she'd had a radical mastectomy. When I asked her about it, and told her I'd have been happy to come to Arizona and help out while she recovered, she said she hadn't seen the need to bother me."

"Yes, that sounds like Violet, although you'd think she'd want to let you know about the breast cancer. After all, as her daughter, you're now at a higher risk yourself."

Liss sent her aunt a fulminating look. "You're a fine one to talk. If you hadn't had a bad reaction to the anesthesia, we'd never have known you had eye surgery."

"You're comparing apples to oranges," Margaret protested. "And aside from your mother's surgery, I doubt she's keeping anything from you."

"Then why are they moving back to Moosetookalook?"

"Sometimes nostalgia is a powerful motivator."

"For Dad, maybe. For Mother? No."

"You are their only child," Margaret reminded her.

"Does that mean they *are* in need of my help? I'll take care of them, of course. That goes without saying. Heck, if it comes to that, we can always add one of those 'mother-in-law apartments' to the house."

Margaret's snort had Liss turning to stare at her aunt.

"Liss, dear, I know you love your parents, but—"

"Of course I do!"

"But there's no denying that you get along much better with them, especially your mother, when there are at least a dozen states between you. Besides, I don't think there's anything serious wrong with Violet. She has high blood pressure, but then she always has."

Liss knew that only too well. When she'd been a small child, she'd thrown the occasional temper tantrum. Every time she did, her mother's response was the same. "You're driving my blood pressure right through the roof," Vi Mac-Crimmon would say. "If I have a stroke and die, *then* you'd be sorry!"

It had been years before she'd realized that although she loved her mother, there were times when she didn't like her very much. Margaret was right. They rattled along well enough when there was distance between them, but any time they were in the same room together for more than a few hours, sparks were sure to fly.

*Don't panic,* Liss warned herself. She took several deep, calming breaths. Just because her parents were moving back to Maine didn't mean they'd need constant care or that they planned to move in with her and Dan.

"Do you know if they're thinking of buying a house?" she asked. "Or will they be looking to rent an apartment?"

The worried look was back in Margaret's eyes. "They're interested in the new assisted living facility that's going to be built on the old Chadwick property."

"I thought you said their health was okay."

"I imagine they're just planning for the future, and the distant future, at that, since the new owner has yet to break ground for the facility."

"So, they'll need a place to live until it's ready." And they were back to the possibility that she'd be living at close quarters with her parents for an undetermined length of time.

*Stop being selfish,* she chided herself. *They took care of you for your first seventeen years. The least you can do is give back a few lousy months.*

It could be much worse. The adult child's worst nightmare had to be the prospect of nursing elderly parents as they descended into increasingly poor physical and mental health.

"I should have gone to see them at Christmas," she muttered under her breath.

"Dan came down with the flu," Margaret reminded her. "No one expected you to abandon him. Not even your mother."

"And they were okay then? Health-wise?" Margaret *had* gone to Arizona for the holidays.

"As far as I could tell."

Liss stared unseeing at the panoramic view. "Somehow, I just assumed my parents would always be there, available to visit when I had the time, paying occasional visits to Maine when the spirit moved them."

Belatedly, she realized that it had been several years since they'd made the trip. When had it become too much for them? And what other clues had she missed? How badly had their health declined while she had been too wrapped up in her own affairs to pay proper attention?

Margaret stood. "We should get going. We still have a drive ahead of us to reach the hotel we've booked for the night."

"Maybe I should call them." Liss fumbled in her tote for her cell phone.

Margaret stopped her with a hand on her shoulder. "It would be best if you just think about what I've told you for a few days. To tell you the truth, I was of two minds about saying anything to you at all."

"Why did you?" Side by side, they headed toward the car park. The clouds that scudded in front of the sun reflected the way Liss's delight in the day had dimmed.

"My brother didn't want to break the news to you over the phone. He was afraid you'd freak out."

"I wouldn't have—"

"You did."

She *had*. She still was. And suddenly she didn't want to talk about her parents anymore.

By Saturday, when Liss and Margaret arrived at the fields set aside for the Highland Games in Antigonish, nothing had been resolved concerning the impending return to Moosetookalook of Mac and Vi MacCrimmon. Liss had, however, found a new kilt maker to handle orders placed at the Emporium. She looked forward to spending the next two days scouting products for the shop, watching competitions, and listening to the skirl of bagpipes.

At the same time, she was beginning to feel a bit homesick. Phone calls and e-mails just weren't the same as being right there with Dan and the cats. It didn't help that their last few conversations had been a bit strained, at least on her end, because of her desire to avoid certain topics. Until she saw her husband in person, she preferred to postpone telling him about the murder of Orson Bailey. Likewise, the news about her parents was something best delivered face-to-face.

The gathering at Antigonish was a welcome distraction. "Business first?" she asked Margaret.

Her aunt nodded. The area designated for merchandise vendors was only a short distance inside the entrance.

Although it was tempting to wander over to watch the Highland dancing competition or visit the cultural and arts workshops, browsing the stock for sale took precedence. They were on the lookout for items that would sell well at the Emporium, particularly those imported from Scotland. Finding them in catalogs was all well and good, but it was always helpful to be able to examine them first-hand.

It did not take long for Liss to spot a potential gem. It was billed as a "DIY Haggis Kit"—hokey, but something that might sell quite well.

On closer inspection, she changed her mind. She snickered as she read the label. The kit contained three synthetic haggis bungs—a bung being helpfully identified in parentheses as skin—together with three lengths of twine, a pack of haggis seasoning mix, and a recipe sheet. It was left up to the cook to add minced beef or lamb.

"Not exactly authentic," Margaret said.

"Authentic would never get past the health inspectors."

According to the label, the haggis seasoning mix wasn't anything special, just oatmeal, salt, rice flour, dried onion, wheat flour, black pepper, vegetable suet, and unidentified spices and flavorings. Since Liss already offered imported canned haggis for sale, she decided to give this item a pass.

Other offerings were more promising. She found a crys-

tal Loch Ness Monster for under twenty-five dollars. Figurines billed as "Clanta Claus" and made in Nova Scotia
were on the pricey side, but definitely collectible. Each
Santa Claus figure carried a bagpipe and wore a kilt made
of 100 percent pure new lamb's wool. A hand-lettered sign
indicated that all clan tartans were available. In the small
notebook she carried with her, Liss scribbled down contact information for the craftsperson who made them.

"Oh, Liss! Look at these." Margaret had moved on to
the next booth.

Liss took one look and started to laugh. "Yes, we have
to have them," she agreed, leaning closer to inspect a se-
lection of tartan dog collars and leashes. She decided to
pass, however, on tartan bow ties for dogs and cats.

And so it went, until they'd examined every vendor's
display. Agreeing to meet later at the area of the grounds
where the food vendors were located, Margaret set off toward the clan tents to pursue the family tree of some obscure Scotswoman who'd married into the MacCrimmon
family and Liss headed for stage where the dancers were
competing. Solo piping competitions were going on at the
same time. Later there would be a tug-of-war, the pipe band
championships, and an afternoon ceilidh, among other events.

The crowds were colorful, noisy, and friendly. Liss was enjoying herself when, without warning, the back of her neck
began to prickle. She looked around, but no one seemed to
be paying any attention to her. Certainly, there was nothing threatening about anyone's demeanor, but she couldn't
shake off the feeling that she was being watched. It grew
stronger as she made her way toward the food vendors. By
the time she reached them, she was moving so fast that she
almost sailed straight past her aunt.

"What on earth is the matter?" Margaret asked. "You
look . . . frightened."

"No! No, of course not. I'm just a little spooked, that's all. I thought someone was following me."

Margaret scanned the crowd, her face a mask of concern, but after a moment she returned her attention to Liss. "I don't see anyone. Maybe you've just been out in the sun too long."

"I didn't imagine it."

"Well, then, it was just someone in the crowd thinking what a good-looking woman you are. Men do stare at pretty girls, you know."

Liss had to laugh at that assessment. "I'm a long way from being a girl and I was never all that pretty."

"Don't sell yourself short."

Liss let the matter drop, but she knew she was right. Today, having dressed for the occasion, she wore traditional Scottish women's clothing—a long tartan skirt and a white blouse. She'd taken no particular care with her hair or makeup. Dan might have admired the way she looked, but she didn't stand out in any way, especially in this crowd, and it wasn't likely she'd attract male attention by her looks alone. If someone *had* been watching her, it had been for some other reason, and that left her feeling uneasy.

Together, Liss and Margaret browsed the food offerings and settled on an item that looked suspiciously like a Cornish pasty, even if it had been given an impressive Gaelic name. To Liss's relief, the sensation of being watched disappeared while they ate and did not return. She and Margaret spent the afternoon watching competitions and performances, had an early supper at a small restaurant recommended by one of the people manning a clan society tent, and returned to their motel just as the sun was about to set. Given the time of year and the time zone, that made it only a little after seven, but Liss was already yawning as she fumbled for her room key.

She froze, staring at the door. It was not all the way closed.

Liss swallowed hard and slowly backed away. She checked the number on the door as she did so. Yes, this was the right room.

Margaret came up behind her, saw what she'd seen, and barged inside anyway.

"You're being overcautious," she said as she flicked on the light. "Housekeeping will have come in to make the beds and leave fresh coffee packets. They were careless when they left and the lock didn't engage. It happens once in a while even at a classy hotel like The Spruces. There's no need to complain to the manager or to call the po—"

She broke off with a gasp.

Whoever had last been in their room, it had not been housekeeping. Clothing was dumped out of suitcases. Papers were scattered everywhere. And Liss's iPad, which she'd left plugged into the charger, was missing.

As Liss had already learned, the RCMP had detachments rather than precincts and members instead of officers. The Antigonish detachment proved to be every bit as efficient as the one that had responded to the murder in Chadwick, especially when it was discovered that Liss and Margaret's room was not the only one that had been broken into.

Their possessions had been thoroughly ransacked. In addition to Liss's iPad, a brooch Margaret had bought during their travels had also been stolen. Liss had to wonder if Canada was as law-abiding a place as she'd been led to believe.

The rest of their purchases had been in the trunk of the car or in the tote Liss was carrying instead of a purse. In addition to her wallet and passport, it contained brochures, the notes she'd made on merchandise that might sell well in the Emporium, and the map she'd brought from Maine to show Orson Bailey.

A good deal of the evening and part of the next morning were spent talking to the police and cleaning up the mess the burglars had left. By the time they were done, Liss had little enthusiasm for returning to the Highland Games.

"At least we don't have to go to the trouble of canceling credit cards and changing passwords." Margaret seemed determined to look on the bright side.

"There is that." She kept nothing on her iPad except books and a few games. She used the device primarily as a reader and to look up things on the Internet. She did her banking in person at the tiny branch bank in Moosetookalook where she knew all the tellers and they knew her.

"It was obviously a random crime," Margaret added. "We shouldn't let it spoil our trip."

Just like Orson Bailey's murder had been random? Liss kept that question to herself. Instead she asked if Margaret wanted to go back to the games.

"Of course." Margaret's voice was firm. "And turn off your cell phone," she added. "If Dan calls you, he can leave a message. The last thing you want is to blurt out what happened. There's no sense worrying him when we'll be home tomorrow evening."

It was good advice and she followed Margaret's suggestion. "One more thing to tell him about as soon as I get home."

Margaret sent her a narrow-eyed look. "Meaning you didn't tell him about the murder? Never mind answering. You couldn't look any more guilty if you tried."

"As you said, why worry him?"

"But it bothers you to keep quiet about it."

Liss shrugged. "Dan and I promised we wouldn't have secrets from each other."

"It isn't as if you're hiding anything. You're just waiting for an appropriate moment."

That was what she'd been telling herself, but Margaret's words did little to ease her conscience. Once they arrived at the field, however, she let the excitement of the Highland Games take her mind off her worries.

Sunday's schedule included many of the same events as the day before. There was also a pipe band competition. The entrants were vying for the championship of all of Atlantic Canada. In the heavyweight athletic events, Canada was competing against the U.S. in both pro and open divisions. Since the annoying sensation of being watched did not return, Liss enjoyed herself more than she'd expected to. She and Margaret stayed through the closing ceilidh and the final performance of the massed bands.

Back at the motel, they found their room securely locked. No one had broken in. Nothing had been stolen. Muscles Liss hadn't realized she'd tensed relaxed as she collapsed into the chair.

When she pulled out her cell phone and turned it on, she found a voice mail from Dan. She was about to return his call when she saw that she had a second message. As she listened to it, her good mood evaporated.

Margaret came out of the bathroom, caught sight of her expression, and sighed. "Now what?"

Liss held up the phone. "Remember Sergeant Childs?"

"That nice Mountie who interviewed us in Chadwick. What about him?"

"He wants us to meet with him tomorrow on our way home." Liss tucked the phone back into her tote, no longer in any mood to talk to her husband. "It didn't sound like a request. It sounded like an order."

# Chapter Five

It was not difficult to locate the headquarters of the RCMP detachment in Amherst. Liss pulled into a parking space and killed the engine. She wished, not for the first time, that Sergeant Childs had given a reason when he suggested they meet at eleven this morning, and that his voice mail request hadn't sounded so ominously official.

"Why is it that cops always make people nervous?" she asked as she unfastened her seat belt. "I know I'm innocent as a lamb, but I still have this awful feeling that I must have done something wrong, because why else would he want to talk to me again?"

"Maybe one of us should have told that nice constable who interviewed us after the break-in that we'd already had dealings with the RCMP," Margaret suggested.

"I would have." It annoyed Liss to hear the defensive note in her voice. "He was too efficient." The truth was, she'd been hesitant to mention the murder and had been relieved when she had been given no opportunity to do so.

Now that they had arrived, she admitted something else to herself. Ever since leaving Chadwick the previous Monday afternoon, she'd been trying to pretend she had no interest in the investigation into Orson Bailey's death. She'd also tried to convince herself that the murder could not possibly have any connection to the map or to the Chadwicks. After all, she knew almost nothing about Orson Bailey. They'd had no relationship beyond an exchange of e-mails, and that had been with her aunt, not her. Bailey could have made enemies left and right while he was alive.

But she *had* been the one who'd found his body. In some inexplicable way, that made it important to her that his killer be caught and punished. With an abrupt movement, she opened the car door and got out.

"Let's get this over with."

Sergeant Childs was waiting for them. "Ms. Ruskin. Right on time. And Mrs. Boyd. I trust you had a pleasant week?"

He listened politely as Margaret recounted some of their successes in finding new suppliers. She was singing the praises of the Highland Games at Antigonish as they settled in around a table in a small meeting room.

"I don't mean to be rude," Liss interrupted, "but we have a long drive ahead of us. Why are we here?"

Childs's infectious grin soothed her jangled nerves even before he answered. Really, she thought, the RCMP was wasting its natural resources if they weren't using him on their recruitment posters.

"I apologize if my message sounded curt or left you with the wrong impression, but since the route you described in your interview indicated you'd have to pass through Amherst anyway, I thought it best not to discuss police business in a voice mail. I won't keep you in suspense. I simply wanted to let you know that we've made an arrest in connection with the death of Orson Bailey. You can return to the States and put this distressing incident behind you. I'm afraid I can't discuss the case in detail," he added when Liss opened her mouth to ask a question.

"Won't we need to return to testify at the trial?" Margaret asked.

"It doesn't seem likely. We have a confession."

Liss told herself she should be relieved. The matter was settled. She could go home and forget the entire unpleasant experience. Echoing Margaret, she thanked the sergeant for keeping them informed. Telling them in person was good public relations, and good international relations, as well.

Sergeant Childs escorted them back to their car and sent them on their way with another of his killer smiles, but as Liss drove off she was plagued by a sense of something unfinished. It didn't take much effort to figure out what it was.

When Liss pulled into the parking lot at the Chadwick Historical and Genealogical Society, Margaret sent her a satisfied look. "I wondered if this was where we were headed when you didn't stick to the main road."

"Just a short detour," Liss said. "I thought we could stop in and ask Cindy if she has the information Mr. Bailey was going to give you."

"She must be relieved that the killer has been arrested." Margaret followed Liss along the flagstone-paved sidewalk, but when they reached the entrance she stopped and pointed to the sign that listed the society's hours. "It's Monday. They're closed."

"Cindy was here last Monday, and I got the impression that it was her usual practice to come in every day."

Liss tried the knob, but the door was locked. She shaded her eyes and peered through the glass. She could see lights burning inside the building. Either the society's secretary was in, or someone wanted to give the impression that the building was occupied. She rang the doorbell. When no one appeared right away, she rang it again and knocked on the door for good measure. Once again, nothing stirred. She was about to give up when she caught a flicker of movement at the entrance to the short corridor, the one off which Cindy had her office.

"Cindy?" she called. "It's Liss Ruskin from last week. If you have a minute, I'd like a word with you."

She'd barely finished speaking when the redhead showed herself. Cindy didn't look enthusiastic about letting them in. Her steps dragged as she circled the reception desk and she took her time to verify Liss's identity before she released the deadbolt. When the door swung inward, she stepped back to allow them to enter.

Cindy had abandoned her "business casual" attire of the previous week in favor of jeans and a peasant blouse. Her shoes were ballet flats instead of three-inch heels, making it necessary for her to look up to meet Liss's gaze. She led them into a small office that was cramped but cheerful, decorated with colorful prints of flowers and supplied with a coffeemaker and mini-fridge.

"Sorry to intrude," Liss said, "but it was material from the society's collections that brought us to Chadwick in the first place."

"You aren't intruding. In fact, I was just putting together a packet of information to mail to you. Having you stop by saves the society the cost of postage."

"Oh, how wonderful," Margaret said. "You must have found the material Mr. Bailey collected for us."

"Oh. Um. Well, not quite." From her cluttered desk, Cindy scooped up a padded envelope that already had Margaret's mailing address written on the front. "But this is everything Orson located. I made copies for you."

"*You* made copies?" Liss asked. "I'm confused. I thought Mr. Bailey had already done that."

Cindy looked apologetic. "Yes, well . . . I expected to

find a folder with your name on it in his office, but there wasn't one, only the record of his research. Fortunately, that had all the citations, so it didn't take long to assemble everything."

"Perhaps Mr. Bailey was planning to make the copies while we were here, so we could see the originals and decide which ones were relevant," Margaret suggested.

"He should have had the copies ready to give to you. I don't understand why he didn't. Orson was always so well organized."

"Maybe the police took the material he collected for us." Liss could have bitten her tongue when she saw Cindy's face crumple.

"It's standard practice to take everything that could possibly be evidence."

Had that explanation made matters better or worse? Liss couldn't tell.

Cindy turned aside for a moment, after which, although there was a catch in her voice, she regained control of herself. "You're probably right. They even took up the carpet in his office, and they confiscated his water carafe and his computer."

"That's pretty typical," Liss said. "They look for fingerprints and DNA evidence from hair or skin cells to help them find the killer. Now that they have him in custody, they'll probably return some of those things."

Cindy abruptly sat down in her desk chair. "I just don't understand why he would murder Orson."

"Do you know the man who confessed?"

"Not personally, no, but I've seen him around." Cindy frowned. "I always thought there was something wrong about him, but I never imagined that he'd turn violent. Orson didn't do anything to him. I doubt he even met him."

"Do you mean he's mentally ill?"

"I think he has PTSD. And he may have been home-less." She managed a faint smile. "U.S. soldiers aren't the only ones fighting terrorism on foreign soil."

While Liss's attention had been on Cindy, Margaret had been going through the contents of the mailer. "Is this from that old atlas Mr. Bailey mentioned?" She placed a photocopy of a map in front of the society's executive secretary.

"That's right." Cindy identified several landmarks, includ-ing the site of the original Chadwick homestead. "There's an apartment complex there now. It was named for Albert Chadwick, who donated the land. There's a newspaper ar-ticle about it in there." She indicated the packet. "Most of the rest record weddings, funerals, and charity events the Chadwicks attended. The family was extremely respectable and very generous to the community."

Maybe they were and maybe they weren't, Liss thought, but she kept that opinion to herself. She swallowed her disappointment at not having a site to explore. "Every lit-tle bit of information helps. Thank you so much for col-lecting all this for us."

"Don't you want to show her your map?" Margaret asked.

"It doesn't match what hers shows," Liss objected, but Cindy's green eyes had suddenly brightened with curiosity and she supposed it wouldn't hurt to let her see it.

She recounted the story of her discovery and what they already knew about the American branch of the Chad-wicks and their highly successful import business during Prohibition.

"If you're assuming that they made Chadwick their base of operations in Canada," Cindy said as she studied the two maps side by side, "I'm pretty sure you're barking up the wrong tree. As I said, our Chadwicks were respectable. Straitlaced would be an even more accurate description."

More to the point, there were no landmarks common to both maps. Liss returned the one she'd found to her tote and handed the other to Margaret to tuck back into the mailer. "We always knew it was a longshot, but since we were going to be in the area anyway, it was worth checking into."

"I'm sorry I couldn't be more help," Cindy said. "I can take you to the Chadwick Apartments if you want, but there's really nothing to see there, and certainly nothing left from the nineteen twenties and nineteen thirties."

Liss glanced at her watch. It was well past noon and they hadn't even had lunch yet. "We have a long trip ahead of us." Without the detours it would still have taken at least nine hours to drive from Antigonish to Moosetookalook. "Is it all right to e-mail you if we think of any other questions?"

"Of course. That's what we're here for." Cindy followed Liss and Margaret to the door, still smiling, but she engaged the lock the moment door closed.

Dan Ruskin was furious and making no effort to hide it. "*Another* body! And as if that wasn't enough, you were the victim of a burglary. If you were a cat, you'd have used up eight of your nine lives by now."

"Don't make a fuss." Liss turned her back on him to trudge up the stairs, hauling her heavy tote and a small roller bag after her.

"Damn it, Liss! You've got to stop taking risks."

She swung around to glare at him from two steps up. Lumpkin, who had been padding along behind her, fled the rest of the way to the second floor, tail fully fluffed. "What risk? I wasn't in any danger."

"You walked into that building right after someone was murdered."

"We don't know that. He could have been dead for hours. Anyway, it was just dumb luck that Orson Bailey was killed that morning, and pure chance that a thief picked our room to burgle."

"Liss—"

"Furthermore, the murderer is in jail. As for the thief, the only thing he got was my iPad and a brooch Aunt Margaret had just bought." She started to climb again, muttering under her breath. "I shouldn't have told you. I knew you'd blow things out of proportion."

"What you *should* have done was call me from Chadwick as soon as it happened. Hell, you should have come straight home at the first sign of trouble."

Again, she turned, her eyes shooting daggers. "Why? Because I'm some frail little female who can't take care of herself. You listen to me, mister. I was on my own for a long time before I came back to Moosetookalook. I don't need some big strong man to watch my back!"

"You need a keeper!"

At that she flew back down the stairs, dropping the tote and roller bag along the way, and got right in his face. Her fist came up and smacked him in the chest. Hard. "You are being an idiot!" she shouted.

"*I'm* an idiot?"

She thumped him again. "Yes!"

She was horrified to feel moisture gathering in her eyes. She didn't want to be the kind of woman who relied on tears to win an argument. But when Dan wrapped his arms around her and held her close, burying his face in her hair, she could only stand stiffly in his embrace, saying nothing, for a moment before she relaxed against him, sniffling a little.

"I'm sorry, Liss. You're right. I am an idiot. But I couldn't stand it if anything happened to you."

"I should have waited till morning to tell you."

"Maybe," he said, "but I'm glad you didn't. I shouldn't have flown off the handle like that. I know you can take care of yourself. Unfortunately, that doesn't keep me from worrying about you."

"I don't stumble over murder victims on purpose."

He gave a wry laugh. "Don't you think I know that? I'm just glad this case has already been solved and that you're safe at home again."

She snuggled deeper into his arms.

"Come on. Let's get your stuff upstairs and you into bed. You look like you could use a good night's sleep."

"I think I'd rather get it all out first," she mumbled into his chest.

"There's more?" He stepped back, holding her away from him so he could see her face.

"Just something else I need to tell you about. Nothing to do with any crime. Do you want me to wait until morning?"

Tension crept back into her shoulders and for a moment the exhaustion born of all those hours of driving threatened to knock her flat. As if he sensed that, Dan slid one hand down her arm until he could fold her fingers into his. With a firm grip, he tugged her down the hall and into the kitchen.

"I'm guessing this means you want to hear it all now." Liss collapsed into one of the chairs at the kitchen table and watched her husband rummage in the cabinets. When he held up a packet of instant cocoa, she nodded.

They didn't talk while he dumped the contents into a ceramic mug, nuked some water in the microwave, and poured it over the powdered chocolate. He prepared a second serving for himself. A quick stir, a dollop of whipped cream, and he carried both mugs to the table, taking the chair opposite his wife.

Glenora had appeared while he'd been busy and was now ensconced on Liss's lap. Holding the small, black feline comforted her, as did the sound of the cat's delighted purring. Lumpkin was nowhere to be seen. As was his habit, he was giving her the cold shoulder for going away and leaving him for more than a week.

"I'm not going to like hearing this, am I?" Dan asked.

"Probably not." Liss picked up her mug, licked at the whipped cream, blew on the cocoa, and took a tentative sip. Finding it too hot to drink, she abandoned it. While she continued to stroke Glenora's soft, thick fur, she blurted out the bad news. "According to Margaret, my folks are planning to move back to Moosetookalook."

Dan stared at her for a long moment. "Why?"

Liss shrugged. "That's what I asked, and I'm still not entirely sure. This is all secondhand information. Dad delegated Margaret to pave the way for their big announcement. I think there are more health issues than they're admitting to. They're investigating assisted living rather than looking for a place of their own."

"Wouldn't they get better care where they are?"

Liss buried her face in Glenora's soft fur. "You'd think so."

"So maybe they just want to be closer to their only daughter."

"I'm being selfish," Liss admitted. "I want them to stay in Arizona so I don't have to see them get older and more frail." Anguish and guilt clawed at her. "What's *wrong* with me? They're my *parents*. I ought to be delighted that they're coming back home for good."

Her agitation made Glenora squirm. Liss released her and picked up the cocoa, sipping without tasting.

"You're not selfish. You're a realist," Dan said. "You know damned well that your mother will drive you crazy if she's living in the same town. I get along just fine with Mac and Vi, but your mother is not the easiest person in the world to tolerate. She's good at handing out criticism and stingy with praise."

Liss's lips trembled and once again she felt her eyes brim with tears. "They might have to live here, at least for a while."

"Tell them we haven't got room."

She had to laugh at that. "We have two guest rooms and a full attic that could be turned into a mother-in-law apartment. And they know that better than anyone since this was their house before it was ours."

Liss stood abruptly and scooped up both mugs, even though Dan hadn't touched his cocoa, to carry them to the sink. She stood there with her back to him, waiting to see what he would say next. Something comforting would be nice.

"Assisted living, huh?"

*Not* what she'd hoped for. She concentrated on rinsing the mugs and placing them on the drainboard. "Margaret says they're considering the place that's going to be built on the Chadwick property."

"It could take a year or more to go from blueprints to finished buildings."

He would know. He'd spent a lot of years in the construction business.

She slumped where she stood, suddenly too weary to talk about it anymore. A moment later, she was once more gathered into Dan's strong arms.

"We'll figure it out," he promised. "Finding solutions to problems is one of the things we do best."

# Chapter Six

Some of the new inventory Liss and Margaret had purchased in Canada arrived in Moosetookalook before
they did. After a short and broken night's sleep, Liss threw
herself into the task of rearranging the shelves in the shop
to make room for additional stock. The job had to be done
anyway, and it had the added attraction of keeping her
mind off all the things she didn't want to think about.

Investigating the contents of the envelope Cindy had
given them was a low priority, especially since Margaret
had already taken a preliminary look. The mailer hadn't
even made it into the house. It was still in the back seat of
Liss's car, where Margaret had tossed it on their way out
of Chadwick. By Wednesday, Liss's second morning back
at work, she had all but forgotten it existed.

She mounted the front steps at Moosetookalook Scottish Emporium at the usual hour, more or less awake after
coffee and toast and the short walk from her house to the
shop. She inserted her key in the lock and froze when it refused to turn. It took her a moment to understand the reason—the door was already unlocked.

"Oh, no," she whispered. The memory of that ransacked
hotel room vivid in her mind, she turned the knob and
stepped into the Emporium.

It looked exactly the same as it had when she closed up the previous evening. The lemon-scented furniture polish she'd used on the shelves still hung lightly in the air, together with a faint whiff of perfume coming from a display of decorative candles. Liss's nose twitched, as it always did. She disliked the smell of those candles. They'd been one of the few mistakes she'd made when purchasing stock. She'd promised herself more than once to lose them if they didn't sell soon. Today might be the day she actually tossed them in the trash. Meanwhile, since no foreign aromas wafted her way and a closer examination of the wares she offered for sale revealed nothing out of place, she slowly began to relax.

At the same time, she gave herself a mental slap upside the head for being so foolish as to rush into what might have been a crime scene. She was relieved that it wasn't, but if no one had broken in, how had the door come to be unlocked?

Liss was positive she had secured the shop at closing the previous day. She was meticulous about locking up, a habit acquired from Margaret, who lived right upstairs. Liss's aunt was even fussier about double-checking doors. Windows, too. She was at heart a trusting person, but she was also a woman living alone. At least, she had been alone until she'd acquired the two Scotties as companions.

Did she rely on them now as watchdogs? Was it possible she'd gone out through the shop and neglected to close up again?

Liss's walk-through to check shelves, displays, and the contents of the stockroom brought her to the stairwell door just behind the sales counter. Opening it, she stood at the foot of the stairs leading up to Margaret's apartment, listening hard. She'd like to believe that Dandy and Dondi would sound the alarm if there was an intruder, but she had no great confidence in their talent as guard dogs. She'd seen how soundly they slept and knew that they were more likely to fawn over a stranger than attack.

Once again she looked around. She saw nothing that was out of place, but she couldn't quite shake the feeling that someone had been in the Emporium before she arrived.

Belatedly, another possibility occurred to her. What if Margaret's apartment and not the shop had been the target? Spurred into action by that thought, she ran up the stairs, her ascent far from silent. Even before she reached the top, a joyful barking came from inside the second-floor rooms, along with the welcome sound of her aunt's voice.

"Hush, Dondi! Settle down, Dandy." Margaret opened the door just as Liss reached the landing.

"Thank goodness you're okay," Liss blurted.

"Why on earth wouldn't I be?"

"Your door wasn't locked." If it had been, she'd have heard the sounds of the deadbolt turning and the chain being lifted out of its slot.

"I've been out already this morning." Margaret sent her a puzzled look. "I took the dogs for a walk."

"Did you leave through the front?" At last—a logical explanation.

"No." With that one word, Margaret dashed Liss's hope of an easy answer. "We went out through the stockroom. Why?"

Liss told her.

Margaret frowned. "I can't swear that door was secure when I turned in last night. I used the outside stairs when I took the dogs for their final run. The back door was definitely locked this morning, though, and I relocked it after we came back in. You know I'm careful about things like that. Is anything missing from the shop?"

"Not that I could see, but I should probably check stock against my inventory lists."

"Sit down and have a cup of tea first." Margaret took a firm grip on Liss's arm and towed her into the kitchen. "Chamomile, I think."

Liss let herself be seated on one of the stools around the center island, but her thoughts continued to race. Why was she so upset? It wasn't as if anything had been stolen. Margaret was fine. The dogs were fine.

"Are you certain you didn't just forget to lock up?" Margaret asked.

Was she? And was she making a mountain out of a molehill? It wasn't like her to get so rattled over nothing.

"I'll feel better when I'm sure everything is accounted for," she said aloud. "And I may have Dan check that lock, just in case there's something wrong with the mechanism." It was a deadbolt. Weren't they supposed to be tamper-proof?

"I'll give you a hand with the inventory," Margaret offered. She set a steaming cup of tea on the counter.

Liss grimaced. "I don't suppose you have any coffee?"

"I do, but you aren't getting any. You're nervy enough already. Drink up."

Three pairs of eyes, one human and two canine, stared at her until she complied. She didn't care for the taste, but she did feel calmer after she'd drained the cup.

"There's no sense in wasting your day catering to my paranoia. I can handle checking inventory on my own."

"It will be no trouble at all," Margaret insisted. "I didn't have a single thing planned for the day, other than taking another long walk with my babies."

As if they knew she was talking about them, Dandy and Dondi performed a fast little jig around Margaret's feet, one that would have sent a less agile woman sprawling.

"Go with Auntie Liss," Margaret told them when Liss got up to leave. "She'll let you out into your yard." To Liss, she added that she'd be down as soon as she'd washed her breakfast dishes.

Having been given their marching orders, all three obeyed.

An hour later, having changed her mind and decided that a complete inventory would be excessive, Liss had given a more thorough eyeballing to every shelf and rack and table in the shop and found not a single shred of evidence to suggest that someone had been inside Moosetookalook Scottish Emporium while it was closed. Was Margaret right? Had she carelessly left that door unlocked when she'd left work the previous evening?

"Are you sure you didn't hear anything odd during the night?" she asked her aunt.

"I'm sure."

"Did you have the TV on?"

Margaret sent her a sheepish look. "All evening, with the volume turned up."

"So, if someone was down here, moving quietly, you might not have heard footsteps?"

"Dandy and Dondi would have alerted me to an intruder."

Liss wished she could share Margaret's certainty, but even if the two dogs were awake and alert, they were accustomed to hearing people walking around below them. They were smart little pups, but they were still dogs. There would have been no reason for them to think anything out of the ordinary was going on.

The sound of the bell over the door had them both looking that way. Beth Hogencamp breezed into the shop, neatly dressed in brown slacks and a white shirt with a name tag pinned to her collar. Was the explanation that simple? She'd given Beth a set of keys before she and Margaret left for Nova Scotia.

"Hello, Beth," Liss said. "Were you here earlier today, before I got in?"

But Beth shook her head, setting long, dark brown hair in motion. "I had to help Mom at the bookstore this morning."

Liss tried not to let her disappointment show, or reveal that she'd completely forgotten that Beth was scheduled to work a half day at the Emporium.

"There now," Margaret said in a cheerful voice. "You don't need me now that Beth's here. I think I'll take my darlings for a walk in the town square."

With that, she was gone, leaving Liss to decide how much to tell Beth. Nothing seemed best. Instead, she complimented her on her outfit.

Beth frowned. "I've been wondering if it wouldn't be better to look Scottish when I work here. Didn't your aunt used to wear the clothes you have for sale? That's a great way to advertise the merchandise."

"Imagine you remembering that. You were just a little girl back when Margaret was in charge."

Liss had fallen out of that particular habit ages ago. When there were so many days with no walk-in customers, jeans and a sweatshirt were better suited to unpacking new stock and preparing items for shipment to customers who ordered by mail or over the Internet.

"If you want, you can pick out something to wear. Maybe I will, too."

As they examined the racks of women's clothing, especially the long tartan skirts, sashes, and frilly blouses, she asked Beth if she was majoring in business. All Liss knew for certain was that Beth had finished her first year at the nearby University of Maine branch at Fallstown, and that she was dating Liss's cousin Boxer. No, she corrected herself. Not Boxer any longer. Ed.

Beth's big brown eyes sparkled when she answered. "No way. I'm a theater major."

"Well, that explains it. You like dressing up in costumes. Did you design the uniform you're wearing now?"

"Of course. This is the work-for-my-mother-in-the-bookstore look." Grinning, she held up a very short tartan skirt. "How about this?"

"I'm sure Boxer—I mean Ed—would love it. Just don't bend over."

"Really? You don't care if I wear a skirt this short?"

"Whatever you feel comfortable in is fine." But she had to smile. Beth had been such a shy child. These days she was still quiet, but she certainly didn't lack self-confidence. "You can go full-out Highland dance costume if you want to."

Leaving her young assistant to mull over the possibilities, reasonably certain that Beth would eventually decide against the miniskirt on her own, Liss selected a more traditional outfit for herself and went into the stockroom to change into it. The skirt was floor-length. The blouse had long sleeves and a demure neckline.

The rest of the day offered few distractions. Too few customers meant that Liss had too much time to brood. Given that she had not an iota of proof that any unauthorized person had entered the shop, she waffled about what to do. It was not until she was ready to close, after double-checking every exit in the place, that she gave up trying to rationalize her way out of her conviction that she had not left the front door unlocked.

Instead of going home, she crossed the town square in

Beth's company. They separated at Main Street. Beth headed for the apartment above Angie's Books while Liss marched into the redbrick municipal building. Her destination was located at the end of the hallway—the Moosetookalook Police Department and the office occupied by Sherri Campbell, Chief of Police.

"Maybe someone's trying to steal your treasure map."

Although Sherri's wry expression and the hint of sarcasm in her voice provided ample evidence that she wasn't serious, Liss didn't dismiss the suggestion out of hand. "Maybe they were. Or maybe someone is after the papers I was given in Nova Scotia. I haven't had a chance to go through them yet."

"Liss, I was kidding. Sheesh! Paranoid much?"

Leaning forward across Sherri's battered Army-surplus-style desk, Liss waited until her friend met her eyes. "It's as good an explanation as any."

"I prefer the one where you're imagining things. People do forget to lock their doors on occasion, even you. It's not a sign of early dementia. It's just plain old human frailty."

"Oh, now you're trying to be philosophical! Thank you so much."

Liss knew her annoyance was way out of proportion to Sherri's attitude, but the more Sherri tried to discourage her from thinking someone had broken into the Emporium, the more convinced she became that it was the only logical explanation for that unlocked front door.

"Okay. Say you're right. What do you want me to do about it? You say nothing is missing, or even disturbed. So if someone jimmied your locks, all they did was come inside, have a look around, and walk right back out again."

"Breaking and entering is a crime." The words sounded

petulant, even to her own ears. "Sorry. I guess there isn't much you can do. I just wanted you to know what happened."

Discouraged, she sank into the uncomfortable visitor's chair opposite her friend and leaned her head back to stare at the tiles on the ceiling. She hadn't told Sherri about the murder in Chadwick or the burglary in Antigonish. This was the first time she'd seen her friend since she'd returned to Moosetookalook.

"Liss?" Sherri's voice broke into her reverie. "Is there something else?"

With a sigh, she launched into the tale of her misadventures in Nova Scotia.

Sherri was shaking her head by the time she finished. "No wonder you're jumpy."

"I'm not—"

"Yeah, you are, but it's understandable. You found your motel room unlocked and someone had been in there. It's only natural you'd wonder when you walked into a similar situation at the Emporium. The thing that puzzles me is why you didn't hightail it over here to get help before you went inside. What if there had been a break-in? What if someone had still been in the shop when you arrived?"

"What if I made a fool of myself crying wolf? And I would have, since there was no one there and nothing had been disturbed. I wouldn't have come to you now if I could shake this feeling that someone did break in, even if he or she didn't leave any evidence behind. Do you think your officers could keep an extra sharp eye on my place for the next couple of nights?"

"That we can do. And I'll ask around at the other businesses on the town square to see if anyone else has recently discovered that they forgot to lock up." At Liss's glare, she held both hands up in the classic "I surrender" position.

"I'm taking you seriously, Liss. I swear it. There just isn't much I can do. Dusting for fingerprints would be a waste of time. Too many people have touched that door handle in the last twenty-four hours."

Liss was far from satisfied, but she had to admit that she could see Sherri's point.

"Margaret will be fine, if that's what has you worried. If your hypothetical thief had been interested in her apartment, he'd have gone on up there last night."

"I do not find that reassuring." Liss hesitated, then put into words the other idea that had begun to nag at her. "A man was murdered in Canada, Sherri. And our room was broken into and ransacked. What if both those things had something to do with our appointment to talk to Orson Bailey? What if he was killed to keep him quiet about something he discovered? What if the map I found really does lead to some kind of treasure and that map was what someone was looking for in Antigonish?"

"That's a whole lot of speculation."

Liss sighed. "You're right. I'm letting my imagination run away with me. After all, they caught the guy who killed Mr. Bailey."

Sherri looked thoughtful. "Where is the map now?"

"At home. And the photocopies I got from the historical society are still in the back seat of my car."

"Just to be on the safe side, you should go through those. Tell you what. If you're willing to spring for pizza or Chinese, I'll round up a babysitter and recruit Pete and we'll help."

"Are you sure?" Sherri had three kids—Adam, Amber, and Christina, who had just had her second birthday two months earlier—and cherished the time she was able to spend with them.

"Positive. We'll go through that material with a fine-tooth comb. If there's anything to find, we'll find it. If there's nothing, that should put your mind at rest."

An hour later, with Pete and Dan set to arrive momentarily, Liss finished scanning all the material in the packet into her computer and printing out copies. She carried them into the living room. She'd already scanned and made copies of the treasure map, doing that shortly after she'd found it.

Sherri sat cross-legged on the carpet, using the coffee table as a desk. At Liss's entrance, she looked up from the printout she'd been studying.

"Thanks for humoring me," Liss said.

"No problem. Your instincts have a tendency to be right on the money. I'd ignore one of your hunches at my peril."

Unsure whether to feel gratified or alarmed, Liss changed the subject. "I asked Margaret to join us but she already had plans. She was very cagey about them too. Wouldn't say where she was going or with whom. She's not dating your father again, is she?"

"If she is, I'd be the last person to know. Dad likes his secrets."

"Does the possibility bother you?" Sherri's parents were divorced.

"Not at all, but I've never been able to figure out what a cheerful, chatty, clever person like Margaret Boyd saw in a super curmudgeon like Ernie Willett."

Liss didn't understand the attraction, either. She left the pages with Sherri and headed for the kitchen. As soon as she returned with a tray of cheese and crackers and placed it on one end of the coffee table, Lumpkin magically appeared. His attention on the cheese, he walked across Sherri's thighs, sharp little claws fully extended. She yelped as they went through the fabric of her slacks to pierce her skin.

"Someone needs his nails clipped," Sherri muttered, "and to go on a diet."

Liss couldn't help but smile. "Lumpkin. Play nice."

Sherri laughed. "He doesn't know the meaning of the word. He was spoiled rotten long before you inherited him."

"At least he's grown out of the habit of leaping out at passersby and biting their ankles."

"Where's the other one?" Sherri sent a wary look around the room.

Liss followed her gaze but saw no sign of green eyes or black fur. "She'll turn up."

"That's what I'm afraid of." Sherri pretended the cats annoyed her, but Liss noticed that she had a sappy smile on her face as she watched Lumpkin steal a thin slice of cheddar cheese from the tray and carry it away to scarf down in private.

The sound of the back door opening told Liss that Dan was home. He didn't have far to travel from his day job—only a few yards across the lawn from his woodworking shop in the former carriage house—but he'd need a little time to clean up. Custom woodworking wasn't a messy occupation compared to some, but there were plenty of days that ended with him covered in sawdust.

Ten minutes later, he joined them in the living room, greeting Liss with a quick kiss and Sherri with a grin. "Roped you into helping, did she?"

"Actually, it was my idea. I needed a break from the kids."

"You ought to bring Adam in on this. He's old enough to appreciate the fun of a treasure hunt."

"This is not a treasure hunt," Liss insisted, giving him a solid thump on the upper arm. "We are simply solving a puzzle." But she was smiling too.

"In that case, I'm getting a beer before we start."

Dan headed back down the hall toward the kitchen. He'd just returned when there was a knock at the door.

"Get it while it's hot," Pete called out.

Liss recognized his voice, but his chunky, linebacker's body was nearly hidden by the stack of pizza boxes and only his dark hair showed above the six-packs of beer piled on top of them. Sherri made room for the food on the coffee table and they settled in to eat. Once they'd made serious inroads into the meal, Liss told Dan and Pete about finding the door to the shop unlocked.

"I know I got way too worked up over it," she admitted. "Chances are good that there's a perfectly logical explanation. Maybe the lock didn't fully engage last night, or maybe I just forgot to lock up."

"Whatever happened," Sherri chimed in, "we aren't going to take any chances. My officers will check all the doors around the town square for the next couple of nights to make certain everything is secure. I'd hate to think that people have to start installing sophisticated alarm systems in their homes and businesses."

Dan took a long swallow of beer. When he didn't look worried, the last of Liss's tension slowly dissipated.

When the pizza boxes were empty and most of the beer had been consumed, along with a bag of baby carrots as their nod to good nutrition, they got down to work. Silence fell as they each read a copy of the material Cindy had given Liss and Margaret in Nova Scotia.

Liss had gone through six newspaper articles before she hit something that rang a bell. *"Miss Euphemia Grant and her parents,"* she read aloud, *"are visiting Mr. and Mrs. Norman Chadwick this week from Yarmouth. Miss Grant attracted much attention at the cotillion Saturday evening by wearing a gown by Jeanne Lanvin that was featured in* La Gazette du Bon Ton.*"*

"So?" Long-dead fashion designers held little interest for Sherri.

"That's from a 1922 society column. During Prohibition. And that godawful painting I bought is of the *Grant* piper. And I think that must be Yarmouth, Maine, not Yarmouth, Nova Scotia." She fumbled for the folder of clippings about the Chadwick family that Margaret had checked out of the Moosetookalook Public Library. "Yes. Look. The portrait must have come into the family with Euphemia. She married Edgar Chadwick and they were the parents of Alison, the last of the line."

"I repeat: so?"

"So that's the link. Euphemia went to Chadwick, Canada, before the marriage. Maybe that's where she met Edgar."

"You're sure she wasn't a Nova Scotia girl?" Dan asked.

Liss nodded. "I've got her obituary right here. It says she was born in Yarmouth, Maine."

"I don't see what difference it makes. Adding Euphemia Grant doesn't change anything," Dan said, "unless you think the place shown on that map is in Yarmouth."

"We need more information on the Grants."

"Why don't you let Margaret handle that," Sherri suggested. "She's already researching the Chadwick family tree. And, really, how hard could it be to track down someone with a name like Euphemia? I think we got stuck with the grunt work. I'm going cross-eyed reading the small, faded print in these clippings."

Ten minutes later, she threw in the towel.

"The Canadian Chadwicks weren't just respectable, they were excruciatingly boring."

Liss had to agree. "Big fish in a small pond. If they hadn't had money, no one would have noticed them at all."

"Is Chadwick as tiny as Moosetookalook?" Sherri asked.

"It's a little larger." Moosetookalook's population was

only slightly over one thousand souls, although that number could nearly double when there was some special event going on at The Spruces.

Pete cleared his throat. "The Canadian Chadwicks may have been dull, but they obviously lived well. Where did the money come from? Are you sure they weren't secretly supplying Canadian booze to their American cousins during Prohibition?"

"Even if they did," Sherri said, "there doesn't seem to be any connection to the map Liss found."

"Why are you assuming someone is after that map?" Pete asked.

"Because we don't have any better explanation for the alleged break-in," Liss answered before Sherri could. "Go ahead and say it. I imagined the whole thing."

"The intruder in the Emporium? Maybe. But there's still a mystery surrounding the map." Dan sent her an encouraging smile. "What does it show? Why was it hidden? That has to mean something."

Liss gathered up the papers spread across her lap and dumped them on the floor, all but the map she'd found. Then, from her perch on the sofa, she addressed the others. "There are no similar landmarks in the map of the Chadwick property in Nova Scotia but they must match someplace. Any ideas?"

Pete consulted his copy of the map. "Odds are good that this is somewhere on the Chadwick property off Raglan Road. Ten Mile Stream runs through there, but . . ." He shook his head as his voice trailed off. "I can get hold of some topographical maps of the area, but it will be like looking for a needle in a haystack. What is that lot? Ten acres?"

"Smaller. Closer to five," Sherri said, "but it's all heavily wooded. I wonder if we're taking this too seriously. What if it's only a game? A kid's game. Why not? The last of the Chadwicks was a little girl. Maybe they threw her a birthday party and a treasure hunt was part of it. I'll have to remember that when Amber's next birthday rolls around."

Liss considered the idea and rejected it, but that led to a new line of thought. "I wonder if there's any way to have the map tested to find out how old it is. It looks like it's been around for at least a century, but what if it's a lot older? There were smugglers in Maine long before Prohibition. Pirates, too."

"Or it could just *look* old." Pete's suggestion put a damper on her enthusiasm.

"How can we find out? Are there tests to tell if paper is modern or not?"

"There are, but they can get pricey."

Liss reminded herself that she didn't have a pressing reason to pursue the mystery of where X was located. Even if her own family had been involved, she'd have a hard time justifying a major outlay of cash to have the paper in the map analyzed. On the other hand, she hated to leave any stone unturned. When Pete and Sherri started to make noises about leaving, she came to a decision. She sent Pete home with a corner of the original map and instructions to see what he could find out about it without breaking the bank.

# Chapter Seven

The next day, when Liss made her regular deposit at the bank, she also paid a visit to her safe-deposit box. She and Dan had rented it to hold birth and marriage certificates, deeds to property, and a few grotesque pieces of Victorian-era jewelry she'd inherited from a great-grandmother. In the cubicle, the box open on the small table provided for customers, she wondered why she kept them. She wouldn't be caught dead wearing a mourning brooch that contained her great-grandfather's hair. The onyx ring was equally off-putting. Neither they nor the necklaces, pocket watches, and stick pins were particularly valuable.

Another decision for another day, she told herself, and retrieved the map from her tote. After placing it on top of the documents and jewelry boxes, she closed the lid. She wasn't sure why she wanted it in a safe place, but she felt better once it was locked away.

Back at work, out of sight was not out of mind. While Liss packaged mail and online orders for shipment, she had plenty of time to wonder whether they would be able to spot any of the same landmarks on her map and the topographical map Pete had promised to produce. When she took a break from her labors to pour herself a cup of coffee, she took out the copy she'd tucked into the pocket of her jeans and unfolded it.

She relished sipping the hot, fragrant brew, even though it was eighty degrees outside and the shop had no air-conditioning. It had never seemed worthwhile to install it when the number of days of oppressively hot, humid weather could be counted on the fingers of one hand. Most of the time, open windows and a couple of fans were adequate to keep the air moving at this time of year.

Bent over the sales counter, she studied the details on the hand-drawn map. They were as vague and unhelpful as ever—generic trees and water. There was a dearth of useful information. Still, it had to show a specific place. Otherwise, why bother to draw it, let alone conceal it behind a painting?

The bell over the door jangled, putting an end to her speculations. Two women staying at The Spruces entered the shop, demanding Liss's full attention. After that, she had a steady trickle of customers and what with one thing and another, she didn't give the map another thought for the rest of the day.

After closing, Liss walked the short distance home and let herself into the front hall. She stopped just inside the door, surprised that neither cat appeared to greet their source-of-all-food. Lumpkin and Glenora were almost always waiting to make sure that her first priority upon entering the house was to refresh the water in their bowls and open a can of cat food. She saw no sign of them on the stairs leading to the second floor nor in the living room to her right.

She started toward the kitchen, straight ahead at the end of the short hallway, her mouth already open to call them. She snapped it shut again at a muffled thump from the direction of the dining room. A few more steps brought her close enough to see that the door into that room from the kitchen was closed. That was unusual enough to have her backtracking. She peered into the living room and stared in disbelief at the pocket doors that separated it from the dining room.

They were closed too.

Liss was positive they'd been open when she left for work that morning. They were *always* left open. Her vague sense that something was wrong solidified when she caught sight of Lumpkin hiding behind the sofa. He wasn't easy to see. The carpet was a pale yellow shade close to the color of his fur. She looked around for Glenora and finally spotted her on the highest shelf of the built-in bookcase. Both cats were staring at the closed pocket doors.

Liss fumbled in her tote for her cell phone as she backed toward the front door. Her hand was shaking as she turned the knob, but once on the porch, she hesitated and stared at the phone in her hand. She was going to feel like a damn fool if she called the police for help and it turned out to be her own husband in the dining room. On the other hand, she'd never seen Lumpkin and Glenora behave in such an odd way before. Something was definitely off-kilter.

Her finger wavered between speed dial numbers. Sherri's office? Or Dan's cell phone? Maybe both. Concern for her husband won out. As she stepped off the porch, heading for the police department, she called her husband. He answered on the first ring, before she was halfway across the street.

"Are you in the shop?" she asked.

"Just about to call it a day." His cheerful voice reassured her as nothing else could have.

"Stay put. I'll be there in a second." Abruptly, she changed direction and sprinted up the driveway that led straight to the workshop. It took all her willpower not to look toward the dining room windows as she passed them. If someone was in there and saw her, she didn't want to alert him to the fact that she was onto him.

Dan already had the workshop door open. His face was a mask of concern. "What's wrong?"

"There's someone in the house."

He took a step toward the back door but stopped when she caught his arm.

"What if he's armed?"

"He? Did you see someone?"

Liss shook her head. "I heard a noise. And the cats are acting strange." Listening to her own words, she realized how foolish they sounded, but her conviction that someone was in the house did not waver. "I heard a thump from the dining room and both the door from the kitchen and the pocket doors are closed. Unless you—?"

Dan's frown deepened. "They were open when I made myself lunch."

Liss and Dan stayed where they were until Sherri responded to Liss's phone call. She brought Officer Mike Jennings with her. He went in the front door while Sherri took the back. Five endless minutes passed, during which Liss clung to Dan's hand so tightly that her fingers went numb.

"Clear," Sherri announced. "No one is in your dining room. No one is anywhere in the house."

Liss didn't know whether to be relieved or dismayed. As had been the case at the Emporium the previous day, it appeared that there was no evidence to back up her suspicion. Together, she and Dan checked every room. Nothing was out of place. Nothing seemed to be missing.

"Someone was in the dining room," she insisted when they rejoined Sherri. "That same someone was probably all over the house. And the only reason I can think of, since the intruder didn't steal anything, is that he was looking for the map."

"That's a bit of a leap," Sherri said.

"Do you have a better suggestion?" Dan asked her.

Sherri didn't need to say anything. Liss could tell what she was thinking.

"It's not all in my head!"

"I didn't say it was." Sherri stood, hands on hips, in the middle of Liss's living room. She huffed out an impatient breath. "Liss, I get that you'd like to find the treasure. I'd like to solve that mystery myself. But you need to consider the possibility that you may be just a tad obsessed with that map."

"I know that!" Liss snapped. "And I know that the odds are against there being any connection between the map and the burglary in Antigonish. And I don't really suppose anyone followed me back home from Canada just to try to steal it. But you didn't see the way the cats were acting. Plus, I *heard* an intruder."

"What, exactly, did you hear?"

"A thump."

"The cats—"

"The cats were here in the living room."

"The house was locked, right?"

"Well . . ."

"We don't lock up during the day," Dan cut in. "Nobody does."

"So someone could have gotten in," Liss said.

Sherri rolled her eyes. "Nothing was out of place in the dining room. Nothing is missing. Maybe the thump came from outside. A bird may have hit a window. It happens."

"Someone was in there," Liss insisted. "He bumped into something, or knocked it over, but he put it back the way it was so we wouldn't notice. I did not imagine that sound."

Sherri rubbed one hand over the back of her neck, as if she had the beginnings of a tension headache. "I'll write up a report. We'll continue to keep an eye on all the buildings around the town square. Meanwhile, why don't you take some simple precautions. Lock your doors, even in the daytime."

"Okay. Thanks." Liss managed not to sound grudging. It wasn't Sherri's fault that she hadn't heard that thump for herself. Of course she had doubts.

Her friend's expression softened. "I wish I could do more, but without evidence, my hands are tied."

As soon as she left, Dan headed for the kitchen and started pulling out pots and pans. "I'll make supper. You've had a rough day."

"*You* believe me, don't you?"

"Of course I do. I'm just not sure that someone being in the house is connected to the map. Maybe Zara came over from next door to borrow a cup of sugar."

"Any of our friends would have stopped in at the workshop or at the Emporium or given one of us a call first. They wouldn't just barge into the house when no one was here. And they would not close the pocket doors. And the cats—"

"Okay. Okay. I agree." He already had water boiling for pasta.

Liss fished a half-full jar of spaghetti sauce and a slab of leftover meatloaf out of the refrigerator. Fifteen minutes later, square "meatballs" were simmering in sauce in the microwave and Dan was getting ready to drain the noodles. A few slices of Italian bread and a bottle of wine completed the simple meal.

Considerably calmer after she had something in her stomach, Liss contemplated the possibility that Sherri was right. She could be letting her admittedly active imagination run away with her. Her life would be much simpler if she could convince herself that was the case.

Then the phone rang. Dan answered and listened in silence for a few minutes. When he hung up, his expression resembled the proverbial thundercloud.

"What's wrong?" Liss asked.

"That was Sherri. She just talked to Sergeant Childs. It seems the Mounties didn't get their man, after all. The guy who confessed made the whole thing up to get a roof over his head and three square meals a day. They have no idea who killed Orson Bailey, or why. For all we know, it *could* be connected to that damn map."

"Thanks for coming in," Sherri said the next morning. "Is Beth minding the store?"

Liss acknowledged that she was and settled into one of the hard plastic visitor's chairs. She folded her hands in her lap and waited.

"Things have been slow in Moosetookalook this summer," Sherri said. "Aside from a few minor traffic accidents, the occasional drunk and disorderly, and that fistfight at the pizza parlor two weeks ago, it's been pretty quiet. I'd like to keep it that way."

Liss felt herself tense. "It isn't as if I *want* my theory about everything being connected to the map to pan out."

Sherri eyed Liss's shoulders. "Relax, will you. You're as rigid as a two-by-four. I'm not about to bring out the rubber hoses." She left her comfortable desk chair, bringing a notepad and pen with her, and resettled herself in the other plastic horror.

"I'm fine."

"You're not fine. You're skittish as a colt and I'm pretty sure I can guess why. Now that you're aware that the police in Canada don't have Bailey's murderer in custody, you're more convinced than ever that all the odd things that have happened to you are linked."

"It's possible. The killer is still on the loose. Maybe—"

"And maybe not. That's what I want to talk to you about. I want you to go back to the beginning and tell me everything."

"You mean finding the body?" Liss repressed a shudder. "To be honest, I'd just as soon not relive that moment."

"If your instincts are on the money, this started at the auction. I was there, too, but I want to hear your recollections. For starters, you weren't the only one bidding on that portrait. Who were the others?"

Liss reached back in her memory and conjured up a dark-haired man and a stocky older woman. She described them to Sherri. "I don't know their names. The dark-haired man bought several other pictures. I saw him with them after the auction. I thought at the time that he must have been after the frames because they were nice, old, hand-carved wooden ones."

Something else niggled at the back of her mind, bringing a frown to her face.

"What?" Sherri paused with the pen poised over the pad.

"It's probably nothing."

"Let me decide that. You know it's the little details that make a difference in an investigation."

"It was when we were in Truro. Margaret and I came out of the shop where we'd been talking to a man about kilts and I nearly collided with a passerby. For just a second I had the strongest impression that I knew him, and a bit later I decided it was because he'd looked a lot like the dark-haired man at the auction. I was sure it was just a chance resemblance. What would he have been doing in Nova Scotia?"

"You say this guy looked a lot like him." Sherri leaned closer, intent on Liss's answer. "Could it have been the same man?"

"The whole encounter was over in a split second. All I got was an impression. The dark hair and the height were right, but I never got a good look at his face."

Sherri sat back and scribbled a note to herself. "I'll see if I can find out who he is. Since he bought things at the auction, there should be a record of his name and address."

"The auctioneer was from away," Liss reminded her. "Maybe even out of state."

"It doesn't matter. The auction itself was held in my jurisdiction and that gives me leverage to persuade the new owner of the Chadwick mansion to hand over contact information."

"I don't know much about the guy who bought the place besides his name. Brad Jardine, right?"

Sherri nodded. "He wasn't at the auction, but he must have raked in a pretty penny from selling the contents of that old house. What about the other bidder?"

Liss shook her head. "I think she must have left before the end of the auction. I didn't recognize her, either."

"Okay—moving on. We dropped the portrait when we were trying to load it into the cruiser, the frame broke, and you found the map hidden between the back of the canvas and the wooden backing. Can you remember if anyone else was nearby at the time? Could someone have seen you find it?"

Liss squeezed her eyes shut and tried to recall the scene. She hadn't been paying much attention to what was going on around them. "There were cars and trucks leaving the auction. People were walking to where they'd parked and loading up. I don't remember anyone in particular, and if someone was watching us, I didn't notice."

"You didn't see anyone you knew?"

Liss started to shake her head, then stopped in mid-movement. "There *was* a woman at the auction who might still have been there. She's just a little bit of a thing—even shorter than you are. She bought that old steamer trunk full of papers and books. It was more than she could manage on her own and I was going to hunt up a dolly for her, but then a good Samaritan came along and helped her haul it to her van."

"And she was around when we dropped the portrait?"

"She might have been. I'm not sure."

"Did you get her name?"

"Beamer," Liss said, and felt her lips twist into a faint smile. "Benny Beamer."

"Funny name for a woman."

"It's short for something. She told me, but I've forgotten. I *do* remember that she said she bought the trunk for the ledgers. She was doing research."

"Writing a book?"

"I don't remember that, either. I do remember thinking what dull reading they'd be."

Sherri wrote Benny's name in her notebook, adding a question mark after it.

"I feel a little guilty calling official attention to a perfectly innocent person," Liss said.

"I'm not going to arrest her. I just want to find out if she saw anything."

"Well, while you're at it, ask her if she found anything in those papers that might relate to our mysterious map."

Sherri duly added another reminder to herself. Then she

pressed on, asking questions about everything that happened in Nova Scotia and making copious notes. By the time they came back to Moosetookalook and the two instances of intruders who might or might not exist, Liss felt as wrung out as a used dishrag.

"Don't take this the wrong way," Sherri said, "but as I pointed out last night, the only thing tying all these things together is you."

"Me," Liss agreed, "and maybe the map."

Sherri sighed, stood up, and stretched. She tossed notebook and pen onto her desk and went to stare out the window that overlooked the parking lot in back of the municipal building. Liss watched her warily.

"Are you having second thoughts?" she asked.

"And third and fourth," Sherri admitted. "But don't worry. I'll check into the people at the auction and I'll follow up with the RCMP. If we're really lucky, the Mounties will find a match for the fingerprints they took at the motel in Antigonish."

"Better yet, maybe Sergeant Childs will call you back to say that the real killer has been caught."

"Wouldn't that be nice!"

Liss heaved herself out of the chair and was about to head back to the Emporium when there was a brisk knock at the door and Margaret Boyd sailed into the office without waiting for an invitation.

"I hope you don't mind," she said as went straight to Sherri's desk, cleared a space, and unrolled a large sheet of paper, anchoring the corners with a stapler, a paperweight, a coffee mug, and a pencil cup. "I thought you should both see this right away. It's the Chadwick family tree."

Liss stared at the names and dates connected by lines. There were a lot more of them than there had been.

Sherri came up to stand beside her. "What am I looking at?"

"This is the Grant line," Margaret said, pointing to the right side of the chart. "Liss was right. They lived in Yarmouth, Maine." Next her finger moved to the far left. "These are the Chadwicks."

Liss was quick to catch on, especially when she realized that the two lines met in the middle with the marriage of Edgar Chadwick and Euphemia Grant. Only one line extended down from their names: their daughter, Alison. Margaret had recorded her marriage to Emmett O'Hare and the dates of their deaths. They'd had no children.

"If you look over here," Margaret continued, indicating the Chadwick side of the chart, "you'll see that the Canadian line also died out, and much earlier than the American one."

"What's this line with the question mark?" Liss asked.

"The younger son went West and was never heard from again." Margaret said. "His father, Norman Chadwick, had three children, a daughter and two sons. The daughter, Daisy, never married. The elder son, Albert, married but had no children. They were still living when Edgar Chadwick was running rum during Prohibition, but if we're to believe our friend from the Chadwick Historical and Genealogical Society, there was never any hint locally that Norman or Albert were in on the scheme. They appear to have lived in genteel respectability, doing good works and leaving their property to the town that was named after their ancestor, Eli Chadwick, who founded the place shortly after the American Revolution."

"What about the Grants?" Liss asked. "Could the map have come from that side of the family, the way the portrait itself must have?"

"Euphemia was the last of her particular line. She brought money into the marriage, maybe even enough to allow her husband to go straight. It was his father, you see, who was the smuggler. I checked the local newspapers here in Carrabassett County as well as reading those articles Cindy copied for us. Like their Canadian counterparts, Edgar and Euphemia Chadwick are mentioned almost exclusively in connection with social events, good works, and civic organizations."

Margaret spoke with so much enthusiasm about her research that Liss couldn't help but be impressed. When she said so, Margaret grinned.

"Someday soon, I'm going to share with you my discoveries about the migration of English colonists from Massachusetts to Canada before the Revolutionary War and the return of many of them to the newly formed United States when the Maritimes failed to become the fourteenth state. Did you know that one of our own MacCrimmon ancestors appears to have crossed paths with a Nova Scotia Chadwick back in Colonial days?"

"I had no idea." And even less interest. Liss felt certain the map she'd found wasn't *that* old.

It was Sherri who stepped in to firmly steer the conversation back to the present. "This is helpful," she told Margaret. "You've eliminated certain possibilities. Now both of you need to leave so I can do my thing."

"I'm going back to the library," Margaret said, rolling up the genealogical chart and departing at warp speed. She was more her old self than Liss had seen in months.

"And I'll head back to work." Liss's voice held considerably less enthusiasm. "I'm expecting a busy afternoon. One of the regional Scottish clan societies is holding their annual conference at The Spruces."

Members would start arriving soon for events, workshops, and panels that would run straight through the next two days, up until the business meeting on Sunday evening. Since no one attended every offering, Liss hoped at least some of the attendees would take the time to come into town—a ten-minute drive—and visit the only shop in the state that specialized in Scottish imports and Scottish-themed gift items.

Poor timing, she thought as she left the municipal building and crossed the town square. If she was honest with herself, she'd have to admit that she'd much rather be spending the time roaming the old Chadwick property to see if she could match the landmarks there to those on the map.

# Chapter Eight

The next day, Saturday, Liss was at work when the phone rang.

"I tracked down the auctioneer," Sherri said. "Your dark-haired man is named Aaron Lucas, but I haven't made contact with him yet. The real question mark is Benny Beamer."

"How so?" Leaning on the counter, Liss watched in amusement as Beth held one outfit against herself, then another, trying to decide which to wear for the day.

"She listed an address in South Portland with the auction house, but it turned out to be a condo that belongs to someone else. They weren't available but the manager had never heard of her. Do you remember anything else from your conversation with her? Any clue to where she might be living?"

"Sorry, no. We didn't talk that long."

*Curious,* Liss thought when they disconnected, but she didn't have time to solve any new mysteries. Customers had begun to trickle in. By noontime, when there must have been a break in activities at the conference, the trickle turned into a flood. It wasn't until around four in the afternoon that the steady stream dried up.

Liss flopped down in one of the comfortable armchairs in the shop's "cozy corner" and put her feet up on the coffee table. The area had been designed as a waiting area for impatient spouses, as well as a place to browse through the Scottish-themed books shelved nearby. "Come and take a load off, Beth," she called as she leaned her head back against the upholstery and closed her eyes.

Days like this were great for the bottom line, but they were also exhausting. She almost groaned aloud when she heard the bell over the door jingle to signal that yet another customer had come in.

"Good afternoon," she heard Beth say to the new arrival. "Welcome to Moosetookalook Scottish Emporium."

A voice that seemed vaguely familiar answered her, asking if the proprietor was in.

With a sigh, Liss got to her feet, but her tiredness disappeared when she saw who had come in. "Ms. Beamer! What a coincidence. I was hoping for another chance to talk to you."

"Really? What about?"

"Come and sit down and I'll tell you all about it. Coffee? Tea?"

A few minutes later, Liss had Benny settled in the cozy corner with steaming mugs of coffee and a plate overflowing with chocolate chip cookies freshly baked that morning by Patsy of Patsy's Coffee House. Benny helped herself to the biggest one and bit into it. An expression of sheer bliss came over her face.

Deciding that no good purpose could be served by being coy, Liss plunged right in. "I've had some peculiar things happen to me since we met at the auction. The police are investigating. The chief has been attempting to locate anyone I spoke with there to ask what they remember seeing at the time. According to her, the manager at the address you gave the auction company has never heard of you."

"That's easy to explain." Benny reached for another

cookie. Once again, she wore a blouse with long, loose sleeves. The butter-yellow color brought out the blond of her curls. "I was only there a short time. I'm a professional house sitter. I was living there, watering the plants and taking care of the pets for the owners while they were on vacation. No one else in the building had any need to know my name or their neighbors' business."

"House sitting. Huh." As an explanation, it made sense, and Liss didn't find it all that hard to imagine not having a permanent address. When she'd been on the road with the dance company she'd spent years without any permanent abode. "Where are you now? Are you currently working for someone in this area?"

Benny grinned. "I've been staying at The Spruces since just before the auction. I decided it was time to treat myself to a vacation." She took a sip of the coffee, meeting Liss's eyes over the rim. "So, how can I help you?"

"I have two questions. First, had you already left by the time I was loading the portrait I bought into my friend's car?"

"Probably." She managed an apologetic look. "Sorry I took off without thanking you for your help, but this nice young man offered to carry the trunk and I was anxious to get it back to my room and start going through the contents."

"No problem. What did you find?"

"Decades worth of ledgers." Benny's eyes twinkled. "A gold mine!"

"You said you were doing research for a book."

"An article. I'm what's known as an independent scholar. The house sitting keeps a roof over my head and gives me the freedom to move around as needed. I also take the occasional job as an adjunct instructor."

"I don't think I know what that means," Liss admitted.

"Part-time and poorly paid. Lots of colleges and universities use them. Saves them money. Even the house sitting is a better deal and living in South Portland was great. I could do research at the Glickman Library at USM as well as at the Portland Public Library."

As she launched into a more detailed explanation of what she was working on, Liss tried to focus. Almost at once, she felt her eyes begin to glaze over. Margaret, she thought, would appreciate hearing about Benny's work much more than she did. Still, the subject gave her an opening to ask her second question.

"So," she broke in when Benny paused for breath, "you bought the trunk for the ledgers, but surely there were other papers in the trunk, as well—letters, perhaps?"

Benny gave an airy wave. "I'm only interested in the ledgers."

Liss took a sip of coffee to allow time to gather her thoughts. How much should she tell Benny? She might have something Liss wanted, but it was doubtful she'd share without an explanation. Liss had heard about the pressure in academic circles to "publish or perish," and she'd read more than one murder mystery in which a college professor was prepared to kill to protect a work-in-progress. Independent scholars must be even more anxious to produce original work. One or two articles in prestigious journals could put Benny on the fast track to full-time employment by a college or university . . . if the fact that she looked and sounded younger than the average student didn't count against her.

She cleared her throat. "About the auction. Afterward, my friend and I dropped that portrait I bought."

"Oh, no!" Benny's hazel eyes widened. "Was it badly damaged?"

"Only the frame. The thing is, there was something hidden behind the canvas. A map. Ever since I found it, I've been trying to determine what location is shown on it. To help out, my aunt has been digging into Chadwick family history."

Ten minutes later, Liss had hit the genealogical high points, repeated the local gossip about smuggling during Prohibition, and produced a printout of the map for Benny to study.

"The most likely location for these landmarks is on the Chadwick property here in Moosetookalook."

Benny giggled. "Oooh—treasure! I love it!"

"It's not likely to amount to anything, but I plan to keep investigating. It occurred to me that since there were papers as well as ledgers in that trunk you bought, some of them might mention the map. Would you be willing to let me take a look at them?"

At once, Benny's amusement vanished. Suddenly, she looked less like a moppet and more like a young woman with a mission. "I can't risk losing valuable information that might have a bearing on my research."

"I understand that. Perhaps, then, you could keep an eye out for anything that might relate to this map."

While Benny considered, she snagged the one remaining cookie. "Sure. Why not?" she said after she'd swallowed the last crumb. "I'll let you know." Tucking the copy of the map into her shoulder bag, she stood. "Anything else you need from me?"

Liss shook her head. She found Benny's lack of curiosity remarkable. The other woman had never once asked what peculiar things had prompted the police to check into the address she'd listed in South Portland. Most people would also have wondered if the cops still wanted to talk to her. Benny was halfway to the door before Liss called her back.

"Wait a minute. If you didn't know anyone was looking for you, why did you come to the Emporium and ask for me?"

The dimple appeared when Benny smiled. "You were so nice to me at the auction that I thought you might like to have lunch with me sometime. I'll be in town a while longer. I still have to check into several local sources of information."

After Benny left, Liss flipped the OPEN sign to CLOSED and locked up. Only when she turned to face the sales counter did she remember she was not alone in the shop.

Beth sat on the high wooden stool next to the cash register, elbows resting on the countertop and chin resting on her fists. Her impish grin told Liss she'd overheard the entire conversation between her boss and Benny Beamer.

"No smart remarks about treasure hunts," Liss warned her.

Beth jerked her head in the direction Benny had gone. "I can't imagine her as a college instructor. She looks about thirteen."

"I just hope appearances are deceiving and she's the serious scholar she claims to be. Right now I'm short on clues. I can go out to the Chadwick mansion, but without a starting point I don't see how I can match any landmarks to the map."

"May I see it?" Beth asked.

Liss produced another copy. She'd made plenty of printouts.

After studying it for a few minutes, Beth said, "You need to get hold of something to compare this to."

"Pete Campbell is working on finding a topographical map of the area."

Beth shook her head. "*Old* maps. From back when the Chadwick house was built. Architect's drawings would be even better. The really good ones show trees and—"

Liss's whoop of delight startled her young friend and nearly caused Beth to tumble off the stool. Thanks to the preparation that had gone into turning the Chadwick mansion into a haunted house all those years ago, she knew exactly where to lay hands on a set of building plans.

The sun was still up when Liss and Dan finished supper.

"The Sox played this afternoon, right?" she asked her baseball-loving husband as they cleared the table.

"Won seven to three."

"So you're free for the evening?"

He sent her a suspicious look. "What did you have in mind?"

Liss produced a large roll of yellowed paper, the edges flaking with age. She'd stopped at the town office on her way home and had been lucky enough to find one of the town's selectmen, Pete Campbell's mother, catching up on some paperwork on the weekend. When Liss had explained her errand, Thea had been willing to let her borrow what she needed from the records room.

"I thought I returned those."

"You did. I checked them out again."

"Sherri had it right. You're obsessed with that treasure map."

Dan said the words lightly, but she gave him a sharp look. She took it as a good sign that he was smiling. Her determination to find answers was a sign of commitment to a goal. Surely that was a good quality.

Fifteen minutes later, Dan signaled for the turn onto Raglan Road. Once they were on the winding drive that led up to the mansion, Liss's anticipation quickened. All her senses were on alert. She was positive that with the help of the sketch that showed the grounds as well as the house she'd be able to spot the markers on the map. She only needed one to start with. The others landmarks would follow.

When Dan's truck rounded the last twist in the driveway, he abruptly hit the brakes. "Well, hell!"

"Oh, dear," Liss murmured.

Where the mansion had been, there was now an empty lot. The new owner had been true to his word. He'd already torn down the entire structure preparatory to building senior citizen housing. There was nothing left except the cellar hole.

Liss hopped down from the passenger seat and picked her way closer. She was mindful of potential debris, but Brad Jardine's crew had done a good job of cleaning up. The basement had been filled in too.

"I wonder if they even noticed the entrance to the old tunnel," Dan said. It had led from the cellar of the house to the bank of Ten Mile Stream.

"Given the condition it was in the last time we saw it, the entire thing probably collapsed the moment the bulldozers went into action. What I don't understand is how he managed all this without anyone noticing."

"He must have brought the equipment in from the other end of Raglan Road." Dan frowned. "Looks to me like he meant to hide what he was doing. He didn't use local labor or I'd have heard about it."

"Maybe he was afraid the historic preservation people would object to his razing the house." She'd heard talk about finding a way to save it, back before Jardine bought the place, but it hadn't come to anything.

"Watch your step," Dan warned as he made his way around the perimeter, heading for the stream. The cleanup hadn't removed rocks or roots, either of which could trip up the unwary.

Reminded of why they'd come, Liss followed him. They hadn't gone very far when she heard the sound of another vehicle approaching. Reluctantly, they turned back.

A shiny blue pickup truck pulled in next to Dan's battered white GMC Sonoma, his truck-of-all-work. Still reliable, it was more than a dozen years old and looked decidedly shabby next to the gleaming monster parked beside it.

The driver was also upscale, dressed in a suit that shrieked custom-made. His long strides ate up the distance until he was face-to-face with Dan and Liss. His body language suggested that he was spoiling for a fight.

"This is private property." The man snarled the words rather than speaking them. "You're trespassing."

Dan shifted position until he stood between Liss and the newcomer. He kept his voice level. "No harm in neighbors taking a look around, is there? After all, we might have an aged parent or two who'd be interested in moving in when the new building goes up."

Liss kept silent. Assisted living was not a topic she wanted to discuss.

The man's eyes narrowed and his gaze fixed on the thick roll of paper Dan held. For a moment his reaction hung in the balance. Then the prospect of future profits won out. He offered Dan his hand. "I'm Brad Jardine. I own this land."

"Dan Ruskin. Ruskin Construction. Perhaps you've heard of us?"

"Can't say that I have. I brought in my own men from Portland for the demolition."

*That figures,* Liss thought. *Some folks just can't grasp the idea that the "other Maine" has as many skilled carpenters, plumbers, and electricians as more affluent places to the south.* Jardine would have done better to support the local economy. He'd have saved himself some money that way too.

Oblivious to Liss's disapproval, the current owner of the Chadwick property began to extol the virtues of the senior living community he had planned. "There will be both assisted living apartments and separate cottages. A clubhouse will offer a place to meet for games and other recreation. Then outdoors," he added, "we'll put in a shuffleboard court and a swimming pool."

"You do know this is Maine, right?" Dan asked.

Despite having mixed feelings about her parents' future plans, Liss barely stopped herself from snickering. She'd seen places like the one Jardine was describing on her visits to Arizona. She'd heard they were popular in Florida, too. In southern states, the design worked with the climate. Here? Not so much.

Jardine ignored Dan's sarcasm, or else it went right over his head. "You said you had an elderly parent?"

"Yes. My father."

Liss glanced at him in surprise before it occurred to her that Joe Ruskin was the same age as Margaret. So was Ernie Willett, Sherri's father, although neither he nor Joe showed any signs of slowing down.

"He's still quite mobile," Dan continued, lying through his teeth. "I expect, if he moved here, he'd want to walk around the property for exercise rather than take a yoga class or swim. Mind if we take a look around? Get the lay of the land, so to speak?"

Jardine didn't look thrilled by the request, but he agreed. Liss could only suppose that he hesitated to offend the relatives of a prospective tenant. If he was sensible, he could also see that they couldn't possibly do any harm. What he thought of the rolled-up plans they'd brought with them was anyone's guess.

"No need for you to stick around," Dan said. "We'll just wander a bit. It will be too dark soon to see much of anything anyway."

Without waiting for agreement, Dan took Liss's arm and guided her around the old foundation, once again heading east from there toward Ten Mile Stream.

"Be careful where you step," Jardine said. "The terrain is still somewhat rough."

Still? What was he planning to do—flatten everything out? Liss glanced over her shoulder in time to see the real estate developer look at his watch, scowl, and head for his truck. She asked the question aloud as the sound of the engine faded away.

"Could be." The grimness in Dan's voice came as no surprise. Ruskin Construction always tried to leave natural features, especially healthy trees, in place.

Picking their way through high grass, underbrush, and pines growing close together, Liss and Dan made their way toward the sound of running water. They came out into the open at the top of a steep embankment overlooking a rock-strewn riverbank. Ten Mile Stream, which formed one of the property's boundary lines, was some twenty feet wide at this point. In the days when the tunnel had been in use, it had been sufficiently deep to allow small boats to navigate it.

Liss took extreme care picking her way down to the water. Once there, Dan went first to look for the old door to the tunnel. It was still there, but beyond it were only fallen support beams and mountains of dirt.

"I bet Jardine didn't even know this was here," Liss said.

"I should probably tell him, so he can fill it in properly. It's impassable the way it is, but kids might still try to crawl through. I'd hate for someone to be injured or be trapped in there."

"Never mind that now. What about the drawings?"

Since what looked like a river or a stream appeared on the map, they had decided that it was logical to start from the same point on the architect's drawings. Liss's hope was that if they stood on the bank and looked toward the house, they'd spot some other landmark from the map.

She removed a copy from the back pocket of her jeans and turned it so that the water feature in the drawing faced her. Looking up, she swept her gaze over rocks and trees, but nothing jumped out at her. Although the sun was low on the horizon, its bright beams still shone through the branches above her head. Shadow and light played on the forest floor, where many a year's accumulation of leaves and pine needles gave the barest hint of a path. The smell of wild roses tickled her nose.

Dan unrolled the architect's plans and looked from the rendering to the reality and back again. Then he moved a little farther along the course of the stream and repeated the exercise. "Huh," he said.

"Got something?"

"Maybe. Let me see your map."

Liss hurried to his side and handed it over, trying to see what it was that he'd spotted. Dan studied the map and the plans for a moment longer, then pointed, first to the map and then into a thickly overgrown area to the northwest of their position. Wild raspberries grew side by side with brambles and sumac and assorted underbrush that Liss could not identify.

"What am I looking at?"

"Sight past the raspberry bushes and squint. See it?"

After a concentrated effort, she did. She looked at the

map again to make certain, but assuming that Dan was standing in the right place by the water, and that the map she'd found showed the Chadwick property in Moose-tookalook, then the spot marked with X aligned with something roughly oblong in shape and located in the middle of that tangle of bushes.

"An old building?" she guessed.

"Part of one. We're only about a hundred yards from the house right now. That's a spot beyond where they planned to put outbuildings when the house was built, as-suming the architect included everything in the plans, but I can definitely see something there that's made of red brick."

"We need to take a closer look."

"Not tonight." He rolled up the plans and offered her his hand to help her up the embankment. "By the time we fight our way to that spot it will be too dark to see any-thing. Besides, we can't do more than look without Jar-dine's permission."

"He isn't going to give it." She was all for investigating now and worrying about ownership later.

"We won't know till we ask." Dan slung an arm around her shoulder, steering her firmly toward his truck. "Maybe he'll be so intrigued by the notion of finding treasure on his land that he'll offer to give us a hand with the search. Besides, unless there's another way to reach that section of the property, we're going to have to uproot a whole heck of a lot of shrubbery just to get at it."

The next day they returned to Ten Mile Stream, but this time Brad Jardine was standing between them as they studied the anomaly they'd identified the previous evening. Jardine held a printout of Liss's map.

In the distance, church bells rang out, signaling the start

of Sunday services. Closer at hand, small critters scurried through the underbrush, disturbed by the presence of the three humans.

"You say you found this behind a portrait you bought at the auction?" Jardine asked.

"That's right," Liss said. "Intriguing, isn't it?"

He made a dismissive sound, but since he'd agreed to come out to the property with them this morning, she was pretty sure he'd already decided to allow them to dig on the site. It was hard to resist the lure of a treasure map. In some ways little boys, and little girls, too, never entirely grew up.

"I can't tell from here if that's a wall or the remains of a building," Jardine complained.

"There are several small structures shown on the original plans." Dan indicated their locations on the unrolled architect's rendering. "I don't know if they actually built all the outbuildings that are shown here, but this is what they intended. There was to be an ice house, since the Chadwicks built their mansion around 1859, well before they had refrigerators. They also planned to put in a smokehouse, so they could smoke their own meat." He tapped the drawing. "This is a chicken coop. Here's the carriage house."

"There's no sign of any of those now," Jardine said, "and that brick wall we're looking at couldn't be any of those. It's in the wrong place."

"It may have been built later."

"Or else they wanted to keep its location secret," Liss suggested. "Maybe it was a still." She'd had all night to imagine about what they might find this morning.

"Unlikely," Dan said. "The Chadwicks were importing, not manufacturing. But it may have been the building where they stored their bootleg hooch." He turned to Jardine. "I imagine you heard all the stories before you bought the place."

"I didn't put much stock in them."

"Maybe you should have." And Dan proceeded to tell Jardine about the tunnel.

Liss couldn't help but grin at the developer's shocked expression and the haste with which he agreed that it should be filled in immediately, before anyone could be injured and sue him.

"Getting back to our brick wall," Liss said. "Is it necessary to cut through all that underbrush to reach it?"

Jardine frowned. "There should be a way in from the other side. I don't recall seeing the remains of a building there, but I haven't been over every inch of the property." He set off at a brisk pace that left Liss and Dan scurrying to keep up with him.

After a few minutes of hard walking through a heavily wooded section of the property, Liss once again caught sight of faded red brick. Reaching what turned out to be a tumbledown wall was easy after that. Too easy. It looked as if someone had taken a machete and whacked a path through the raspberry bushes to their goal.

Dan fingered a broken branch. "This was done recently."

"During the night, do you think?"

"I wouldn't be surprised."

Jardine's scowl could have soured milk. "What the hell is going on here? First you people come up with this cockamamie story about a treasure map and then someone else trespasses on my property and—" He stopped short, breaking off in mid rant, to stare at the ground beside the remains of the wall.

Someone had dug a series of holes. They extended the length of it, each one about a foot deep.

"I guess we aren't the only ones hunting for treasure." A

chill raced along Liss's spine at the possibility that someone had followed them the previous night and watched
where they went. Had that person crept close enough to
listen to their conversation . . . and was that someone the
same person who killed Orson Bailey? Sherri would say
she'd just made a huge leap in logic, but Liss was not
about to discount any possibility.

One section of brick wall was all that was left of what
had once been a small building. Whatever it had originally
been used for, it appeared to have been a ruin for a long
time. Weeds, underbrush, and even a small tree grew close
to it.

"Do you suppose they found anything?" Dan asked, indicating the holes.

"If they did, they're guilty of out-and-out theft." Jardine's face darkened in anger. "Anything buried on this
land belongs to me."

Liss couldn't look away. Jardine's nostrils flared like
those of an enraged bull. Then and there she decided that
any clever quips or smart-ass comments would be best
kept to herself.

Having knelt to examine the holes more closely, Dan
shook his head as he rose. "I don't think whoever dug these
had any luck. Look at the pattern. Down about a foot, then
on to the next one." He peered over the wall. "There are
holes on the other side, too. If he'd found something, he'd
have stopped digging, but these go right up one side and
down the other."

"Maybe he didn't dig deep enough," Liss suggested.

Jardine snorted. "You talk like you think this person believed a shallow hole would be sufficient to find what was
buried at X."

"Maybe he knows what it is. We sure don't."

Liss joined Dan beside the wall. She was surprised at its thickness. Why would anyone want walls like that in an outbuilding? Tentatively she ran her fingertips over the uneven surface on the side nearest her. This *was* the location shown on the map. There was no question in her mind about that.

She stared at her hand, resting lightly on a broken brick. What if no digging was required? What if the X indicated a hiding place inside the wall?

Her spirits sagged at the possibility that the "treasure" had been destroyed along with most of the old building. The other three sides and most of this one had crumbled decades ago. The odds against finding anything in the section that remained were enormous. Despite that, she began to search brick by brick. Using slow and careful sweeps, she ran her fingers over the rough surface. She could hardly believe it when she felt one of the bricks shift at her touch.

She warned herself not to get her hopes up. Of course some of the bricks were loose. They were old. The mortar had fallen out. The entire wall was in danger of collapsing from sheer age. But when she explored further, she realized that the thickness of the wall was significant.

"Can you say *cliché*?" she murmured. Finding a hiding place behind loose bricks was a hackneyed plot twist, but that didn't mean it wasn't possible.

Liss pushed and pulled and tugged on the loose brick. At first nothing happened. Then, as if her efforts finally struck just the right spot, four bricks still mortared together abruptly popped out from the rest of the wall.

With only a two-inch projection to grab hold of, Liss needed Dan's help to pull the section free and set it on the ground. A gaping hole was left behind. She'd found a hiding place right where X marked the spot.

Eagerly, heedless of spiders and other creepy crawlies that might be inside, Liss thrust out a hand. Dan caught it before she could plunge it inside.

"Wait." He unhooked a flashlight from his tool belt and turned it on.

Liss bent closer as the beam illuminated the interior. When she drew back, disappointment put a catch in her voice. "It's empty."

Dan took a turn to look, but he was shaking his head when he stepped away from the wall.

"I can't believe we went through all this for nothing!" Liss grabbed the flashlight. Holding it in one hand, she extended the other into the hole. The sides were smooth beneath her fingers, making it all too obvious that she'd been right the first time. There was nothing inside. She felt every inch of the hiding place before she gave up, but in the end she had to admit defeat. If there had ever been anything hidden where X marked the spot, it wasn't there now.

# Chapter Nine

It took Liss a full twenty-four hours to snap back from her disappointment. On Monday, the one day of the week that the Emporium was closed, she tried to cheer herself up after her morning workout with next-door neighbor Zara at Dance Central by having a late breakfast of blueberry muffins and coffee at Patsy's Coffee House.

It always felt good to exercise the muscles in her long dancer's legs. She didn't need that strength for much these days, but she was determined to stay in shape. Besides, she had to counteract the calories she packed on at Patsy's somehow. When the last crumb was gone, she headed for Sherri's office to report on the dismal end of the quest for X. She rapped on the door and let herself in just as Sherri was finishing a phone call.

"How's it going?" Liss asked.

"You see before you the exciting life of a cop—telephoning, online searches, and paperwork. But I did turn up a few interesting details about your friends from the auction."

Liss plunked herself down in the uncomfortable visitor's chair. "Tell me. I need cheering up."

Sherri gave her a questioning look but obliged. "You remember that I was able to find out the name of your dark-haired man?"

Liss nodded. "Aaron Lucas, right?"

"Yes. And he listed a home address in Connecticut. With that information to go on, I did some more digging. I wanted to see if any red flags came up in a background check, in particular if he'd ever been arrested. I also sent a query to find out if Lucas crossed the border into Canada at around the same time you did. The results have started trickling in. Lucas is ex-military and currently works for a company called Cornwall Pharmaceuticals."

"Never heard of them," Liss said.

"Me, neither, but I figured nothing ventured, nothing gained, so I gave them a call. I was on the phone with them just now. I learned a bit more about Aaron Lucas but I'm not at all sure what it means. Cornwall Pharmaceuticals is a small Connecticut-based drug company. Lucas works for them as head of security. I wasn't able to talk to the man himself because according to what a helpful personnel officer told me, Lucas is on vacation. He's walking the Appalachian Trail."

"And therefore almost impossible to reach," Liss finished for her.

"Yup."

"Wasn't there a politician a few years back who claimed he was hiking in the wilderness when he was really meeting his mistress somewhere in South America?"

"You have an even more suspicious mind than I do," Sherri said. "My first thought was that even if the information on Lucas is correct, it doesn't necessarily put him in the clear. The northern end of the Appalachian Trail runs fairly close to Moosetookalook."

Liss frowned, wondering if they'd just solved the mystery. "No way is he out there with only a backpack, not if he was buying all those framed pictures at the auction."

"What did he want with them in the first place?" Sherri asked.

"That's easy. He was looking for something hidden in a frame. He didn't find it in any of the ones he purchased because it was behind the painting I bought."

"That fits." Sherri allowed herself a small, self-satisfied smile. "I bet it won't surprise you to hear that someone dropped off a half dozen framed pictures at the Share Shack at the Moosetookalook transfer station the day after the auction. They're in good condition but the backing has been removed on each and every one of them."

"He took them to the *dump?*"

"Either that or he abandoned them by the side of the road and someone else picked them up and disposed of them properly."

"So he was looking for the map and he may still have been looking for it when my motel room, my shop, and my house were searched."

"It's certainly possible, but all we know for sure is that Aaron Lucas isn't just an innocent bystander who collects picture frames for a hobby. If I can get confirmation that he followed you to Nova Scotia, then I can issue a BOLO. If I can find him, I can bring him in for questioning."

"How long before you have that information?" Liss shifted uncomfortably in the hard plastic chair. "And when are you going to get decent furniture for this place?"

"Go to the next town meeting. Vote for a bigger budget. As for my query, an answer should come in today or tomorrow. Every time someone crosses the border, their name is collected, along with a lot of other information. It goes into a database other law enforcement officers can access *if* they've been approved and certified. Unfortunately, certification costs money and Moosetookalook is too small to consider the expenditure worthwhile. I had to call in a favor from a friend. He's checking for me, but it isn't a high priority for him."

Liss got up and began to pace. "If this guy has been fol-lowing me since the auction, is it possible he got to Chad-wick first? Do you think he could be the one who killed Orson Bailey?"

"Why would he, Liss? You're the one with the map."

"I don't know, but then I don't know exactly how Bai-ley died, either. If Lucas is ex-military, maybe he just snapped. You hear about that sort of thing a lot. In fact, that was what the woman at the historical society thought must have happened when we believed that the man who confessed was guilty."

Sherri was shaking her head. "Don't go off half-cocked. If it was Lucas you saw in Truro, then he could certainly be the one who broke into your motel room, but how could he know you were stopping in Chadwick on your way there? To have killed Bailey, he'd have had to get there ahead of you."

Deflated, Liss sank into the slightly less uncomfortable chair behind the second desk in Sherri's office. She used one foot to swivel slowly from side to side as she thought that over. "You're right. If he followed us, he'd be behind us. But he has to be the one who let himself into the shop last week, and into my house, too. And if he trailed Dan and me out to the Chadwick property on Saturday evening and saw us spot that brick wall, then he could easily have returned later that night to dig those holes."

Sherri sent her a blank look. "Holes? What holes?"

"That's what I came in to tell you." Liss filled Sherri in on what they'd discovered on Sunday morning. "Do you think he found what he was looking for?"

"I hope he did, and that he's long gone."

Liss bristled. "You can't mean to let him get away with it!"

Sherri sighed and stated the obvious. "As far as anyone can prove, Lucas hasn't done a darned thing he can be prosecuted for. Even if he followed you to Canada, that isn't a crime."

Liss was still sputtering over the injustice of that situation when Sherri's phone rang.

"Go home, Liss," she said as she reached for it. "It's too soon for this to be my friend with the information on Lucas. Odds are about equal that I either need to go round up somebody's runaway cow or that I'm wanted to direct traffic at the scene of a jackknifed pulp truck."

Liss was at the door when Sherri called her back.

"It's none-of-the-above. Pete's been looking for you. He says he tried the house and the Emporium and got answering machines and that your cell went straight to voice mail."

"I turned it off when I was at Dance Central." Liss reached for Sherri's phone but her friend refused to relinquish it.

"Tell me first," she instructed her husband.

Liss thought about trying to punch the speaker button but decided against engaging in an undignified tug-of-war. Instead, she waited, watching Sherri's frown deepen as she listened a few moments longer and then disconnected.

"Well?" Arms crossed, stance hostile, Liss glared down at her friend from the other side of the desk.

"Your map isn't old enough to have anything to do with Prohibition or rum running."

"But—"

"Prohibition lasted from 1920 through 1933. Pete consulted an expert. He says the paper the map is drawn on was made in the 1940s or later."

"It looked a lot older than that."

"Maybe it got wet or muddy before it went into the picture frame." Sherri shrugged. "Who knows? Pete says the expert, who didn't charge him, by the way, told him it's easy to identify modern paper because it fluoresces much brighter than older paper. All they had to do was use a blacklight on it. Paper from the 1920s or earlier would have had a darker appearance and look dull in color."

Liss took a moment to process this information and to remember that they'd never known exactly what they were looking for. "If the map didn't have to do with smuggling," she mused aloud, "could it still have been put there by one of the Chadwicks?"

"Why not?" Sherri tapped the end of her pencil on the desk, a sure sign she was growing impatient with the subject.

"But why?" Liss made an inarticulate sound and stamped her foot. "Ooh! I *hate* not knowing."

Sherri chuckled. "Let's think this through. Maybe you've been on the wrong track. Maybe the map has nothing to do with the Chadwicks at all."

Liss stared at her. "You may be onto something. There was another owner, right? Someone bought the mansion from the town and then, apparently, did nothing with it but install better locks before selling it to Brad Jardine. I can go check the registry of deeds and find out who else owned the place."

Sherri glanced at her watch. "How about I treat you to lunch—egg salad sandwiches at my place?"

"Thanks, but—"

"You want answers? The quickest way to get them is to ask my mother-in-law and this is her morning with the grandkids."

They walked to Sherri's house, since it was only a few blocks from the municipal building, and found the normally prim and proper Thea Campbell, Moosetookalook's longest-serving selectman, playing Barbies on the floor with her granddaughters. If she was embarrassed to be caught in such an undignified position, she shrugged it off with a self-deprecating grin.

"Do you two want to join us?"

"You're doing a great job on your own." Sherri's lips twitched when she tried to contain a smile. "Why don't I handle making lunch?"

Sherri's formidable mother-in-law appeared to have mellowed in the last couple of years. Liss hoped that relaxed attitude would extend to an informal sharing of information. She could find the buyer's name in the record books, but Sherri had been right—it was much easier to ask Thea. The added benefit was that she'd know any good gossip associated with the sale.

The sandwiches went together quickly, since Sherri had made the egg salad before leaving for work that morning. Within ten minutes of arriving at the house, everyone was gathered around the kitchen table, even two-year-old Christina.

The toddler sat on a booster seat in order to reach her plate. Acting very grown up at nearly six, Amber announced that she wanted tea with her sandwich and that she wanted the crusts cut off her bread.

"I was reading them a story—"

Sherri held up a hand to stop her mother-in-law's explanation. "I know the one." She fixed Amber with a stern look. "Does your ladyship thinks she's a princess who was kidnapped by gypsies?"

Widening her eyes to achieve a look of greater innocence, Amber nodded earnestly and held up her plate. Sherri obligingly trimmed off the crusts. Then she ate them herself. "What?" she demanded when she saw Liss shaking her head. "I hate to waste food."

Liss was not always comfortable around children and had opted not to have any, but today she got a kick out of Amber's antics. Once the little girl reached the age of twelve or thirteen, Liss might even feel comfortable talking with her. By the time they were teenagers, kids wanted to be treated like adults. That thought reminded her that Sherri also had a son. "Where's Adam?"

"Off with his friends," Thea said.

"What friends?" A worry line appeared in Sherri's forehead.

Thea sighed. "He has too many of them for me to keep track. Stop fussing, Sherri. The boy is fifteen years old. He doesn't need a babysitter anymore."

Sherri looked as if she wanted to disagree but not if it would irritate Thea. They finished eating in silence.

Pushing her plate to one side, Liss cleared her throat. "Thea, we were wondering if you could do us a favor?"

The request earned her a suspicious look before Thea shifted her focus to her daughter-in-law. "I can't stay later than one. I already told you that."

"That's fine," Sherri said. "I have an afternoon sitter lined up. I'll even stay till she gets here if you want to leave early."

"This isn't about the kids," Liss interrupted. "It's about the town."

Thea's eyes narrowed even farther. Despite the impression she'd given while playing with her granddaughters, she was tightly wound. "What about the town?"

"Do you happen to remember who owned the Chadwick mansion before Mr. Jardine bought it?"

"Is that all you want to know? I thought you were leading up to something difficult. It was a man named Lester Widdowson, an older gentleman. After all the trouble we had with that property, the board of selectmen was anxious to unload it. Maybe too anxious. He bought it for a fraction of what it should have sold for."

"Did he ever live there?" Liss asked.

"Not that I know of. Perhaps it was in worse shape than he'd anticipated, although if he had a contractor take a look at the place, it was no one local. I do know that he never applied for any building permits."

When Thea had left and Sherri's sixteen-year-old baby-sitter had arrived, Liss and Sherri walked back to the police station.

"Now what?" Liss asked.

"Now I do some checking on Lester Widdowson. More of the glamorous life of a law enforcement officer!"

"Back to the computer?"

"Back to the computer," Sherri agreed.

Liss veered off toward her house when they reached the town square. She was still there, enjoying her day off by sitting on her front porch and reading the newest mystery in the Mistress Jaffrey series, when Sherri emerged from cyberspace and stopped by to share what she'd found.

"Lester Widdowson died last year," she reported after she'd accepted a tall glass of lemonade and a comfy seat on the porch swing. Liss perched on the wide railing, her back propped against one of the roof supports. "It was his son, Sean Widdowson, who sold the property to Jardine."

"You're grinning like the cat that swallowed the ca-nary," Liss observed. "What else did you find out?"

"Oh, nothing much." Sherri took a long sip of her drink before she deigned to satisfy her friend's curiosity. "Only that, by a rather remarkable coincidence, Lester Widdowson once worked for Cornwall Pharmaceuticals, the very same outfit that now employs your mysterious dark-haired man."

\* \* \*

"Tell me again why you were in such a rush that we had to drive all the way to the coast to talk to this guy."

Dan sounded disgruntled, but that was an improvement over the near silence of the earlier part of their trip from Moosetookalook. After a couple of hours cooped up together in the cab of his truck, bouncing over a variety of winding, two-lane roads, they'd hit U.S. Route 1 for a blessedly short stretch, given summer traffic, and now sat at the Cook's Corner intersection waiting for the light to change.

Liss sighed. "We're here because Lester Widdowson's son and heir wouldn't agree to answer questions over the phone."

At the time, it had seemed simplest to agree to meet Sean Widdowson at his summer place in Harpswell, but when she'd told Dan where she was going, he'd insisted on dropping everything to accompany her. Now that they were getting close to their destination, Liss was glad of his company, but she could have done without the surly attitude.

"You didn't have to come."

"Yes, I did. You don't know anything about this guy."

"I'm pretty sure he's not an ax murderer."

The light changed and Dan drove straight through the intersection. They didn't have much farther to go. Liss dug in her tote for the directions Widdowson had given her. He'd called his place a cottage. That could mean anything from a rustic cabin to a palatial mansion like the ones in Bar Harbor.

She glanced at her watch, surprised to see that it was not yet five in the afternoon. It seemed eons ago that Sherri had stopped by with her news about Lester Widdowson. Things had moved swiftly after that. Armed with the phone number Sherri had unearthed, Liss had made the initial contact with Sean. When he'd stated his conditions for discussing his father and the house in Moosetookalook, she'd seen no reason not to agree. It was her day off, after all.

Lost in her own thoughts, she was startled when Dan asked for landmarks. He veered right, following the signs to Harpswell.

"After a boathouse with a green door, it's the second drive-way on the left." She consulted her notes. "There should be a sign that says 'Widdowson' and the house number." She gave him the latter and startled looking for the boathouse.

The driveway was short and sloped steeply upward. The garage was to their right. Trees boxed in the area on the other two sides, but straight ahead she could catch glimpses of glistening blue water. When Dan parked and they got out, Liss could not, at first, see either a house or a path through the mini-forest.

"Someone likes his privacy," Dan said. "This way."

A gap between two pines brought them to the top of a series of wide brick steps cut into the hillside. These wound back and forth and ever downward. There was no railing. "Not exactly handicapped accessible," Liss muttered.

"Not exactly a public building, either."

At the bottom stood an ordinary house with blue shut-ters. Flowering shrubs had been planted in the tiny yard, but Liss had a feeling that the primary appeal this "cot-tage" held for Sean Widdowson was the view from the back. There, undoubtedly, he'd have a deck that looked out over the cove.

"Isolated," Dan said.

"Not an ax murderer," Liss repeated under her breath. She raised her hand to knock.

Widdowson must have been watching for her. The door

opened almost before she had time to take a step back. He
was short, slender, and twentysomething, wearing khaki
shorts, a Red Sox T-shirt, and a neatly trimmed beard.

"Ms. Ruskin?"

"Yes. Thank you for agreeing to meet with me, Mr.
Widdowson."

He gave a curt nod and shifted his gaze to Dan. "And
you are?"

"*Mr*. Ruskin."

Widdowson gave a short laugh. "I'm flattered that you
think she needs a bodyguard."

"You wouldn't be if you knew what's been going on
lately."

Widdowson's finely shaped eyebrows lifted in a question. "I'd like to hear that story. It's all grist for the mill."

With that rather enigmatic statement, he led them along
a hallway to the open space at the water side of the cottage. To the right was a living room with an enormous
fireplace and even bigger windows. A dining area and
kitchen were to their left, the former boasting a spectacular view of the island on the other side of the cove. Widdowson waved them toward the door to the adjoining
deck rather than into the chairs around the table. Liss
couldn't help but notice that there was no room on top of
the table for food or drink. Except for the space occupied
by a laptop, the entire surface was covered with papers
and books. The arrangement screamed "writer."

A few minutes later, settled in cushioned Adirondack
chairs and supplied with cold drinks, Liss asked him what
he was working on. Widdowson's answer confirmed Liss's
guess. He wrote science fiction under a pseudonym, and
was fairly successful at it too.

"I don't even know why I answered the phone when

you called," he admitted. "I usually let it go to the answering machine and I was in the middle of a particularly thorny scene at the time."

"I can understand why you wouldn't want to be interrupted, especially by snoopy questions from a perfect stranger." Liss tried to sound sympathetic, but it struck her that it would have been much more convenient for both of them if he'd simply set a time for her to call him back.

Dan sipped his soda and said nothing, but he kept a wary eye on their host.

"You said this is about my father?" Widdowson asked.

"Your father and the property he owned for a few years in Moosetookalook. Do you know why he bought it?"

"He didn't need a reason. The old man was batshit crazy."

Liss blinked at him in surprise. "I beg your pardon."

"My father was a research scientist who worked for a drug company until they fired him. Among other things, he'd been using himself as a guinea pig for some of the wonder drugs he was working on."

Having no idea how to react to that information, Liss simply nodded for Widdowson to continue.

"There's not much else to tell. We weren't close. He and my mother divorced when I was just a kid. By the time I found out what he was up to, he was on his deathbed and making even less sense than usual."

Widdowson watched a lobster boat slowly chug past on the water, but Liss had a feeling his thoughts had drifted far away from the peaceful scene before his eyes. She hesitated to pry into private memories, especially painful ones, but that *was* why they'd come.

"Did he ever mention a portrait?"

Widdowson gave a start and turned to stare at her. "Do you mean a painting, framed and all?"

"Yes." She leaned toward him. "It was in the house in Moosetookalook, left there by the former owners."

"Well, well."

Liss waited.

"It wasn't anything specific. Sorry to disappoint you. Just the incoherent, unconnected ramblings of a dying man who wasn't entirely sane to begin with."

"But he mentioned a portrait?"

"Not exactly. A couple of times he mumbled the word *frame*. Just that one word, out of context. Maybe you can explain what he meant?"

Although Liss was disappointed that Widdowson had no more to offer, that tidbit did seem to connect his father to the map. She produced the copy she'd brought with her.

"What the hell?"

Briefly, she told him how she'd come to discover the map hidden behind the portrait and that they'd determined it showed a portion of the Chadwick property in Moosetookalook. "We found the spot marked by the X. There was a hollow space behind some bricks in a falling-down wall, but it was empty."

"Well, I'll be damned. Looks like the old boy *was* a crook." He returned the map.

"You want to explain that?" Dan's thundercloud expression was back. Liss could almost hear him asking himself if this was a case of "like father, like son."

"After my father died, the company he used to work for contacted me. They claim he walked off with the formulas for several drugs he'd been working on. Not to put too fine a point on it, they accused him of industrial espionage. I was certain the claim was bogus, or else they were as crazy as he was, and that's what I told them. Then I let my lawyer handle it. I haven't heard from them since."

"Did you tell them about your father's mention of the word *frame*?"

Widdowson ran a hand through his hair, leaving it standing on end. "Yeah, I did, but I wasn't thinking picture frame. At the time, given the accusations they were making against him, I figured the old man must have been trying to tell me *he'd* been framed—that he'd been fired by the company and then framed for something he didn't do." He shrugged. "That interpretation was the only one I could come up with."

"How did they react when you told them that?"

"Hard to tell. There were two guys who came to talk to me. One of them never said a word. The other acted like he was convinced I was trying to hide something. He was a long way from satisfied that I'd told him all I knew."

"The quiet one—was he tall? Dark-haired?"

"Yeah. You know him?"

"Depends. Did you get a name?"

Widdowson closed his eyes for a moment. When he opened them, he said, "Lucas. Arnold . . . no, Aaron Lucas." He shrugged. "I collect names. I never know when I might want to use one for a character. The other guy, the one who did all the talking, was Kelsey. Maurice Kelsey."

"How long ago was it that you talked to them?" Liss asked.

"It was right after my father died, so that makes it almost a year ago. I haven't heard from them since, but that's probably because my lawyers warned them I'd sue for harassment if they showed up here again."

"When did your father leave Cornwall Pharmaceuticals?"

"I'm not sure. Like I said, we weren't close. But it couldn't have been more than a few months before his death."

"He already owned the Chadwick mansion by then," Liss murmured, "but why did he buy the place to begin with?"

Widdowson gave a snort and polished off his drink before he ventured an answer. "I can't say for sure, but I can make a guess. He was always obsessed with his research, and paranoid about other scientists beating him to a discovery. This house—it's off the beaten path, right?"

"Secluded," Liss conceded.

"Then my money is on him planning to set up his own lab there."

"It's not all *that* remote," Liss objected. "It's part of the village."

Dan spoke for the first time since settling into his chair. "Our permanent population is around a thousand people, but we have a thriving tourist industry. If not for all the trees surrounding it, the Chadwick mansion would have a clear view right down to the town square."

"Let me guess—picturesque and rustic as all get-out? You're lucky my father didn't go through with his plans. If this guy Kelsey is to be believed, then at least one of the formulas he was working on turned out to be highly explosive. If he'd blown himself up while conducting one of his experiments, it's likely he'd have taken half the village with him."

# Chapter Ten

Although it was getting late and the children would already be in bed, Liss insisted upon stopping at Sherri and Pete's house on their way home. Pete was working, since he was a patrol deputy for the county sheriff's department and changed shifts every week or so, but Sherri was home. In short order, Liss and Dan were settled on the sofa in the living room and Liss was telling their tale.

"Interesting," Sherri said when Liss had repeated everything Sean Widdowson had told them.

"I'd call it downright scary," Liss said.

"Relax." Dan grinned at her. "If anything was going to explode, it would have blown up when Jardine demolished the house."

Liss repressed a shudder. "Just thinking about what could have happened gives me the willies."

"Widdowson thinks that if his father hid something in that wall, it would have been a formula, not an explosive," Dan reminded her.

"But if Lucas found it—" Liss broke off when Sherri abruptly stood.

"You've established another link to Aaron Lucas. That's the good news." She retrieved a laptop from among the coloring books, alphabet blocks, and a grubby ball cap with the name of the local Little League team emblazoned on the front—the usual clutter on top of the small desk tucked into one corner. "I've been doing a little snooping of my own, semi-officially, since I came home."

Squeezing in on the sofa between Liss and Dan, she booted it up and opened a file. A photograph filled the screen.

"That was taken at the auction," Liss said in surprise.

"I remembered that there was a photographer there and tracked her down. She's doing a feature story for one of the antiques magazines down on the coast. She mostly took pictures of the items up for sale, but she e-mailed me all the ones that showed bidders." She tapped a finger on the screen. "That's Lucas, right?"

"That's him."

It was a nice, clear shot, showing him with his hand raised to bid on an item. The focused, determined look on his face might be mistaken for some as that of an avid collector, but Liss had a feeling it was more than that. To her, it looked as if he was going in for the kill.

She shook off the too-vivid impression when Sherri pushed slide show and asked who else she recognized.

"You look good," she said with a laugh when a picture of the two of them came up on the screen.

Sherri squinted at the screen. "My eyes are closed and my mouth is open."

"So are mine. Can we delete that one?"

"Pay attention. I need you to identify the other person bidding on the portrait of the piper."

Two more photographs faded in and faded out before Liss spotted her. "There. The older woman in the short-sleeved blue shirt."

"Oh, good," Sherri exclaimed. "We can eliminate her. That's Claire Mortimer. She has a small farm near where my mother and I were living when I first came back to Moosetookalook."

That was roughly halfway between the village and the county seat at Fallstown and provided at least a partial explanation of why Liss hadn't recognized her. "What was her interest, I wonder? If she's into Scottish heritage, I'm surprised I never ran into her before."

"She makes a pretty good living as a picker. She finds odds and ends locally and resells them at one of those auction sites online. I expect she thought the portrait was unusual enough to attract buyers."

"And she dropped out when the bids got too high." Satisfied, Liss returned her attention to the screen.

She identified Benny Beamer, easily recognizable by her corkscrew curls, and picked out several local people she knew. Sherri and Dan spotted others. There was a second picture of Aaron Lucas that showed him walking away from the camera. Liss couldn't decide if he looked furtive or if that was just her active imagination once more coming into play.

Bright and early Tuesday morning, before it was time to open Moosetookalook Scottish Emporium for the day, Liss took a slight detour and entered the municipal building. She waved to the town clerk as she passed the town office. Farther along the hallway but short of the door into the police department, a steep flight of stairs led to the second floor, where the Moosetookalook Public Library was located. Tucked under one arm, she carried the file of clippings on the Chadwick family, the one Margaret had checked out for her.

From the street, Liss had seen light coming from inside the library, but she was unsurprised to find the door locked. Dolores Mayfield was particular about adhering to posted hours. According to the schedule etched in the glass section of the door, the facility would not be open until noon.

Liss rapped impatiently on the heavy wooden door frame. "I know you're in there, Dolores," she called. "It's Liss Ruskin and I need to speak with you."

From the other side, she heard a sharp intake of breath. Yes, Dolores was there, all right. If Liss knew the other woman at all—and she thought she had a pretty good handle on her, having known her all her life—the librarian was in a quandary. It was second nature for her to get on her high horse, offended and affronted at Liss's audacity, and refuse to break the rules. On the other hand, Dolores Mayfield lived for gossip. She must have guessed by now, since she had a clear view of both Liss's house and the Emporium from the library windows, that something was up. Sherri was a friend and often visited both places, but two of the most recent visits had been official.

That Margaret had borrowed the Chadwick file would have told Dolores that whatever Liss was involved in had to do with the old Chadwick mansion, a place rife with secrets and skullduggery. Would she stick to her petty regulations and end up dying of curiosity? Liss was betting that she would bend the rules, just this once, for the chance to get an insider's scoop on the latest developments at the most notorious location in the village.

A loud click, the sound of the door being unlocked, had Liss fighting the urge to pump her fist in the air. She managed to assume a bland expression by the time Dolores stuck her head out. The librarian looked both ways, to make certain there were no witnesses to this breach of the rules, before she grabbed Liss's arm, hauled her inside, and locked up again.

"This better be important." Dolores's scowl was impressive.

Without giving Liss time to answer, she stalked away from her, heading for the enormous check-in desk situated in front of a bank of tall windows that overlooked the town square. From behind this highly polished barrier, Dolores ruled her library with an iron hand.

No one ever questioned her right to do so. She was, in her own way, a treasure. Although the facility was only open twenty hours a week, Dolores spent at least another twenty making certain that the two large rooms contained the best offerings the town budget would allow.

These days, the library provided far more than books and magazines. For some residents, it was the only place they could go to access a computer. For them that meant they had a way to look for jobs. Others, like Sherri's friend Claire, sold items at auction sites on the Internet. A few came to the library to receive and send e-mail, their way of keeping in touch with loved ones, especially those serving in the military. Students, who were bused to Fallstown to attend the consolidated school, also relied on the local library, not only to do research for term papers but for a quiet place to study when there were another half dozen kids at home. On the one evening a week the library was open, the place was packed.

"You're looking well, Dolores." Liss placed the file folder full of clippings on the desk.

Dolores's small, rimless glasses had slid partway down her long, thin nose. She gave them a poke to return them to their proper place and regarded Liss through eyes of the same steely gray as the roots of her improbably dark hair.

"You didn't check this out," she said. "Margaret did."

Liss wasn't surprised that Dolores remembered that detail. She and Margaret went way back. They'd graduated from high school in the same year, along with Dan's father and Sherri Campbell's dad. If age was starting to slow any of them down, Liss saw no sign of it.

Liss was struck by that observation. Most of the senior citizens in Moosetookalook seemed to be in remarkably good shape for their age. Maybe her folks were onto something, after all. She did not, however, have time to ponder that idea any further.

Dolores spoke again, demanding her attention. "What was so important that you couldn't wait until the library was open?"

Liss nodded toward the bulging folder. "Chadwick business."

"There aren't any Chadwicks left." But she leaned closer, her gaze avid.

Twenty minutes later, Liss had given the librarian a capsule account of the auction, the search for the location marked by X on the mysterious map, and the discoveries she had made in both Nova Scotia and, more recently, in Harpswell. She did not mention the murder of Orson Bailey, but she did share her suspicion that the break-in at the motel in Antigonish and the intrusions into her shop and her home might be connected to the map.

For a long moment, Dolores said nothing. While she mulled over Liss's story, Liss considered how best to pry information out of the librarian if she did not volunteer it. That Dolores knew something that would be helpful went without saying. Sooner or later, Dolores knew everything about anything that happened in their little town.

"Lester Widdowson was in here right before he bought the Chadwick mansion," Dolores announced.

"Here? At the library?"

"He wanted to know the history of the property, so of course I told him all the about rumors—the smuggling during Prohibition and the wild tales about Blackie O'Hare's buried treasure. By then, of course, we knew there wasn't any treasure, but Mr. Widdowson wanted to hear all the theories anyway."

"Did he say why?"

Dolores's smile was smug. "Looking back on it in light of what you've just told me, I'd say he was after information on potential hiding places on the property. Industrial espionage! Who would have thought it of such an ordinary-looking man? He was just a little squirt of a fellow with big glasses and one of those pocket protectors only the brainy kids used to wear when I was a girl." She shook her head. "I thought to myself at the time that he was a caricature of a scientist."

Liss let that observation slide, taking it with a whole handful of salt. Hindsight was always twenty-twenty. "He told you he was a scientist?"

"Not in so many words, but I looked him up after he left and found out that he worked for a drug company in Connecticut."

If the faraway look in Dolores's eyes was anything to go by, she was imagining Widdowson as the hero of some cloak-and-dagger spy thriller—an undernourished, bespectacled James Bond, cleverly arranging drop sites for his confederates.

"I don't suppose you were able to tell him where those hiding places were?" To the best of Liss's knowledge, Dolores had never been inside the Chadwick house.

"Well, no." The admission came out reluctantly, as if it pained the librarian to admit it. "But I did point out to him that if the Chadwicks really did smuggle booze into the country during Prohibition, they must have had large storage areas somewhere on the property. Otherwise, where would they keep it? And I did know to tell him about that old tunnel you and Dan discovered, the one that used to run down to the edge of Ten Mile Stream."

"How did he react to that information?"

"His eyes lit up like it was Christmas and his birthday and the Fourth of July all rolled into one."

"Is there anything else you can remember about him?" Liss asked when Dolores fell silent.

"Not about him, no."

Liss waited.

"As soon as he left, I went to the window." She gestured behind her.

"Of course." Liss sent her an encouraging smile.

"I watched him come out of the front of the building. There was a car parked at the curb, waiting for him. The driver was leaning against the hood, watching kids play on the merry-go-round in the town square. Widdowson got in on the passenger side."

"He had a driver?" That was new. "Did you get a good look at him?"

Dolores shook her head. "Just a glimpse from above, but it wasn't a him. It was a her."

By the time Liss was certain Dolores knew nothing more about Lester Widdowson, she had to cross the town square at a jog to open the shop on time. It wasn't that she expected much in the way of walk-in traffic, but it didn't do to post business hours and not keep them.

She had plenty to think about as she checked on orders that had come in overnight and began her usual routine of

packing and shipping. Dolores had never seen Lester Widdowson after that day, but she had been nosy enough to
read up on him. She'd uncovered the connection to Cornwall Pharmaceuticals, quite possibly *before* Widdowson
and the company parted ways.

Still, the only entirely new bit of information was that
he'd been accompanied by a woman. Dolores believed she
was a real estate agent, since Widdowson was looking to
buy property. It sounded as if she'd been dressed like one.
Most Realtors Liss had encountered went for the professional look—high heels and a power suit for the women.
The anomaly in this case was that the woman had been
wearing a hat. Dolores had been unable to see what color
her hair was or get a glimpse of her face.

Liss counted on the bell over the front door to warn her
if a customer came in while she was in the stockroom. She
was not expecting anyone to rap on the small window in
the back door. She was elbow-deep in bubble wrap when
she looked up and saw Benny Beamer standing on the
other side of the glass.

For a moment, Liss simply stared at her. The bright,
mid-July sun turned her pale yellow hair almost colorless,
what could be seen of it under a floppy hat designed to
project the super-pale skin of her face. She must burn as
badly as a redhead, Liss thought as she took off the security chain and unlocked the deadbolt. Once again, Benny
wore a gauzy blouse with long sleeves and a high neck.

"Hi, there." Benny's greeting was bright and friendly.
"Got a minute? I wanted to bring you up-to-date now that
I've had time to go through the papers in that trunk."

"You found something?" Liss couldn't quite keep the
anticipation out of her voice.

Benny sniffed the air. "Is that coffee?"

Resigned to playing gracious hostess in return for answers, Liss relocked the door. Benny eased herself onto one of the tall stools beside the worktable, watching as Liss filled two mugs and doctored each with a generous dollop of creamer and two packets of sweetener. She remembered how Benny liked it.

"I'll just clear a space for those, shall I?"

Liss turned to find her uninvited guest shoving boxes and packing material aside with reckless abandon. When a ceramic bagpiper took flight, Liss barely managed to set Benny's coffee in front of her and use her newly freed hand to catch the figurine before it hit the floor and shattered.

Oblivious to the damage she'd nearly caused, Benny lifted the mug and took a long swallow of hot coffee. Liss sent her an incredulous look before placing her own mug on the tabletop. Swiftly and efficiently, she finished wrapping the piper and settled it into its mailing carton. She shifted the box to another, smaller table where it would be safe until she had time to add the packing slip, seal the package, and affix a mailing label.

Choosing to stand beside the worktable instead of seating herself on the other stool, Liss took up a position directly opposite Benny. The other woman offered her a tentative smile.

"It turned out to be fascinating stuff, all those letters and papers, although not as interesting as the ledgers, but there wasn't anything in them about treasure or a map. I want you to know that I went through *everything* with a fine-tooth comb." Eyes big, voice earnest, she looked like a puppy waiting for approval.

"I appreciate that you tried."

Benny took another sip of coffee, watching Liss over the rim of the mug. "I really wanted to find something. After all, who doesn't love a good treasure hunt."

"No treasure, I'm afraid."

"No? From what little you told me the other day, I thought there must be *something* to find. Do you mean to tell me that you've already located the spot marked with the X?"

Liss couldn't think of any reason not to answer. Benny already knew a good deal of the Chadwick side of the story.

"We did. There was a hidey-hole in a brick wall. Smallish." She used her hands to indicate the size. It had been plenty big enough to hold a stolen chemical formula.

"*That* was the spot marked by the X?" Benny's face fell. "Just a hole in a wall?"

"Looks that way."

"What was in it?"

"Nothing. It was empty."

"Do you think there had been something there?"

That was the million-dollar question. Liss settled for a vague answer. "Hard to tell." She wondered if she should share the information Sean Widdowson had given her.

"Maybe someone used to leave love letters there," Benny suggested.

Liss couldn't help but smile. "Could be. Certainly nothing much larger would fit."

Benny took another sip of the hot coffee and sighed. "Buried treasure would have been nice. Do you think it's possible that something else could be hidden on the property?"

"Doubtful," Liss said, but Benny's question reminded her of that series of holes they'd discovered on both sides of the wall.

Had it been Aaron Lucas who'd dug them? It seemed obvious to her that he'd been the one after the map—the person who had ransacked their room in Antigonish and searched the Emporium and her house. She wondered if Sherri had managed to find out if he had been in Canada at the same time she and Margaret were there.

"Liss?"

Benny's soft voice brought her back to the present with a start. "Sorry. Wool-gathering."

Liss blinked and brought the other woman into focus, her gaze coming to rest on Benny's fingers, tightly clasped around the coffee mug. Whatever she'd been about to say next flew out of her head.

The otherwise immaculate Benny had dirt under her fingernails.

# Chapter Eleven

Liss burst into Sherri's office at the PD only minutes after Benny left the Emporium. She'd had a tough time getting the other woman to go without letting on that anything was wrong. Then she'd had to wait until the coast was clear to dash across the town square to the municipal building. She was slightly out of breath by the time she skidded to a halt.

"You've got to investigate Benny Beamer," she blurted.

Sherri looked up from the paperwork covering her desk, brow furrowed. "Why?"

"Because I think she's the one who dug all those holes at the Chadwick place. She certainly didn't get dirt under her fingernails from gardening! Not if she's been staying at The Spruces."

"Okay," Sherri said slowly.

She didn't look convinced, but Liss knew she'd take a look at Benny's background anyway. "You'll be able to find out if she went to Canada after the auction, right?"

"Yes, but it will take time. I still don't know if Aaron Lucas was there."

Liss sank into the visitor's chair and scrubbed her hands over her face. "This is getting complicated. Before Benny

showed up this morning, I was sure Lucas was behind everything. And then there's what Dolores told me earlier today. I
was going to tell you next time I saw you. It's probably not
that important, but it does back up what Sean Widdowson
told us."

"Slow down. Tell me what Dolores said."

"But Benny—"

"Dolores first."

While Liss did so, Sherri scribbled down notes.

"So Lester Widdowson was looking to buy a place with
secret hiding places." She leaned back in her swivel chair,
thinking that over. "Combined with what you and Dan
learned from Widdowson's son, it adds up to the picture
of a man with a fragile grasp of reality."

"Does the map I found have to do with Widdowson or
the Chadwicks?" Liss asked aloud. "I keep changing my
mind about that. After all, the hiding place in the brick
wall existed long before Widdowson came along."

"That house was riddled with hidey-holes. Don't forget
the tunnel that went from the cellar to the banks of the
stream, and wasn't there a hidden panel in the living room,
too?"

"I'd forgotten all about that one," Liss admitted. "So
who knows what other secrets there were, dating back to
Prohibition and even earlier?"

"If there was anything else, it's not there now. The
wrecking ball took care of that when Jardine demolished
the house."

"He was awfully quick off the mark to get that done,"
Liss murmured. "Maybe you should be looking into him."

Sherri did not look enthusiastic about that prospect, but
she was spared having to answer by the creak of the door
in the outer room. The entire police station consisted of a

small reception area, the office with its two desks and assorted file cabinets and communications equipment, and a miniscule holding cell that had originally been a closet. Footsteps were clearly audible as they crossed to the inner door, which stood open. After a tentative knock, a man stuck his head inside.

"Excuse me," he said in a mellow baritone. "I'm looking for Chief Campbell. Is he in?"

"*She* is," Sherri said.

Liss was quick to vacate the hard plastic visitor's chair and settle into the marginally more comfortable wooden swivel chair behind the other desk. When Sherri beckoned, the man eased the rest of the way into the office, revealing himself to be a well-dressed gentleman of medium height and rigid posture. What there was of his thinning hair was mud-colored, but it was difficult to discern what shade his eyes were. They were hidden by thick glasses. Liss's best guess placed him in his mid-forties.

"I'm Maurice Kelsey," he announced, producing a business card.

Liss's interest sharpened at the name. This was the man Sean Widdowson had told them about—the one Cornwall Pharmaceuticals had sent to talk to him about his father.

"Vice president, hmmm?" Sherri read his title off the card for Liss's benefit. "What can I do for you, Mr. Kelsey?"

After a moment's hesitation, he perched on the edge of the plastic chair, shoulders stiff and hands resting somewhat awkwardly in his lap. He ignored Liss. She imagined that he took her for a secretary, therefore dismissing her as unimportant. Let him enjoy his misconception, she thought, since it gave her an excuse to stay put and hear whatever he had to say to Sherri.

"I have been sent here to find out why you are looking for Aaron Lucas."

Sherri's eyebrows shot up. "Your company sent an executive all the way from Connecticut to Maine just because I was inquiring about an employee?"

"It involves a rather sensitive matter." His fingers drummed on the knee of his perfectly tailored slacks.

Poor guy, Liss thought, although without any real sympathy. He was completely out of his element. She could almost feel sorry for him. Almost.

"I think you need to answer some questions for me first, Mr. Kelsey," Sherri said. "Your Mr. Lucas may have followed a resident of my town into Canada. If so, it is possible he committed at least one crime while he was there."

"Impossible!" Kelsey started to stand.

"Sit down!" Sherri snapped out the order in a voice that brooked no disobedience and Liss silently applauded.

Kelsey subsided into the chair.

"Bluster won't do you any good. If Mr. Lucas was in your employ, acting on your company's behalf, then you are liable for his actions."

Liss was pretty sure her friend was bluffing, but she didn't think Kelsey realized it. She pegged him as the type who underestimated women. Given Sherri's small stature and the fact that she was a blonde, he had been unprepared for her to throw a bucket of cold reality his way. It took him a moment to recover from the shock.

He cleared his throat. "I do not know where Lucas is."

Hearing the note of desperation in his voice, Liss believed him. Even more telling was the way his shoulders slumped as he made the claim. That was one worried man!

"All right," Sherri said, speaking more gently, "let's try this. We already know that Lester Widdowson was employed by Cornwall Pharmaceuticals, that he was fired, and that there was a lawsuit pending against him when he died. Why don't you tell me your side of the story?"

"The man was mad."

"So I understand."

Kelsey worried his lower lip. Then he took off his glasses, produced a handkerchief, and spent an inordinate amount of time cleaning lenses that already appeared to be perfectly clean. Sherri waited him out without fidgeting. Liss found it harder to sit still.

The glasses back in place, once again hiding eyes that had turned out to be a rather nice shade of blue, Kelsey wasted a few more seconds repeating the finger-drumming bit. At last, he spoke. "Lester Widdowson stole proprietary information from my company when he left."

"Formulas he worked on?" Sherri asked.

"Well, yes, but he didn't own them. We did. He'd become increasingly paranoid in the last few years he worked for us, imagining all kinds of conspiracies. He decided we were evil—his word—and that we intended to misuse the drugs we were developing. He got it into his head that if he stole the formulas and gave them to rival companies, they would be used wisely—his word again."

"Did he succeed?"

"In walking off with company secrets? Yes. But as far as our investigation has been able to determine, he only persuaded one manufacturer to deal with him. Cornwall Pharmaceuticals has since sued that company to get our rights back."

"What about the lawsuit against Lester Widdowson?" Liss asked, startling Kelsey. He'd forgotten she was there.

"It was dropped when he died."

"Even though you also accused him of stealing a formula for an explosive?"

Kelsey's eyes went wide. "Where did you hear that?"

"Does it matter? I want to know if it's true."

"That's what he claimed, but I assure you the man was not rational. There is absolutely no evidence to suggest that he was working on anything that wasn't medical in nature."

"Let's get back to the main point," Sherri interrupted. "You dropped the suit. Does that mean you believe the matter is settled?"

After a brief hesitation, Kelsey shook his head. "Widdowson took one formula that might lead to a major breakthrough. A cure for a disease that currently doesn't have one. I can't say more than that, except that we are most anxious to recover it."

"You couldn't duplicate what he was working on?" Sherri looked skeptical but she kept her tone of voice carefully neutral.

"We've tried, believe me, but so far we've been unsuccessful."

"Yes," Sherri said slowly. "I gathered as much from the fact that you sent Aaron Lucas, from your security department, to the auction of the contents of Widdowson's house here in Moosetookalook. He slipped up, letting a possible clue to the whereabouts of your missing formula go to another buyer. It's what he did next that I'm investigating."

"I know nothing about anything illegal!" Kelsey sprang to his feet and made tracks for the exit. "And you'd better be careful about flinging around false accusations, Chief Campbell!"

Liss half expected him to threaten to sue Sherri, or the town, or both, but he surprised her by turning tail and fleeing without another word. All the way back to Connecticut, she wondered, or would he book a room at The Spruces and stay a few days to see what developed?

By the time she turned to ask Sherri that question, her friend was already punching a number into the phone. From her end of the conversation, it was obvious that she'd called the hotel switchboard. When she disconnected a few minutes later, she was smiling.

"He's registered?" Liss asked.

"He is. And all paid up for a three-day stay. I have a feeling I'll be talking to Mr. Kelsey again before long. Now, back to what we were talking about when we were interrupted. Why do you think dirt under Benny Beamer's fingernails proves she was the one who dug the holes at the Chadwick mansion?"

"What else could it mean?" Liss blinked, bewildered by the question.

"You're overlooking one significant fact," Sherri said. "The digging was done Saturday night. This is Tuesday. Do you really think she hasn't washed her hands since then?"

Liss had put out the BACK IN FIFTEEN MINUTES SIGN before her visit to the PD. She'd been gone much longer than that. Although she doubted she'd missed much in the way of business, it went against the grain to take off willy-nilly. That was no way to stay in the black.

With her bottom line in mind, she took a short detour, stopping in at Angie's Books before she returned to the shop and opened up again. Ten minutes later, Beth took over for her, leaving Liss free to go home, get her car, and drive out to The Spruces.

Moosetookalook's turn-of-the-nineteenth-century grand hotel was well over a hundred years old. The building had long dominated the village's skyline with its towers and cupola, and after renovations by Ruskin Construction, it once again offered first-class accommodations to travelers vacationing in Maine's beautiful inland mountains. Liss's aunt Margaret had been events coordinator for nearly ten years and had loved every minute of her second career. Dan still helped out when his father needed him. As a result, Liss felt right at home on the premises.

She found Joe Ruskin in his office, a small, cluttered space hidden away behind the luxurious public rooms of the hotel. Margaret's old office was located off the same corridor, but now its occupant was a much younger woman named Tricia Lynd. She'd come to work at The Spruces as an intern at the same time Margaret took the job, back when the hotel was surviving on a wing and a prayer. Since then, Tricia had done just about every job in the place, making her ideally suited to pitch The Spruces as the perfect setting for small conferences, mini-conventions, weddings, and other gatherings.

"Gimme a minute," Joe said without looking up from the spreadsheet displayed on his computer monitor.

Liss plopped herself down in the straight-back wooden chair in front of his desk and waited for him to stop glaring at the screen. She had to smile as she listened to him mutter to himself. He'd always hated the accounting end of running a business, but he was too stubborn to hire someone else to do what he felt he was perfectly capable of accomplishing on his own. It was a stance she could appreciate because it was one she shared.

Joe loved everything to do with this old hotel he'd brought back to life. He'd bought the property when everyone else thought the building was a white elephant that should be torn down before it collapsed. Through dogged determination, he'd restored the place to its former glory. It had been touch and go the first few years, but by establishing a reputation for excellence, the business had turned a corner. These days it was making a small but steady profit.

As for Joe himself, he always said that running the hotel kept him young. He'd built up a fine physique as a construction worker in his younger years and showed no sign of letting himself go. There was no paunch visible, no stoop to his shoulders. That boded well for Dan's future. If someone saw Joe and Liss's husband from a distance, they'd be hard put to say who was who. Joe, Dan, and Dan's brother, Sam, were all over six feet tall and they all had lovely thick hair. In Joe's case, the sandy brown color was gray at the temples. Together with a few lines around the molasses brown eyes his sons also shared, that was all that marked him as a senior citizen.

Liss listened to him grumble for a good five minutes more before she finally interrupted. "Your face is going to freeze into a permanent scowl if you keep carrying on like that."

Joe laughed, pushed back in his desk chair, and gave her his full attention. "How are you doing, Liss? I hear you've been treasure hunting."

*Got to love the Moosetookalook grapevine*, Liss thought. It saved time on explanations. She got right to the point. "I need a favor."

"Name it."

"Don't be too quick to agree. What I'm asking is that you give an unauthorized party permission to examine the hotel guest records."

"You?" At her nod, he grinned. "No problem. You're family and this is a family business." He swiveled around in his chair to reach the computer keyboard and held one finger on each hand poised above it. "Does this have anything to do with Sherri asking about some guy named Kelsey?"

"Maybe." Rising, she came around his desk and stood at his shoulder. "I need you to look up a guest named Beamer."

Joe's brow furrowed, but he obliged. "There you go. Benedicta Beamer? What's she got to do with anything?"

"I don't know for certain, but when I talked to her earlier, she had dirt under her fingernails. You haven't started letting guests dig in the flowerbeds, have you?"

His incredulous look was enough of an answer.

She studied the record. Benny Beamer had checked in at The Spruces right before the auction and she'd been in residence ever since. If she made a side trip to Nova Scotia, she hadn't checked out while she was gone, even though it was costing her a fortune to keep her room for such a long time.

"Credit card okay?" Liss asked.

"No flag." Joe sent her a sharp look. "Should I be worried about getting stiffed?"

"I just find it odd she can afford The Spruces. She claims not to be gainfully employed at present."

She reached over Joe's shoulder to type in another search. There was nothing under Lucas, but she hit pay dirt when she tried Cornwall Pharmaceuticals. The company had booked a room for three days, the middle one being the day of the auction. It had been paid for with a corporate credit card, saving Aaron Lucas the necessity of registering under his own name.

"Do you still have guests sign in at the old-fashioned register out front?" Liss asked.

"Of course. Go ahead and look at it. I'll let the desk know it's okay." He was reaching for the phone as Liss left his office.

Emerging from the corridor, Liss was struck, as she always was, by the feeling of having stepped back into the past. The lobby of The Spruces was a marvel of late Victorian elegance with its white pillars, its polished wooden floors, and its high ceiling carved with animals and flowers. Large plush rugs made seating areas into cozy meeting places, especially those near the enormous fireplace directly opposite the main entrance. She couldn't help but spare an admiring glance for its ornate mantel and the beveled mirror above. In winter, there was always a fire going. Now that it was high summer, the tile-lined hearth was full of fresh flowers.

In the leather-bound register kept on the big, nineteenth-century check-in desk, a guest could sign in under any name he liked. Liss was half expecting to find "John Doe" on the date in question, but Aaron Lucas had instead chosen to be "Lucas A. Cornwall."

"He probably thinks that's clever," she muttered under her breath.

The desk clerk gave her a funny look. "Anything else I can do for you, Ms. Ruskin?" He was young, probably a summer intern, and eager as a puppy to please.

"Just a second." She flipped to the current page, easily finding Maurice Kelsey, the nervous executive who'd just paid a visit to the police department. "What can you tell me about this guy? Is he traveling by himself?"

The clerk checked the computer record, just as Joe had, and looked rattled when he couldn't find Kelsey's name.

"Try Cornwall Pharmaceuticals," Liss suggested. "Today's check-in, not an old entry."

"Oh, here it is! I remember now. Mr. Kelsey had a corporate credit card."

"Single room?" That's what they'd provided for Aaron Lucas.

"Nope. Two-bedroom suite. One of the really nice ones, too."

That could mean he'd brought his wife. Or a girlfriend. But Liss couldn't see Kelsey as the type to come to Moosetookalook for a romantic rendezvous. Besides, if that were the case, he wouldn't need two bedrooms. Had he come to town just to talk to Sherri, or was he planning to meet his confederate, Aaron Lucas, during his stay in Moosetookalook? Unfortunately, the only additional information the clerk could provide was the make, model, and license plate of the car Kelsey was driving.

It came as a considerable shock to turn away from the check-in desk and immediately catch sight of the very man she'd just been asking about. Maurice Kelsey was seated in a quiet corner of the lobby. From the way he kept looking at his watch, it appeared he was waiting for someone. Lucas? There was only one way to find out.

Liss stationed herself in the lobby, half hidden by a pillar. There she lurked, keeping an eye on the man from Cornwall Pharmaceuticals.

A half hour passed. Kelsey glanced at his watch with greater frequently but showed no sign of giving up and moving on. Her neck stiff from craning it to peek out at him, the rest of her protesting because she'd stood still for so long, Liss risked sidling from the cover of one pillar to the next. At just that moment, Kelsey looked up.

He sprang to his feet to confront her. "Are you following me?"

"Of course not. Why would I be?" Liss backpedaled only far enough to keep him from stepping on her toes.

"Who the hell are you, anyway?" His face had turned an ugly shade of red and his narrowed eyes and fisted hands suggested he wanted to throttle the answer out of her.

"That's none of your business."

Liss held her ground. She was in no danger. They were

standing in the hotel lobby in full view of several other guests and the clerk behind the check-in desk. If Kelsey's temper got the better of him, that young man could be relied upon to call for help.

She was a trifle disappointed when Kelsey abruptly turned and stalked away from her. She hadn't deliberately tried to provoke him, but if he had exploded, she'd have been able to file a complaint against him. With an excuse to make an arrest, Sherri might also have been able to search his room. Who knew what, or who, she might have found there?

A moment later, Liss answered herself—she'd have found nothing. Kelsey had been waiting for someone. Someone who had not kept their appointment. That had to have been Aaron Lucas, which meant that he was not sharing Kelsey's suite. Not yet, anyway.

Still pondering the situation, Liss headed for the staff parking where she'd left her car. She locked herself in and turned on the air to cool the interior, but she was in no hurry to make the five-minute drive back to the Emporium. Something was nagging at her, buzzing in her mind like the most annoying of flies. Something about the hotel records she'd just seen. Not Kelsey or Cornwall Pharmaceuticals or Lucas, she thought. And then she had it—Benny Beamer.

*Benedicta* Beamer.

Seizing the tote she'd tossed onto the passenger seat, Liss rummaged through it for the Chadwick family tree Margaret had given her. Wasn't there something . . . ?

Yes, there it was, in the Canadian line. Norman Chadwick, father of Albert, the last Canadian Chadwick, had married a woman named Hazel Benedict. Of their three children, Daisy and Albert had stayed in Nova Scotia and neither had produced offspring. The third, Harold, was the one who'd left home as a young man, eager to find his fortune, and had never been heard from again.

She studied the dates. Harold had been born in 1910. Assuming he married and had a daughter, might he have named her Benedicta after his mother? Benny Beamer was too young to be his child, but if there was one Benedicta in the family, why not another? If Benny was Harold's granddaughter, the dates could work.

With great care, Liss folded the family tree and tucked it back into her tote bag before pulling out of the staff parking lot and heading home. Her brainstorm was a long shot, such a long shot, in fact, that she hesitated to mention it to Dan or Sherri. Sherri had already punched holes in her theory that Benny had been the one digging for treasure.

She winced at her inadvertent play on words, but kept thinking. Just because she'd been wrong on one count didn't mean all her ideas were worthless. In fact, if it turned out that Benny *was* a Chadwick descendant, it made sense that Benny had been the culprit on Saturday night. The number and placement of the holes suggested that the digger had not found anything . . . including the hiding place behind the bricks. Had she gone back, perhaps on Monday night? Maybe even on Tuesday morning, if no one was working at the property?

Liss refused to rule out the possibility.

When Liss and Dan were first married, he and his brother had turned what had been open space in the attic into a combination office and library with plenty of room for all of Liss's books. After stopping briefly at the Emporium to make sure Beth didn't need her help, Liss retreated to this haven for a good think. She turned off her cell phone and the ringer on the landline and didn't even turn on the new iPad she'd bought to replace the one stolen in Nova Scotia. With only the two cats to distract her, she settled in at her desk with an eight by eleven lined tablet in front of her.

Creating lists had always been Liss's way to make sense of events. She started with her purchase of the portrait of the Grant piper and wrote down everything else that had happened in chronological order. Some of the items would turn out to have nothing at all to do with the things currently puzzling her, but at this stage she had no way of knowing what was important and what wasn't.

First on the list was the auction and the fact that Aaron Lucas bid against her for the painting. Not only Aaron Lucas, she reminded herself. There had also been Claire Mortimer. Was Claire as innocent as Sherri believed? Liss hoped so, because the last thing she needed was another suspect.

She continued with her list. Item two was "met Benny Beamer." Liss tapped her lips with the eraser end of her pencil. Benny hadn't shown any interest in the portrait, but that could have been because she expected to find the map in the steamer trunk with the ledgers. Why had she bought it otherwise? That story about writing an article could be just so much hogwash.

So—she'd met two viable suspects on the same day. Both had an interest in items that came out of the Chadwick house. Lucas had been looking for something Lester Widdowson might have hidden. Benny, if she really was a Chadwick, was probably looking for something connected to her family.

Remembering the family tree Margaret had drawn, Liss couldn't quite see what that would be. The Moosetookalook Chadwicks had been in the U.S. for a long time. If Benny was related to them at all, she was a very distant cousin, surely too distant to have any legal claim to an inheritance.

The digging suggested a belief in buried treasure. She was as deluded as Lester Widdowson if she thought it was a Chadwick who'd left something valuable hidden on the property. According to local legend, the loot had belonged to Blackie O'Hare.

"Good grief," Liss said aloud. "You don't suppose it was Blackie who made that map and hid it behind the portrait?"

Lumpkin woke up from his nap long enough to send her a contemptuous look.

Liss laughed. "You're right. No need to come up with fresh theories. We have far too many already."

She went back to her list. A short time later, she read over what she'd written.

1. won portrait bidding against Aaron Lucas
2. met Benny Beamer
3. found map
4. showed map to Dan and Margaret
5. Margaret suggested trip to Nova Scotia
6. Margaret contacted Orson Bailey and set up appointment
7. discovered Orson Bailey's body

Liss paused for a moment to contemplate that item. Everything else was minor compared to murder, but was Bailey's death connected to the rest? It didn't have to be.

8. motel room burgled in Antigonish
9. given copies of information Bailey was supposed to have ready for us

10. found door unlocked at Emporium
11. found intruder in house
12. Benny reappeared; agreed to look through papers; took copy of map
13. located X on map
14. discovered someone had been digging near spot marked by X
15. saw dirt under Benny's fingernails
16. Kelsey admitted Lucas was sent to look for a formula

Liss tossed the pencil down in disgust. For once, making a list wasn't helping. Nothing had become clearer. No brilliant new conclusions had leapt out at her.

She needed more information. It would help if Sherri's contact found evidence that either Aaron Lucas or Benny Beamer was in Canada at the same time she and Margaret were. That would at least narrow down the number of suspects. Unless the two of them were working together . . .

She didn't even want to think about that possibility!

# Chapter Twelve

A landline served as Liss's primary phone at the house, cell phone service in rural Maine having been unpredictable for so many years that most people in Moosetookalook refused to risk relying on it. The phone and answering machine combination sat on an end table in the living room with an extension in the kitchen. Having forgotten that she'd turned off the ringer, it was some time before Liss noticed the red message light blinking to signal a missed call.

She expected to hear political propaganda or a request that she participate in a survey when she hit the play button, since those calls were always more frequent than legitimate messages from friends. A hesitation came first. She could hear someone breathing. That happened a lot too.

Then her father's voice issued from the speaker. "You know I hate these things. Call us back when you get a minute. Use this number." He rattled off a series of digits.

Liss felt like thumping her head on the hard wooden end table. For the first time in ages, she didn't answer her phone, so of course that was when her father called! What was especially frustrating was that she'd been trying to reach her parents, on and off, ever since her return from

Nova Scotia. She'd tried both the landline at the house in Arizona and her mother's cell. Every single time, she'd been sent straight to voice mail. No one had returned any of those calls.

As she stared at the unfamiliar numbers she'd written on the notepad by the phone, she wondered if her father had finally broken down and bought his own cell. She took a couple of deep breaths before attempting to return the call and almost dropped the receiver when he picked up on the second ring. She'd been positive she'd be connected to a recorded message and have to talk to a machine after the beep.

"Daddy? Are you and Mom okay?"

"Why wouldn't we be?" He sounded puzzled by her question.

"This isn't your regular phone number."

"It's my new smartphone. Your old dad's decided to get with the times. I'm even thinking I might learn how to text."

"Knock yourself out, but first tell me why you haven't returned any of my calls." Liss settled herself on the sofa. She had a feeling this wasn't going to be a short conversation.

"What calls?"

Liss was glad she was sitting down. "The dozen or so I've made in the last week, ever since Margaret and I had a little chat about your future plans. I left messages."

"Huh," her father said. "I guess Vi forgot to tell me about them."

She *forgot*? Liss's heart sank. Her thoughts leapt at once to the fear that haunts all children of parents over the age of sixty-five—could Violet MacCrimmon be in the early stages of Alzheimer's? "Are you *sure* you're both okay?"

"Right as rain."

He sounded so cheerful that she knew he believed it. It remained to be seen whether or not he was deceiving himself.

"As a matter of fact," he went on, "the reason I called was to let you know that we're on our way north."

"So soon?" Listening more closely, Liss could hear traffic sounds in the background and a car radio playing softly. A more immediate concern grabbed her by the throat. "Please tell me you're not talking on the phone while you're driving. You need to keep both hands on the wheel!"

He laughed. "I'm not such a fool. Your mother is spelling me."

Liss held the receiver away from her ear and stared at it. Surely she hadn't heard correctly. While it was true that her mother had a driver's license, she never voluntarily drove if she could get someone else to play chauffeur. She'd barely absorbed that detail when she suddenly saw the bigger picture.

"Are you *driving* all the way from Arizona to Maine?" The last few times they'd come to visit, they'd flown into Portland International Jetport. Liss and Dan usually met them there and brought them the rest of the way to Moosetookalook.

Her father cleared his throat. "I thought you said Margaret talked to you. We, ah, have some extra baggage with us this time."

Did that mean they'd already sold their condo in Arizona and were heading north with all their possessions crammed into a rented trailer? Before she could find the right words to ask, her father spoke again.

"Anyway, we're taking our time on the road, but we expect to be there to help you and Dan celebrate your anniversary."

"Daddy—"

"And we're looking forward to those cooler tempera-tures in Maine. You wouldn't believe the heat wave we've had to endure lately!"

"I watch the news, but I thought all that dry heat was good for your arthritis." Liss leaned her head against the back of the sofa. She needed the support. This conversation was making her dizzy.

He chuckled. "I'm on some really good drugs."

That was *not* reassuring. She tried again. "Daddy—"

"Got to go now. We're coming up on a good place to stop for an early supper. Love you."

Without waiting for her response, he ended the call.

Liss swore under her breath. She considered hitting re-dial, then thought better of it. Either he wouldn't answer or he'd pick up and give her the runaround all over again.

Wednesday morning dawned as one of those bleak, drizzly days that sometimes engulf Maine in July, even the Maine that is far distant from fogs that come in off the ocean. Liss dragged herself to work, tempted to leave the CLOSED sign up and concentrate on updating the Emporium's Web pages. The sense of responsibility hammered into her from an early age would not permit such a lapse. With a long-suffering sigh, she flipped it around to read OPEN.

No one came in until two hours later, and then it was only Sherri, but Liss was glad to take a break from her self-imposed task. Adding items and their prices to the store's online inventory and making sure they could be moved seamlessly to the "shopping cart" function by cus-tomers was a picky and time-consuming process. Once, she'd accidentally priced an item at $10.99 instead of $110.99. She'd been obliged to honor the lower price, even though that was far less than what each one had cost her. She'd been able to fix the problem fairly quickly, but the mistake had taught her a valuable lesson. She now proofread every bit of copy at least three times before letting it go live.

"Coffee?" Liss offered.

"Love some. Do you have a minute?"

"I have way more than one."

Liss disappeared into the stockroom and returned a few minutes later with two steaming mugs and the last two jelly doughnuts from the half dozen she'd bought at Patsy's Coffee House on Tuesday.

Sherri had made herself comfortable in the cozy corner. She looked tired, Liss thought. No surprise there, not when she worked full time at a stressful job and was a full-time mother to three active children, one of them a teenage boy. Pete was a great father, but he worked full time, too, and his job as a patrol deputy for the sheriff's department meant he was often called upon to work extra hours.

After gulping down the first few swallows of coffee, Sherri perked up. "I finally have some news to report. This morning, I received confirmation that Aaron Lucas did enter Canada, and on the same day you and Margaret did, too."

"Now what? Arrest him?"

"*Talk* to him."

Liss placed her almost-full mug on the coffee table, sloshing a little of the hot brew over the side as she did so. She was surprised to note a slight tremor in her hand, a sure sign that she already had way too much caffeine in her system. She couldn't remember how many cups of coffee she'd downed since coming into work. She hadn't slept well the night before for worrying about her parents and their imminent arrival in Moosetookalook.

Sherri handed her a napkin to mop up the spill. "You okay?"

"Sure." Embarrassed by the irritation she heard in her own voice, Liss was quick to turn the conversation back to Aaron Lucas. "What else do you know?"

"Not much. He crossed the border at Calais at two in the afternoon. That would be three New Brunswick time."

Liss stared at her. "But that's hours after Margaret and I entered the country."

"I think you'd have noticed if he was in the car behind you the whole way."

"Yes, but . . ."

Her voice trailed off as she realized that a part of her had truly believed that Lucas had been responsible for Orson Bailey's murder, as well as for the lesser crimes tied to the map she'd found. *Was* there a way he could have killed the archivist? From the border, he'd have had to drive across New Brunswick into Nova Scotia. He couldn't have known where she and Margaret would stop for the night. They hadn't made reservations in advance. In order to kill Bailey, he'd have had to arrive in Chadwick first thing the next morning. But how could he have known what town they were headed for, let alone that they had a meeting scheduled at the historical society? As far as anyone but Dan had been aware, their only destinations in Nova Scotia had been Truro, a couple of places on Cape Breton, and Antigonish.

"Lucas was in Canada," she said slowly. "He was the man I saw in Truro. He was probably the one who broke into our motel room in Antigonish."

"Looks that way," Sherri agreed, "but that's still just

speculation. Speaking of which, I asked my contact to find out if Benny Beamer was north of the border on the dates in question. He'll check, but it could be a few more days before I hear anything back from him."

Liss nodded her thanks, but her enthusiasm for investigating Benny had waned. Although she'd already shared her theory about a Chadwick connection with both Sherri and Margaret, in the murky light of this new day the possibility seemed at least as far-fetched as her conviction that Aaron Lucas had murdered Orson Bailey.

Sherri stood. "I've got to get going. Just before I came over here, I talked to Maurice Kelsey on the phone and persuaded him that it would be to his advantage to produce Aaron Lucas." She looked well pleased with herself. "I may have led him to believe that someone actually saw him with Lucas at The Spruces. Anyhow, he caved. Lucas will meet me at the hotel in half an hour for an informal interview."

Liss's answering smile was weak but genuine. "I don't suppose you'd let me come with you? If I see Lucas close up, I should be able to confirm that he's the one I saw in Truro."

Sherri hesitated. "You're a civilian."

"I'm a witness." Liss crossed to the phone on the sales counter and punched in the number for Angie's Books. A few minutes later, she'd arranged for Beth to take charge of the Emporium.

"This isn't a good idea," Sherri warned her.

"It's a great idea," Liss insisted, as much to convince herself as to get Sherri to agree. "Lucas will assume I know more than I do and you'll get more out of him."

"I do all the talking," Sherri stipulated.

"Of course."

Although Sherri still looked doubtful, she agreed to the revised plan.

Sherri had arranged to meet Aaron Lucas in the staff conference room at The Spruces. In contrast to the meeting rooms in the rest of the hotel, this one was exceedingly plain, furnished with nothing more than a long wooden table, several chairs, and a smaller side table that held a coffeemaker and containers of sugar and creamer. Aaron Lucas had already fixed himself a cup and taken a seat. His eyes—rather nice, bright blue ones—narrowed when Liss and Sherri came in. He took note of Sherri's uniform, acknowledging her authority with a curt nod, but he regarded Liss with obvious suspicion.

"What's she doing here?"

"Concerned citizen," Liss said.

"Interested party," Sherri answered at the same time.

Lucas grunted and took another swallow of his coffee.

Sherri took the seat opposite him while Liss remained standing near the door. She produced a notebook and a pen, flipping open the former before she looked her suspect straight in the eye. Liss had to admire her style.

"Mr. Lucas, I must inform you that you are a person of interest in an investigation now being carried out by Canadian authorities. It would be to your advantage to cooperate by helping to clarify certain matters."

His look was cool and assessing. He did not seem at all intimidated by the possibility of arrest. Not a good start, Liss thought, especially when he knew that he was not obligated to answer Sherri's questions.

"Mr. Lucas," Sherri said, "I was under the impression that you had agreed to cooperate."

"Kelsey's idea. Not mine."

"Yes, well, the company you both work for no doubt prefers to avoid bad publicity."

Liss studied Lucas as he maintained a stubborn silence. His expression gave away nothing of what he was thinking—a good "cop face." That was a skill Sherri had yet to master. Liss could see her friend's patience begin to fray as the silence lengthened.

Impatient herself, Liss put an end to it by breaking her promise to Sherri and thrusting herself into the interview. She plunked herself down next to Sherri, glared at Lucas, and demanded, "Did you kill Orson Bailey?"

"Liss!" Clearly appalled, Sherri glared at her.

Liss swallowed hard. That wasn't what she'd meant to ask. The question had just popped out, as if it had been lurking in her subconscious, waiting for the opportunity to escape.

Lucas's voice rose to a bellow. "Who the hell is Orson Bailey?"

Liss stared at him. His stone face had cracked to reveal a combination of bafflement and outrage. His blue-eyed glare was leveled at her with laser precision, demanding an answer. She had to swallow again before she could oblige.

"He was murdered in Chadwick, Nova Scotia, just before he was scheduled to meet with me and my aunt. You entered Canada the same day we did. You could easily have gotten there ahead of us."

"Listen up, lady, and listen good. I didn't go near Chadwick. I didn't even know there was such a place."

Lucas's hands clenched into fists on the tabletop. In her peripheral vision, Liss saw Sherri shift slightly to give herself better access to her utility belt. Belatedly, it occurred to Liss that Lucas might be armed. He was in the security business, after all.

Even without a gun or a knife, he was dangerous. He was a big guy in good physical condition. If he was the violent type, he was capable of doing considerable damage with only his fists.

Sherri spoke in a soft voice, her demeanor calming. "We're attempting to get at the truth, Mr. Lucas. Mr. Kelsey seemed confident you have nothing to hide. If you'll just answer a few simple questions, we can settle this matter."

"Simple? She just accused me of murder."

"She will stay out of it from now on or be evicted from the room."

Liss, watching Lucas, saw the tension in his shoulders ease a fraction, but he still had her in his sights.

"As far as I can see," Sherri continued, "you had no reason to kill anyone, but if you did follow Ms. Ruskin and Ms. Boyd to Nova Scotia, it is possible you have information that will help the RCMP find out who did murder Orson Bailey."

Without looking away from Liss, Lucas addressed Sherri. "You're lousy at this."

Sherri blinked in surprise. "At what?"

"Interrogation. If I had killed this guy, Bailey, you'd be doing a good job of lousing up the investigation for the Mounties."

The accusation made Sherri bristle and caused Liss to suspect that Aaron Lucas might have more experience questioning suspects than her friend did. That shouldn't have surprised her, she supposed. After all, when a murder occurred in rural Maine, the state police took over. Town cops were pushed out of the loop.

"I would appreciate your cooperation," Sherri said, "without the critique."

At last Lucas took his eyes off Liss, swiveling toward

Sherri so fast that she jerked back in reaction. Her hand went to her holster. Liss held her breath, but all Lucas did was slowly unclench his fists until his fingers lay flat on the tabletop. His lips curved into something that was more smirk than smile.

"You really should be recording this," he said.

"Are you planning to confess?" Sherri shot back.

"I'm planning," he said in icy tones, "to exonerate myself."

Lucas's shift from obstructive to cooperative didn't make him any less dangerous, but Sherri, too, placed both hands in plain view.

"Joe has one of those memo cubes," Liss offered. "Shall I borrow it?"

At Sherri's nod, she left the room, returning a few minutes later with a small electronic device that was years out of date. It had been designed to let busy people record reminders like "buy milk" and "call Mom about babysitting," but it would work well enough for Sherri's purposes.

In her absence, Sherri had apparently identified Orson Bailey.

"He couldn't have had the map," Lucas said. "I wouldn't have had any interest in him."

When Liss set the recording device on the table between Lucas and Sherri, Sherri turned it on and gestured for him to start talking. Wearing a long-suffering look, he picked it up and held it like a microphone.

"Lester Widdowson stole formulas he'd been working on from Cornwall Pharmaceuticals, my employer. They have been anxious to get them back, one of them in particular. After Widdowson's death, his son consented to be interviewed. That's how we learned that his father, on his deathbed, mumbled something about a frame. At first we thought Widdowson was claiming he'd been framed. It was only when I dug deeper that I found a connection between the word *frame* and a house Widdowson owned."

"The Chadwick mansion," Sherri murmured.

"Right. By then the house had been sold and the new owner had scheduled an auction of the contents. On the strength of my theory, the company sent me to Moosetookalook to buy up anything with a frame—photos, paintings, mirrors."

"But you let the Grant piper go," Liss said. "Why?"

Sherri sent her a quelling look, but Lucas didn't seem to mind the question, now that the accusation of murder had been dismissed.

"I didn't want to call attention to myself by bidding any higher. I was planning to contact you later to see if I could take a look at the frame, assuming I didn't find anything in the ones I purchased."

"What about the other bidder?" Liss asked.

"Someone else just liked the painting, I guess. I didn't see who it was."

"Go on," Sherri interjected, shooting Liss a glare she interpreted as "don't interrupt with any more questions."

Lucas leaned back in his chair, giving every indication of being perfectly relaxed as he continued his tale. "I confess I was still around when you were loading the painting into the car. I saw you drop it and I saw you find something behind the backing. It wasn't in the frame, but it was close enough. I figured it had to be the formula we were looking for."

"You could have approached her then and there," Sherri said. "Why didn't you?"

He shrugged. "Do you want to hear my side of things or not?"

"Go on."

"I followed you two back to town. It wasn't hard to figure out where Ms. Ruskin here lived, or why she'd bought the portrait. And it didn't take much more effort than that to discover that what she'd found was a map."

"You *spied* on me!" Liss was halfway out of her chair before Sherri grabbed her arm and jerked her back down.

Lucas seemed amused by her outrage. "People leave their windows open in the summer. Voices carry."

It must have been that same evening, Liss realized, when she'd told Dan and Margaret about her find at the auction. The dogs had known there was someone out there. They'd barked and she'd foolishly ignored them.

"I'm surprised no one saw you lurking," Sherri said. "This is a small town. Neighbors look out for each other."

"No one was home on that side. There were no lights on in the house or in the downstairs dance studio. Besides, I'm good at what I do. I listened, but what I heard didn't seem relevant." He shifted his gaze back to Liss. "It wasn't a formula you'd found, unless it was in the scribbles on the back."

"Faint markings," Liss murmured, remembering the conclusions they'd drawn at the time. "Hardly noticeable and nothing we could make sense of."

"From what I overheard, the writing on the back had to relate to the map, if it meant anything at all, and the map didn't seem to have any connection to Lester Widdowson. Not then. You were convinced it was *old*." His tone implied that he blamed her for steering him wrong.

"What did you do then?" Sherri asked.

"Since I'd already checked the frames I'd bought at the auction and come up empty, I headed back to Connecticut. I figured I'd been barking up the wrong tree."

"When did you tell Kelsey about the map?"

He had the good grace to look sheepish. "Not right away. It wasn't until he insisted on going over every detail of my trip to Maine that it came out. He was fit to be tied. He told me to get hold of that paper, whatever it was, preferably without letting on that it might be valuable. He didn't want to have to pay through the nose for it."

"So your job was on the line?" Sherri asked.

"I doubt it. And given that you folks thought you had a treasure map, I was pretty sure the paper hadn't been tossed out in the trash. The only trouble was, by the time I got back here, Ms. Ruskin had already left for Canada."

"You followed pretty fast," Sherri said.

He shrugged. "It didn't take me long to find out she was heading for Truro. I didn't even have to ask questions, just listen while I had breakfast at the coffee shop. Word was that the ladies were on a buying trip but that they were also going to do some research into the family that owned that house. It made sense that they'd take the map with them."

"So you followed her to Nova Scotia to steal it?" Sherri's voice was dangerously quiet.

Lucas ignored the question. "I went hunting for a kilt maker in Truro, since that was the only lead I had. I staked out the shop until they showed up. *Then* I followed them." He held up a hand, palm out. "Not a crime, Chief Campbell."

Liss was starting to believe him. He'd ducked out of the way so she wouldn't get a good look at him and then he'd trailed them to Cape Breton. It made sense, except for one thing. "Why didn't you approach me? If you'd asked to look at the map, especially if you'd explained why, I'd probably have shown it to you."

He laughed. "I don't think so."

"So you just assumed you'd have to steal it?"

"My plan was to find an opportunity to take a gander at the back of that map. One good look would have told me whether or not to offer to buy it from you."

A glance at Sherri told Liss that her friend had serious doubts about this part of his story.

"I agree it's unlikely that you killed Orson Bailey," Sherri said, "but that doesn't mean you didn't commit a crime."

Lucas shifted his steady blue gaze her way. "What, exactly, are you accusing me of now?"

"Someone broke into Ms. Ruskin's motel room in Antigonish. Were you hoping to find the map?"

"You stole my iPad," Liss put in, "and my aunt's brooch."

Even more relaxed now, Aaron Lucas leaned back in the chair and stretched his legs out beneath the table. "Nope. Wasn't me."

Liss hastily shifted her feet.

"Are you denying you were in Antigonish?" Sherri asked.

Moving slowly to avoid alarming anyone, Lucas turned off the recorder and set it back on the table. "This whole thing is making me look bad, but I'll tell you God's honest truth. I admit that I went to the motel Ms. Ruskin and her aunt were staying at. I meant to take a look around while they were busy at the Highland Games. But if I'd broken into that room, no one would ever have known I was there."

"Someone burgled the place," Sherri said, "and not just that one room, either."

"Exactly. Someone burgled the place. It wasn't me. By the time I got there, the door to Ms. Ruskin's room was standing open and the thieves had been and gone. I took a quick look around for the map. Then I got out of there."

"I'm right here! Talk to *me*." Liss didn't try to hide her annoyance.

"You have a question?"

"Darned right I do. You just admitted you're good at sneaking into places. It was you in the Emporium and in my house, wasn't it? You were still searching for the map."

Lucas looked amused again, and declined to respond to the accusation.

"You see, Mr. Lucas, a crime was committed, after all," Sherri said, "and those two break-ins took place in my jurisdiction. He's not going to confess to them," she added in an aside to Liss. "If he did, I'd have to arrest him on the spot."

Aaron Lucas didn't seem overly concerned by the possibility. After a moment, he shifted position again and leaned across the table until he was nearly nose-to-nose with Sherri. "Here's the thing. I already *know* the copies Ms. Ruskin made of that map show only one side. And I watched her go to her bank the other day. I saw her pay a visit to the vault where they keep the safe-deposit boxes. It didn't take much of a leap to figure out that those scribbles I'm interested in are currently out of my reach."

"So why haven't you offered me big bucks to take a peek at them?" Liss asked.

Turning his head a fraction of an inch so that his gaze fell on her, he chuckled. "Maybe I just like making Maurice Kelsey run around in circles." With that, he backed off and stood, sending Sherri a mock salute. "If that's all, Chief Campbell, I'm thinking I'd like to leave your pretty little town. I'll be taking Kelsey back to Connecticut with me."

Sherri watched in silence as he left the conference room.

"Why don't you stop him?" Liss hissed at her.

"I haven't got grounds to arrest him. Not on any charge."

"Couldn't you warn him not to leave town?"

"And just why would he listen? That order has never had more legal force than a suggestion, no matter how many times someone says it on TV."

Liss slumped forward, resting her head in her hands, and tried to think if there was anything she could do to stop their prime suspect from leaving Moosetookalook. She could get the map and show it to him, but then he'd see that the squiggles were too faint to read and leave anyway. That might be best in the long run, but it would leave her with unanswered questions. She *hated* unanswered questions.

"Did you buy his story?" Sherri asked.

"I don't know. And we forgot to ask him if he dug those holes."

"Do you think he was responsible for the thefts in Antigonish?"

"I'm beginning to doubt it. I did believe him when he said he could have searched our motel room without leaving behind any trace that he'd been there. He had no reason to make a mess or steal my iPad, let alone break into other rooms. Maybe it was just a random burglary, after all."

But she didn't like coincidences.

Haunted by a vague sense of stones left unturned, Liss followed Sherri back to the lobby. She waved to Joe as they passed the check-in desk. Outside, the rain had stopped and the sun glistened on the wet grass. While they waited for the parking valet to bring the cruiser around, Liss studied the view to the southeast. A faint rainbow had formed . . . ending right over the Chadwick property. Liss's smile was sour. At this point, she had serious doubts that *anyone* was going to find a pot of gold.

She turned toward Sherri, meaning to point out the

many-colored arc, but at that moment Benny Beamer came out of the hotel and passed through her line of vision. Pleased recognition flared on Benny's face when she caught sight of Liss, but an instant later, when she spotted Sherri's uniform, it was replaced by a look of panic.

# Chapter Thirteen

Liss was nearly running by the time she skidded around the corner into the short hallway that opened into the vestibule in front of the main dining room. The only people in sight were a couple of tourists, casually attired in shorts and T-shirts, and the luncheon hostess who was assuring them that they didn't have to dress up to enjoy fine dining at The Spruces. She probably wished they would, since knobby knees and hairy white legs weren't a particularly appetizing sight for the other patrons, but Joe Ruskin had long ago decided that his luxury hotel would be welcoming to everyone. While snootier places offered to loan a tie, and even a jacket, to a gentleman who came into the dining room in more casual attire, Joe limited his dress code to requiring a shirt and shoes.

"Drat," Liss muttered. Two directions to choose from and she'd picked the wrong one.

She retraced her steps to the lobby and trotted across it to the grand staircase that led up to the mezzanine. There was no sign of anyone on the steps but some group or other was using the meeting rooms above. She could see men and women in business suits and hear the dull roar typical of a large group of people all talking at once.

That left the corridor that led into the west wing of the hotel. Without much hope of success, Liss made her way along it, stopping just outside each door to peer in. There was no sign of her quarry in the business center, the gift shop, the game room, the library, or the music room. As a last resort, Liss entered the lounge. At this hour, there were few patrons. The hotel employee behind the bar gave her a friendly wave, recognizing her as the owner's daughter-in-law. She was about to ask him if he'd seen a small blond woman when Sherri caught up with her.

"What on earth are you up to?" she asked. "I thought you were right behind me until the kid brought the cruiser around and I realized you'd vanished."

"Apparently, I'm up to running around like a chicken with its head cut off."

"Lovely image!"

Distracted by the windows that looked out over the indoor pool, Liss said, "My grandmother used to say that."

She peered down into the sparkling blue water but did not see anyone she recognized. Her nose wrinkled. Even at this distance and with solid glass in the way, she could smell the chlorine. It was not one of her favorite scents.

"Want to tell me what you're looking for?" Sherri asked.

"Who."

"Okay—*who* are you looking for?"

"Benny Beamer. She stepped out of the hotel while we were standing there waiting for the car. I would have spoken to her, but the minute she saw you, she turned tail and fled back into the hotel."

"Why?"

"I assume because she knew you're a cop."

"So, naturally, you had to follow her."

"Easy on the sarcasm. You'd have done the same thing."

Together, they walked back toward the lobby.

"Probably. So where do you think she went?"

"No idea. She was moving too fast for me to catch up to her."

Emerging from the corridor, Sherri waved a hand toward the elevators to their left. "Maybe she just forgot something and went back to her room for it."

"She may have gone to her room, but it was to get away from us. She was trying to give me the slip and she definitely didn't want you to catch sight of her. She's hiding something, Sherri."

Liss endured her friend's long-suffering look. Sherri's curiosity was as great as her own. As she expected, they didn't leave right away. Instead, Sherri crossed to the check-in desk and asked Joe Ruskin for Benny's room number.

"You want me to call up there and see if she's in?" he asked after he'd supplied it.

"We'd rather surprise her," Sherri said.

A few minutes later, Liss and Sherri stood in front of the open door of a double room on the third floor. A housekeeping cart blocked the entrance. When Liss started to move it aside, Sherri caught her arm.

"Uh-uh. I can see from here that she's not in there."

"But—"

"You are not going to go poking around in her belongings. And I am definitely not setting foot inside."

"Maybe she's got illegal drugs in there."

"Don't sound so hopeful. Even if she does, if I can't see them from the doorway, I can't go in. Give it up, Liss."

Attracted by their voices, the housekeeper came out of the room's bath.

"Hello, Rhonda," Liss said.

"Something I can do for you?" Rhonda sent them a suspicious look. She was a worn-down woman in her fifties who had the triple misfortune to marry a total loser and give birth to two equally worthless sons.

"The woman staying in this room," Liss said. "Have you seen her in the last few minutes? We need to talk to her."

Rhonda's gaze shifted from Liss to Sherri. She was no rocket scientist, but neither was she stupid. "What'd she do?"

"Nothing." Sherri snapped out the word, surprising Liss and making Rhonda jump.

"Have you seen her or not?" Liss asked.

Rhonda chewed thoughtfully on a wad of gum. The distinctive scent of Juicy Fruit drifted Liss's way. "She was in the room when I got here but she was on her way out. Seems like a nice enough lady. Good tipper. Why're you bothering her?"

"We're not bothering her," Sherri said through clenched teeth.

"We just need to speak with her." Liss forced herself to smile. "Any idea where she was going when she left?"

"Like she'd tell me!" Rhonda pulled fresh towels off the cart and returned to the bathroom.

Sherri grabbed Liss's arm and tugged her away from the open door. "Enough," she whispered. "Let's not give Rhonda any more gossip to embroider."

Liss allowed herself to be led away, but only under protest. "Local gossip isn't likely to reach the ears of a guest at The Spruces. Besides, Rhonda could probably use some excitement in her life."

"A lot you know."

Liss stopped and stared at her friend. "What's going on? Don't tell me you're investigating Rhonda Snipes for something."

"I don't intend to tell you anything." Sherri kept moving, heading for the elevator.

Liss felt her jaw drop. It must be serious if Sherri wasn't

willing to share. She wasn't particularly worried about Rhonda, but family connections were complex in a tiny place like Moosetookalook. Liss's cousin Boxer was also Rhonda's nephew by marriage. Her husband and Boxer's mother were siblings. Boxer—no, she remembered, he wanted to be called Ed now—was fond of his aunt Rhonda, even though he didn't much care for his no-good uncle or his ne'er-do-well cousins.

Back outside, Sherri's cruiser was waiting for them. Liss slid into the passenger seat and buckled up. She and Sherri didn't speak as they left the hotel property and headed for town. It took only a few minutes before the town square was visible dead ahead, but instead of continuing to the municipal building, Sherri flipped on her turn signal and swung into the parking lot at the bank.

"I've been mulling over what Aaron Lucas told us," she said. "I think it's time we took a good hard look at what's written on the back of that map."

The Moosetookalook branch of Carrabassett County Savings Bank provided a tiny room with a wide shelf and two wooden chairs for the convenience of those who wished to add items to or remove them from a safe-deposit box. It was a tight squeeze as Liss and Sherri bent to examine the back of the map.

"See?" Liss said. "Illegible."

Sherry leaned closer. Then she picked up the paper and held it up to the light. "It might have been something once."

"A squiggle."

"We need a magnifying glass."

"Thank you, Sherlock Holmes. And, by the way, you're just lucky I didn't remember to take the key back out of my wallet after the last time I was here. Ordinarily, it would be at home, cleverly hidden in my jewelry box."

Sherri ignored the aside. "Maybe a microscope would be more appropriate. Widdowson was a scientist, right?"

"This is not a spy movie." For once, Liss was the one trying to be practical.

"I don't know, Liss," Sherri said. "There could be something to this 'secret agent' thing. I have to admit that the term *industrial espionage* doesn't have quite the same ring, but you know I've always gotten a kick out of James Bond films, not to mention having a special soft spot for Bruce Willis in *RED*."

"Trust me, Lester Widdowson doesn't measure up to anyone's idea of a superspy."

"But he did leave behind an intriguing puzzle. What you think is just a squiggle could very well be important."

"Fine. I'll get the bank to make a copy of this side of the map."

Sherri shook her head. "We need to take the original to an expert. There must be some way to clear up what's written here."

Liss gave the page a doubtful look. "It looks pretty darned illegible to me."

"It could be in code."

"Or it could be the place Widdowson tested his pen to make sure it had ink in it before he drew the map on the other side."

Sherri conceded the point, but she stood firm. "It would be irresponsible to overlook any possibility and this is definitely a clue."

They took the map with them when they left, returning with it to Sherri's office. She made copies of the back of the page and then, while Liss listened in, she made a few phone calls to friends with more knowledge of forensics than either of them possessed. It didn't take long to come up with someone with the expertise to do exactly what Sherri wanted.

"Well?" she asked. "Your map. Your call. He has to see the original. I'll take it to him personally."

Liss handed it over. She wanted to know too.

It was several hours later when Margaret appeared at the foot of the stairs that led from her apartment into Moose-tookalook Scottish Emporium. She made a beeline toward the front door.

"I'm off to the library," she called out as she passed the sales counter.

Liss looked up from her computer screen. "Let me know if you find anything."

She assumed her aunt meant to continue her research into the Chadwick family, since Liss had asked her to see if she could pin down a relationship between Benedicta Beamer and Hazel Benedict, wife of Norman Chadwick of Nova Scotia. It was a long shot, but it was worth looking into. Besides, Margaret seemed to enjoy climbing family trees, even if they weren't her own.

*Better her than me,* Liss thought. Never in a million years would she have imagined her dynamo of an aunt turning into a genealogy nerd.

When the bell over the door rang again just a few minutes later, she smiled to herself and called out, "What did you forget?" The last two times Margaret had gone to the library, she'd been back just that quickly to grab one thing or another she'd meant to take with her.

"I never forget anything," said a voice Liss did not at first recognize.

Startled, her gaze flew from the customer e-mail she'd been answering to the small woman standing just inside the entrance. "Benny!"

"In the flesh."

Her response drew Liss's attention to Benny's size and general appearance, and what she saw gave her pause. When she stopped and thought about it, Benny seemed an unlikely candidate to spend an entire night digging for treasure. The role of Canadian cat burglar didn't fit either. And why would she murder someone she didn't even know? That was the most preposterous idea of all.

On the other hand, according to every classic mystery novel Liss had ever read, the least likely suspect usually *was* the guilty party. Better to err on the side of caution, she decided. She pasted on her "shopkeeper" smile. "Welcome back to Moosetookalook Scottish Emporium."

Benny giggled again. "Say that three times fast."

"Funny."

"I thought so."

"So, what brings you into my humble shop today?" Liss came around the counter, still smiling, but not before she surreptitiously checked to make sure her cell phone was in the pocket of her slacks.

"I heard you were looking for me."

Bold as brass, Liss thought. Was that a sign of innocence or of cunning?

"I thought I saw you when I was at the hotel this morning, but you disappeared before I could speak to you."

Benny drifted from shelf to shelf, running idle fingers over the merchandise. She picked up a stuffed Loch Ness Monster toy to examine more closely, then put it back. "That must have been when I went for a walk. The hotel grounds are lovely at this time of year."

"They're lovely all year round."

"I'm sure you're right. I'll have to come back in the winter for the skiing." She met Liss's gaze with big, wide, innocent-looking hazel eyes.

That look, combined with the turned-up nose, fair skin, pale hair, and small frame gave her the appearance of an elf maiden. Elves, Liss reminded herself, were sometimes portrayed as benign, even helpful creatures . . . but not always. Sometimes they were tricksters. And sometimes they were warriors. She could not afford to trust Benny farther than she could throw her. Given Benny's size, Liss imagined that she could throw her a considerable distance.

Darker suspicions surged to the surface once more when Liss remembered the way Benny had reacted to seeing Sherri. On the other hand, by this time Sherri had surely done a background check on Benny and obviously hadn't turned up a criminal record. To be fair, the only thing that had made her suspect Benny of being deceitful was the dirt she'd seen under her fingernails. Time to bite the bullet.

"I have a question for you," she said as she followed Benny toward the cozy corner.

The grin on Benny's face vanished, but she sounded game. "Well, sure. What do you want to know?"

"The other day you had dirt under your fingernails. How did it get there?"

Benny looked stricken.

Liss waited.

"Promise you won't set the law on me?" Benny asked.

"No promises." One hand slid into the pocket containing her cell phone.

"I dug up a yellow lady's slipper."

Liss stared at the other woman with a blank expression on her face as Benny plopped down into one of the two comfortable chairs in the cozy corner and curled her legs beneath her.

"It's a rare plant, one of the orchid family. You're not supposed to collect them. No picking them. Definitely no digging them up."

Sinking into the other chair, Liss sat stiffly, both feet flat on the floor and hands clasped in her lap. "And you dug one up?"

Benny nodded, an earnest look on her face. "It was just so pretty that I couldn't resist. I mean, there it was, blooming in the wild like there was no tomorrow. I was on my way to talk to you when I saw it and gave in to temptation. That's why there was still dirt under my fingernails. I didn't even notice it until I got back to the hotel."

"I see." And she did. The story was just bizarre enough to be true.

"I've been keeping it in my room at The Spruces," Benny continued. "I'm taking good care of it. As soon as I get back home, I'll plant it in my own garden. If it flourishes, well then I'll actually have helped preserve the species, right?"

Liss hesitated, still uncertain what to believe.

"So why do you ask?" Bright-eyed, Benny waited for an answer.

"You remember that map I found?"

"Oh, yes." Benny's expression became even more avid, reminding Liss of the faces of little kids as they waited for story time to begin.

The image had her unbending enough to lean toward the other woman. "The spot marked by X turned out to be a brick wall with a loose section that had a cavity behind it."

Benny nodded. "You told me that the other day. Oh—I see. You think because the treasure wasn't *in* the wall that maybe it's somewhere else? Buried next to it, do you suppose?"

"Someone apparently had that bright idea. They dug a series of holes on both sides of the wall, but if they found anything, they took it away with them."

"So *that's* why you wanted to know about the dirt under my fingernails? You thought I was the one who'd been digging?" Benny gave a snort of laughter. "Can you really see me doing manual labor? Believe me, transplanting a flower is as physical as I get!"

With a sheepish smile, Liss acknowledged her point. Hadn't she already worked that out for herself? She offered to make amends with coffee and some of the chocolate chip cookies she'd been unable to resist buying after lunch at Patsy's.

Benny glanced at her watch and shook her head. "I have too much research to do to stay longer. That article I'm working on won't write itself."

"Is it for a magazine?" Liss asked.

"Scholarly journal. Or so I hope. I've been trying to get a full-time job teaching at the college level for ages, but all I ever land is temporary adjunct instructor positions." She grimaced. "Poor pay, no benefits, and no hope of tenure. The only way out of that spiral is to publish. That impresses the people who do the hiring."

"That sounds like a tough way to make a living." And it went a long way toward explaining why Benny took on house-sitting assignments.

"No kidding. And it makes it harder for me to get to source materials, too. If you aren't already affiliated with an institution of higher learning, the major research libraries don't want to let you in. I can call myself an independent scholar, but sometimes that isn't enough."

"Well, I hope those ledgers give you all the information you need for a killer article," Liss said.

"Thanks." Benny bounced up out of the chair and headed toward the door.

When she'd gone, Liss returned to her computer. A quick search for lady's slippers informed her that several kinds grew in Maine and most were still flowering in July. The yellow ones were rarer than the pink, but none was listed as endangered. It turned out that Benny was half right—digging one up was discouraged, but it wasn't illegal. Had she really thought that "the law" was after her that morning, at the hotel? Did that explain why she'd taken off at the sight of Sherri's uniform? Looked at closely, that excuse didn't stand up very well.

*Maybe it was your imagination that took off,* Liss warned herself. If she'd added up a couple of random facts and jumped to a foolish conclusion, it wouldn't be the first time, but she had the strongest feeling that there was something she'd missed. Something Benny had told her didn't jibe with the rest of her story, but try as she might, that vague something eluded her.

# Chapter Fourteen

When Margaret hadn't returned by closing, Liss tracked her down at the library. Dolores Mayfield was just locking up for the day. Grudgingly, she let Liss in.

"I suppose you've got a right," she said, "since you're the one who started this."

"You've found something?" Liss could feel her eyes light up at the thought.

"Come and see," Margaret called from beside one of the library's long wooden tables. She'd spread out the chart she was making. It took up nearly the entire surface. "The older Chadwicks were easy enough to track using census records and I filled in a lot of the blanks with the help of the newspaper articles we got when we were in Nova Scotia. The obituaries were particularly helpful."

Dolores Mayfield made a derisive sound. "Obituaries are full of lies."

"Don't start, Dolores," Margaret warned the librarian. Shifting her attention back to Liss, she added, "It's only natural that surviving relatives would try to make the deceased sound as good as possible. Speak no ill of the dead and all that."

Dolores had never been easily silenced. Figuratively buttonholing Liss, she launched into a lecture. "More people than you'd think make up connections to famous people when they're eulogizing Dad or Mum. Got the same last name? Go ahead and claim direct descent from Ralph Waldo Emerson or George Washington, never mind that in reality there aren't any descendants."

"Well, that's not the case here," Margaret interrupted. "Come and take a look."

Detaching herself from Dolores, Liss studied the Chadwick family tree. "You still have a lot of blank spaces," she observed.

"Not as many as there were when I started." The way Margaret snapped out the words made Liss realize she'd touched a tender spot.

"That's why she needed my help." Dolores sounded smug. "The library has access to resources Margaret lacked. She'd already tapped into the major genealogy sites online, but they don't cover everything, especially if no Chadwick family member ever joined up and provided information."

The longer Liss studied the chart, the clearer it became. The research Margaret had done still only went back to one Eli Chadwick, born in 1750, but now she'd added that his place of birth had been Boston, Massachusetts.

"Why did he leave there for Canada?" she asked.

"My best guess is that he backed the losing side in the Revolutionary War. Lots of Loyalists moved to Nova Scotia afterward. Their neighbors made it rather uncomfortable for them to stay where they were. Eli was lucky. He did well for himself in Nova Scotia. You already know that he was one of the founders of the new settlement that was later named after him."

"Chadwick," Liss murmured. Using one finger to trace the descent, she went from Eli to his son Jedediah and

Jedediah's two sons, Lawrence (1797–1875) and Jeremiah (1799–1866).

"Jeremiah is the one who returned to this country, settled in Moosetookalook, and built the Chadwick house around 1859," Margaret said, "but Lawrence's descendants are the ones who interested me. And look at this. Lawrence had a daughter named Maud and her husband's brother married the sister of the wife of an early MacCrimmon."

"So we're related to the Chadwicks?"

"Well, no, but there's a *connection*."

Underwhelmed, Liss shifted her attention to the section of the chart where she'd thought Margaret might find a link to Benny Beamer. Lawrence's son Chester was the one who'd had a son named Norman, the one who'd married Hazel Benedict.

Margaret tapped Norman's name on the chart with her index finger. "This is the line I've been following with Dolores's help. As you already know, Norman had three children. Daisy, the eldest, never married. Albert, the older son, had a wife but no children. That left us with the youngest child, Harold, born in 1910. He's the one who left home as a young man and was never heard from again."

"Can you speed this up?" Dolores nodded toward the clock over her desk, reminding them that it was now well after closing time.

Margaret ignored the hint.

"When Hazel Benedict Chadwick died in 1950, no one knew where her son Harold was. If he had a daughter, whether he named her Benedicta Chadwick or something else, whoever wrote Hazel's obituary—probably her son Albert—didn't know about her. However, that doesn't mean there was no daughter. The difficulty lay in pinning down a location for our search. Birth, marriage, and death certificates are available, but it helps to know in what state, or better yet in what county, those events occurred. Otherwise, you're left with a general search that will turn up every name in the U.S. and Canada that even remotely resembles the one you're looking for."

Liss appreciated the problem. Wading through dozens of wrong entries must be frustrating, mind-numbing work, but she couldn't help wishing that her aunt would get to the point. Had she and Dolores made a significant discovery or not?

"It's rather like going on a treasure hunt." Margaret said.

By now Dolores was tapping her foot, accurately reflecting Liss's growing impatience. The librarian interrupted before Margaret could draw things out any further. "For goodness' sake, tell the girl what I found."

"*You* found?" Liss asked in surprise.

"Which one of us is the trained researcher here? Of course, I'm the one who found the probate record for the estate of Harold Chadwick. He died in Kansas, of all places."

"You're sure he's the right Harold Chadwick?" Liss's enthusiasm for the project returned in a rush.

"Oh, yes," Margaret said. "Born in Canada in 1910. When he died, in 1990, his heir was his daughter, Hazel B. Beamer. It stands to reason that the B. in Hazel B. stands for Benedict or Benedicta and she named a daughter after herself—"

"Then that's our link." Liss could hardly believe it. Her wild theory about Benny had turned out to be true.

"Once we knew to look in Kansas, there was a lot more information to be found."

Liss barely listened as Margaret detailed all the evidence she and Dolores had accumulated to prove that Benedicta Beamer was the granddaughter of Harold Chadwick. Her mind was busy working out the significance of their discovery. She felt certain of only one thing—Benny herself could hardly fail to be aware of the connection.

"Does she think she has a claim on the property?" she asked aloud. "The relationship is pretty distant."

"Fourth cousin once removed, I believe," Dolores said.

"I'll take your word for it."

"Not a bit of family resemblance that I could see," the librarian added.

"You've met Benny Beamer?" Liss asked.

"Why so surprised? She came in looking for material on Moosetookalook in the nineteen twenties. Spent most of her time at one of the microfilm readers looking at old newspapers and taking notes. Very dedicated researcher from what I could see. I bet it's hard for her to be taken seriously, looking the way she does." Dolores shoved at the glasses slipping down her nose. "Nothing she can do about being short, but if I were her, I'd change my hairstyle."

"I don't suppose she said anything to you about the Chadwicks?" Liss asked.

"She barely said anything at all. A stuck-up little miss, I thought."

Liss was surprised Benny hadn't played the frail-and-helpless-female card, but she supposed that wouldn't have worked very well with someone like Dolores Mayfield.

As soon as Liss and Margaret arrived back at Moose-tookalook Scottish Emporium, Margaret scurried up the stairs to her apartment to collect the dogs. "Come on, kids!" she called out as she entered her tiny foyer. "Walkies!"

Dandy and Dondi came barreling through the living room to greet her. They danced with excitement when she took their leashes out of the coat closet.

"Poor babies," Margaret cooed, snapping leashes onto collars. "You haven't been outside all afternoon, have you? Want to visit the town square?"

"They were out in the dog run for an hour before closing." Liss entered the apartment just behind her aunt, shaking her head at the performance the two Scotties were putting on. To look at them, one would think they never got a bit of attention from anyone but their owner.

People could be just as deceptive.

"It isn't just exercise they need. They crave company, just like humans do."

As she spoke, she reached for the scoop and the plastic bag she'd need to clean up after her charges. Liss wrinkled her nose, hoping the fact that she had let the dogs out earlier in the afternoon would mean Margaret didn't have to deal with that unpleasant task. Cats were much simpler to care for . . . most of the time.

The Scotties were little but strong, dragging Margaret after them as they raced back downstairs. "Slow down, you little demons! Do you want me to break my neck?"

"Question," Liss said when she'd locked the front door behind them. "When you were at my house with the dogs the day I found the map, do you remember that they started barking?"

"I can't say that I do."

"It turns out that there was someone sneaking around outside the house. I think they must have heard him."

As they crossed the street and entered the town square, Liss filled her aunt in on what she and Sherri had learned from Aaron Lucas. By the time she was done, Margaret was shaking her head. "We were concentrating on that mysterious map. I probably just told Dandy and Dondi to hush up and they did."

"It's too bad they didn't kick up more of a fuss. If they'd kept barking, we might have investigated."

"I've been trying to train them *not* to bark at every strange sound. When I first brought them home, the bell on the shop door used to set them off every time a customer came in. They finally adjusted to that, thank goodness, and to hearing the other normal comings and goings in the Emporium."

"That explains why they didn't sound the alarm when someone, probably Aaron Lucas, came into the shop during the night." At Margaret's crestfallen expression, she added, "It's okay. I never expected your Scottish terriers to do double duty as guard dogs."

Margaret had to chuckle at that. "The worst a burglar would have to fear if he broke into my place is that they'd lick him to death."

They followed the flower-lined paths that wound their way around a gazebo-style bandstand, a monument to the Civil War dead, a flagpole, and a playground complete with jungle gym, slide, merry-go-round, and swings big enough for adults. By ignoring the KEEP OFF THE GRASS signs, someone could cross the square in less than two minutes. The meandering route they chose allowed them to keep strolling as long as they liked.

Margaret slowed her steps to allow Dandy and Dondi to examine a tree that had caught their canine fancy. In the branches above, a squirrel chattered, setting off a spate of barking. After a bit, Margaret jerked gently on their leads and they continued walking. Through all the subsequent stops and starts, they discussed the significance of Benny Beamer's Chadwick heritage.

"I wish I'd known about it earlier," Liss lamented. "The

last time I talked to Benny, she had an explanation for the dirt under her fingernails. I almost believed it."

"Almost?" Margaret's eyebrows shot upward.

"There was just something that seemed . . . off about her story." Liss shrugged. "I couldn't put my finger on it. I still can't."

And then, out of the blue, she could.

"She said she was going to take the lady's slipper home and plant it in her garden. Margaret, she doesn't have a garden. She doesn't have a permanent home. She was lying to me."

"Surely she washed her hands and cleaned under her fingernails between the time someone dug those holes over the weekend and the time you noticed the dirt."

"She went back. That's the only explanation. She's still searching on the Chadwick property for . . . something."

"That man from the pharmaceutical company seems a much more likely suspect to me. After all, he's admitted to spying on us, and to following us in Nova Scotia. He even admitted to poking around in our room in Antigonish. Are you certain he wasn't the one who broke into it?"

"I don't entirely believe his story, either."

They had reached the playground. Three middle-grades youngsters were on the merry-go-round, shrieking with delight as they made it spin faster and faster. Dandy strained at her leash, eager to join the fun, but Margaret firmly pulled her away. Side by side, Liss and Margaret sat on the adult-size swings while the dogs explored a nearby bush.

"I hate to raise the possibility," Margaret said, "but do you suppose one of them could have murdered Orson Bailey?"

"I can't think of a good reason why either one would. Besides, as far as we know, Benny wasn't in Canada at the time."

"As far as you know?" Margaret queried.

Liss shrugged. "Sherri's contact, the one who can get information from the border patrol or immigration or whatever branch of government it is that keeps records of that sort of thing, hasn't gotten back to her yet about Benny." She glanced toward the municipal building as she gently set her swing in motion. "I should go over there now and bring her up to speed on what you and Dolores discovered."

With a final pat for each of the dogs, Liss suited action to words.

It took a bit of persuading, but Sherri eventually agreed that it was worth another trip to the hotel to talk with Benny Beamer. By the time they walked into the lobby it was late afternoon, but Joe Ruskin was still on duty at registration.

"Do you know if Benny Beamer is in her room?" Sherri asked him.

"I know she's not," Joe said. "She checked out a couple of hours ago."

Liss bit back a curse. "That must have been right after she talked to me."

"Sounds like it," Sherri said. "What did you say to send her running?"

"Nothing. I've already told you about our conversation. When she left, she said she was going to come back here and work on her article."

Joe had been listening to their exchange with unconcealed interest. "Maybe she found a cheaper place to stay," he suggested. "Aren't writers always strapped for cash?"

"Some of them are." Liss based that belief entirely on interviews with mystery writers she'd read in online blogs. "Unless they're really, really successful. But Benny isn't a professional writer. She's a part-time college instructor who house-sits on the side. Maybe she found a job in the area."

"Carrabassett County doesn't exactly run to people who hire house sitters."

Sherri's skepticism reflected what Liss was feeling. If Benny had lied about the lady's slipper, she'd probably lied about other things, too.

"So where would she go?" Liss asked. "Surely not to the Day Lily Inn."

Besides The Spruces, accommodations in Moosetookalook consisted of that one small, slightly sleazy motel and an up-scale B&B where the rooms were even more expensive than those at the hotel. There was nothing to say that Benny couldn't have resettled farther afield, except that her interest centered around the Chadwick property. Surely she wouldn't want to be too far away.

"Is she really writing an article?" Sherri asked. "I know that's what she told you, but she hasn't exactly been truthful with either of us."

Joe answered before Liss could. "I've seen her sitting in the lobby and typing on a laptop. Of course, I have no way of telling what she was writing. For all I know, she could have been answering e-mail."

"One part of her story did check out," Sherri said.

"Which part?" Liss asked.

"She has worked as adjunct faculty. After you passed on what she said about that, and told me that she mentioned the Glickman Library, I got in touch with the folks at USM. She taught a couple of freshman composition courses there about four years ago, but she hasn't been employed by them recently and no one there could tell me much about her. And before you ask, I checked with personnel and with the department she taught in. They had difficulty even remembering who she was."

"Except for her size and those curls and the giggle, she is kind of forgettable." Liss thought for a moment. "Did they have an address for her?"

"An old one. It appears to have been another house-sitting job. Ditto the more recent one listed on her driver's license, but the DMV also provided me with her license plate number."

"This it?" Joe asked.

While they'd been talking, he'd looked up Benny's registration. The make, model, and license number of her car were listed there, along with a street address in Cape Elizabeth, one of the swankier areas close to Portland.

"The information on her car is right," Sherri said, "but that's an address I haven't seen before. I wonder if this one is current."

"She moves around a lot," Liss said in a dry voice. "Joe, is there any chance her room hasn't been cleaned yet?"

He was already holding out a key card. "No reason you can't go in, now that she's checked out."

The subtle emphasis he put on the last phrase made Liss painfully aware that he must have known about the occasion a few years back when she'd entered a guest's room uninvited, unauthorized . . . and illegally. Until now, she'd thought Joe was unaware of the incident. Had his son told him, long after the fact? Or had he somehow found out on his own? She decided not to ask. At the time, she'd felt her actions were justified.

Sherri took the key card and led the way to the elevators for their return trip to Benny's room. This time they went in.

At first glance, the interior looked as if a tornado had touched down. The sheets, pillows, summer-weight blanket, and goose-down comforter had all been tossed on the floor and the mattress was half off the bed. The closet door stood open, revealing fallen hangers and a single overlooked white crew sock, the top folded over and the discolored sole suggesting that Benny wore a pair of socks instead of bedroom slippers. The desk and desk chair, easy chair, hassock, and reading lamp were in better shape, but they, too, showed signs of a hasty departure. Everywhere Liss looked, items were just slightly askew.

"She left in a hurry."

"Looks like it," Sherri agreed. "And she was keeping something under the mattress. Either that or we aren't the first people to take an interest in this room."

"It looks a lot like our motel room in Antigonish." The words were scarcely out of Liss's mouth before she realized the similarities might be significant. "Could Benny have been the one who broke in and searched it?"

"Why would she steal your laptop?" Sherri retrieved a pair of latex-free vinyl exam gloves from a pocket and slipped them on before pulling out one of the half-open dresser drawers to make certain it was empty.

"Maybe she thought there was information about the Chadwicks on it. Or a copy of the map. That must have been what she was after, right?"

"How did she even know about the map at that point?"

"What if—" She hesitated, then just blurted it out. After all, Margaret had already had the same thought. "What if she murdered Orson Bailey?"

Sherri stopped what she was doing to stare at her. "Why?"

"To get the articles he collected to give to Margaret. We thought he must have made copies, but they were missing after the murder. The society's secretary had to make new ones for us."

"You're jumping to a lot of conclusions. Assuming

Benny was in Nova Scotia, all she'd have had to do to get her own copies of those articles was ask for them. Heck, she had a better right to them than Margaret did, since it turns out that she's a Chadwick descendant. And even assuming that she might have had a reason to take your laptop, thinking there was more information stored there, why would she burgle those other motel rooms?"

"To confuse the issue, of course." That seemed simple enough to Liss. "Doesn't the fact that she's run away prove she's guilty of something?"

"Not necessarily, and it certainly doesn't give me grounds to arrest her." Sherri continued to search the room.

"How about issuing a BOLO? Can't you at least haul her in for questioning?"

Ignoring Liss's question, Sherri picked up the wastepaper basket and stirred the contents. She pulled out a crumpled receipt and squinted at it. After a moment, she gave up. "Can you make out what this says?"

Liss reached for it, but Sherri pulled back her hand. "Don't touch. Just read."

"What are you after? Joe has her credit card number and you don't need to ID her. You already know her name. Heck, we already have all the names in her family tree!" Liss had to hold her head at an awkward angle to read what appeared to be a receipt that had come out of a cash register that badly needed to have its ink changed. Squinting, she made out the date, but the amount of the transaction was illegible. "It's from early June. The seventh."

"Is it?" Sherri asked. "Or does it say July sixth?"

Liss only needed a moment to catch on. 6/7 or 7/6? In Canada, both formats were in use. Newspapers preferred month-day-year and that was what was on customs stamps, too, but immigration records used the day-month-year order and so did a lot of businesses. If this receipt came from one of them, it was proof that Benny had been on that side of the border at the same time as Liss and Margaret.

Sherri tucked the receipt into an evidence bag that had come out of the same bulging pocket as the gloves. "We may be reaching," she warned. "Could be an old receipt from right here in the U.S. of A."

Liss didn't reply. She'd had a thought and was stepping over the twisted sheets to get to the window. The room boasted a splendid view of distant mountains, but her interest centered on the wide sill, the most likely place for someone to put a pot with a flower in it. She was not surprised to find no evidence that such a thing had been placed there while Benny was in residence. The story about digging up a lady's slipper had most likely been a complete fabrication.

She turned to find that Sherri had moved on to search the closet. "Was there anything else in the trash?" Liss asked.

"Only what you'd expect—the wrappers from two of the water glasses, a used basket from the coffeemaker, and a whole bunch of empty creamer and sweetener packets. Since only one mug was used, I'd say our missing friend has a sweet tooth."

Liss opened the mini-refrigerator hidden in a cabinet. If Benny had stored any leftovers there during her visit, she'd taken them with her. In the bathroom, Sherri inspected the cabinet and even pulled back the shower curtain, leaving it open when she returned to the bedroom.

"That's it," she announced, removing the gloves. "There's nothing else to find. Her behavior is suspicious, especially given her distant connection to the Chadwicks and her sudden departure for parts unknown, but I don't have compelling evidence that she's guilty of any crime. I have no reason to go looking for her, let alone to arrest her. It isn't illegal to keep information from strangers—that would be you, Liss—or to lie to them. And Joe is right. If she plans to stay in the area for some time, whether to do research or for some other reason, it makes sense that she'd move somewhere cheaper. The cost of a room in this place would strain most people's budgets."

"Can't you at least check around? See if she is staying somewhere else in town?"

"Officially? No." Sherri opened the door to the hallway and held it ajar, waiting for Liss to take the hint.

Reluctantly, she left, but she was not done searching. Sherri couldn't help. Liss understood why her friend's hands were tied. But there was nothing to stop Liss from looking for Benny on her own. She'd just have to make the rounds herself . . . *un*officially.

# Chapter Fifteen

Liss mulled over ways to find Benny Beamer for the rest of the day, but that evening all thoughts of the other woman were wiped from her mind when Lumpkin, in search of something edible, decided to investigate the plates of salad Liss had just placed on the kitchen table. She'd turned her back on him to collect the rest of their meal from the kitchen counter, unwittingly giving him time enough to catch a claw in a placemat and pull both it and one of the salads to the floor. A dinner plate in each hand, she swung around at the sound of ceramic clattering on tile. It was already too late to avert disaster.

Lumpkin, happily chowing down on scattered bits of romaine, was unaware that a healthy dollop of cottage cheese that had, until a moment earlier, been nestled on top of the lettuce, now decorated his back, the curds actively embedding themselves in his long, luxurious fur. Frozen in place, Liss stared the sight in horrified fascination for far longer than she should have. Mind and body simply refused to take in what she was seeing.

She snapped out of her trance when Lumpkin waddled toward a second shred of lettuce and the cottage cheese started to move down the side of his body. Four steps brought her to the table to set down the plates she was still holding. Then she scooped up the big Maine coon cat and carried him straight to the sink. Caught by surprise, he didn't try to squirm out of her grasp until she turned on the cold water. Keeping a firm grip on Lumpkin, Liss tried to scrub the cottage cheese out of his fur, but all she succeeded in doing was grinding it in more deeply. It wasn't until he was soaking wet that she made any progress with cleaning him.

Drawn by the promise of supper, if not by the commotion in the kitchen, Dan turned up during Lumpkin's impromptu bath. When Liss at last turned off the water and lifted the cat out of the sink, he was waiting with a bath towel to help dry the protesting feline. It took both of them to keep hold of him until he was no longer dripping.

Once he'd been set free, Liss grabbed a handful of paper towels and attacked the mess on the floor, grateful that it was tile and not carpet. With Dan to lend a hand, they were able to eat before their meal had gone completely cold. They split the remaining salad between them.

It was not until after they finished supper that Liss thought of Benny again, and only then because Margaret stopped by to see if there was any news. Liss took the opportunity to bring both her aunt and her husband up-to-date.

By the time she finished, they were seated in the living room, Liss and Dan on the sofa and Margaret in an easy chair. Lumpkin, having forgotten the indignities he'd suffered less than two hours earlier, hopped into Liss's lap. When she automatically ran a hand over his back, she found his long hair dry but stiff and there were still a few tiny white bits of cottage cheese caught in the fur. Reaching into the drawer of the end table, she fished with her fingers until she found the cat brush she kept there. The arrangement of its bristles made it function more like a comb and she began, slowly and methodically, to groom her cat.

Margaret's brows were knit together in consternation. "Seems to me you'll do nothing more than waste a lot of time by looking for her. By now, she could be anywhere."

"With any luck," Dan said, sotto voce, "she's far, far away and won't be coming back."

"I have to try," Liss said without looking up from her task, "if only for my own peace of mind. It's way too unsettling *not* to know where she is."

"Digging holes isn't exactly a major crime," Margaret said. "If she's even the one responsible for that. You said yourself that you have no proof."

"She lied about the lady's slipper. That's suggestive. Who knows what more she's capable of?"

Dan put a hand on her arm, arresting the next stroke of the cat brush. "If you really think she murdered that man in Nova Scotia, you shouldn't go anywhere near her."

He sounded testy and Liss couldn't blame him, but it wasn't as if she planned to put herself in danger. She resumed brushing the cat, a remarkably soothing pastime . . . so long as Lumpkin cooperated. At the moment he was signaling his contentment with a loud purr.

"I'm just going to make a few phone calls. Ask around." *Maybe pay a few visits here and there, Benny's photograph in hand,* she added to herself. She could ask Sherri to make her a copy of that picture taken at the auction, enlarged so that it gave a clearer view of Benny's face.

"I don't suppose it's any use telling you to leave this to the police," Margaret said, "but at least promise us you'll be careful."

"I promise. The only thing I've thought of to do so far is to make a list of all the hotels, motels, and B&Bs in the surrounding area." She paused to glance at the clock and then gave Dan a pointed look. "Isn't it time for your game?"

When he took the hint, reached for the remote control, and turned on the Red Sox, Liss transferred Lumpkin to his lap, along with the brush, after which she and Margaret retreated to the kitchen. Glenora was in her accustomed spot on top of the refrigerator, making Liss wonder if she'd been there all though the cottage cheese debacle.

She busied herself slicing cheddar cheese and collecting crackers and store-bought cookies while Margaret made lemon and ginger tea. In short order, they were seated at the kitchen table. Margaret had also unearthed one of Liss's college-ruled legal pads and a rollerball pen with red ink. It took them less than ten minutes to compile a list of all the lodgings in the area.

"Are you going to start calling tonight?" Margaret asked.

"I'd rather stop by in person." Liss lowered her voice, even though she was sure the sound of the television blaring in the living room would keep Dan from overhearing. "Benny could be using an assumed name. It would be best to show people her picture, don't you think?"

Margaret pursed her lips. "I wasn't kidding when I made you promise to be careful. If there's even the slightest chance that she's the one who killed Mr. Bailey, then she's too dangerous for you to confront."

"Have you seen her? She's just a little bit of a thing. Besides, I'm not going to do anything foolish." Liss took a tentative sip of her tea, found it scalding hot, and got up to get a bottle of cold water from the refrigerator. A dollop would cool the beverage down enough to drink.

"From everything you've told me, that girl is a loose cannon."

"In that case, it would be even more foolish *not* to find her." Liss opened the refrigerator and stood there, staring into the depths, momentarily at a loss. "What did I come here for?"

"I haven't the foggiest." Margaret calmly sipped her tea.

The way her aunt drank beverages that were so hot they were almost boiling had often made Liss wonder if she had asbestos lining her throat. Abruptly, she remembered why she was standing in the open refrigerator door. She grabbed the small bottle of Poland Spring water sitting on the top shelf next to a carton of half-and-half.

"Had myself worried for a minute there." Liss's smile was sheepish as she resumed her seat at the table.

Margaret quirked a brow.

"I thought my memory was going."

Margaret chuckled. "You know what they say—if you stand in front of an open fridge and can't remember what you're looking for, that's okay, but if you stand in front of one and can't remember what a *refrigerator* is for, *then* you should worry. Or words to that effect." Frowning, she peered more closely into Liss's face. "Whatever is the matter? You look . . . stricken."

Liss took a hasty swallow of the cold water before dumping a little of it into her teacup. "It's nothing."

"It's not nothing. Tell me."

With a sigh, Liss capitulated. "It's Mom. Bad jokes about Alzheimer's aside, I'm worried about her. Dad says she forgot to tell him about my phone calls. I must have left a half dozen messages. How could she forget all of them?"

Margaret gave a ladylike snort and settled back in her chair. The frown lines vanished from her forehead. "That's easy. We are talking about your *mother*, Liss. She is a law unto herself and always has been. I imagine she simply decided not to tell him you'd called. Why bother when they'll be seeing you soon enough?"

"I'd have liked to talk to them about their plans to move north *before* they left Arizona."

"Exactly why Vi would have preferred to avoid contact."

"They're on their way." Liss stared glumly into her teacup.

"I know. Donald phoned me yesterday."

"How did he sound?"

"Tired. It's a long drive."

"Mom is driving part of the time." Liss took a sip of tea, grimaced at the taste, and moved the cup and saucer to one side. A mug of hot chocolate would have better suited her state of mind. That, or a stiff drink. "I can't help but worry about them. Their decision to move back to Maine came out of the blue."

"Did it?"

"It looks that way to me. Something must have happened to trigger it."

Margaret finished her tea and set the cup carefully back into its saucer. "Try not to jump to any unfounded conclusions, Liss."

"I prefer to call it extrapolating from the facts."

The smile her aunt sent her in return was tinged with sadness. "Whatever name you give it, be careful. So very often, things are not entirely what they seem."

And with that enigmatic pronouncement, she went home to her dogs.

The next morning, Sherri showed up at the front door of Moosetookalook Scottish Emporium shortly after Liss opened for the day. She brought with her a bakery bag from Patsy's Coffee House and one of Patsy's go-cups. Since Liss had just topped off her mug, the big white one with BOSS emblazoned on it in red letters, they headed straight for the cozy corner. Even before Liss saw what was in the bag, she smelled the cinnamon. Sherri had brought a half dozen freshly baked, cinnamon-sprinkled doughnuts. Liss had scarfed one down and was reaching for a second before she asked her friend if she'd brought the photo of Benny she had asked for.

Sherri produced it. Enlarged, it wasn't as clear as Liss had hoped, but it was better than nothing.

"I also have news," Sherri said. "I spoke to Sergeant Childs on the phone this morning."

Liss couldn't respond verbally—her mouth was full of doughnut—but she knew her eyes lit up. Heck, she was probably as bright-eyed as a puppy catching the scent of a squirrel.

"Don't get too excited," Sherri warned. "There hasn't been an arrest, but I did persuade him to tell me a few more details about the case. I think we can rule out Benny Beamer as a suspect."

Liss swallowed the last of the second doughnut. "Why?"

Sherri dipped into the bakery bag to extract a doughnut of her own. "Did anyone in Nova Scotia tell you how Orson Bailey died?"

"He was murdered."

"I meant do you know what means was used to kill him?"

Liss stopped with her third doughnut halfway to her mouth, her appetite for the sweet pastry suddenly gone. She returned it to the bakery bag untasted.

Sherri looked as troubled as Liss felt. "I'll take that as a no."

"I found the body in a break room. From the door, it was mostly hidden under a round table. The tablecloth reached almost to the floor, so I wouldn't have noticed him at all if his shoe hadn't been sticking out." She swallowed convulsively and her vision was unfocused as she visualized what she had seen that day.

"Did you check for a pulse?" Sherri asked.

"I didn't have to. When I lifted the tablecloth, I could see his face. Nobody who's still alive has wide staring eyes like that." She shuddered. Using both hands, she picked up her mug and took a long swallow of coffee.

"Blood?"

"I didn't see any. I didn't look very hard. I backed out of there at warp speed and waited for the police."

"Okay, here's the thing—Bailey's body had been moved. He wasn't killed in the break room, just hidden there. He died in his office."

"And that brings us back to how?"

"I'm afraid so. You know those spikes people used to use to hold notes? I'm talking about way before computers. Nineteenth and early twentieth century."

"Mounted on a base with the pointy end up?"

Sherri nodded.

Liss felt her face go cold and imagined the color had shifted from merely pale to dead white. "*That's* how he was killed?"

"It was still in his back, plunged in all the way to the base." Sherri looked a bit green herself as she relayed the information. "The thing is, Liss, it took a blow with some force behind it to kill him that way and then the killer had to be physically capable of moving him to another room and stowing him under that table where he'd be more or less out of sight."

From what little Liss had seen of Bailey, he hadn't been obese, but he hadn't been a lightweight, either. It would have taken considerable upper-body strength to drag or carry him from his office to the break room. "Benny's just a little bit of a thing. Even shorter than you are."

"Exactly."

"Adrenaline?"

"Maybe, but it's a stretch."

Liss stood, suddenly too restless to sit still. She didn't go far, stopping at a nearby display to fiddle with clan crest patches and tartan ribbons. Anything to keep her hands busy. "Killing him didn't make any sense in the first place, but killing him with something picked up off his desk? Stabbing him in the back?"

"Maybe he turned away from his killer to reach for the phone and call the police," Sherri suggested.

"Then it would have made more sense for whoever he was talking with to leave while his back was turned. Homicide is a much more serious charge than robbery."

"You're assuming he was robbed."

"The file he'd promised to make for Margaret didn't turn up afterward."

"You said yourself that the police probably took it. I should have asked when I had Sergeant Childs on the line. But whether he has it or not, the fact that Bailey's office was tossed, as if the person who killed him was looking for something, has them thinking the murderer was looking for drugs or money to buy them."

"Did you tell Sergeant Childs our suspicions about Benny?"

"Yes, and about Aaron Lucas following you to Canada too. I figured I'd better bring him up to speed, even though there's nothing solid to connect either of them to Bailey's murder." She hesitated. "You do realize that meant I had to explain the whole map-hidden-behind-the-portrait and treasure-hunt thing? You really should have told him about that yourself."

"At the time, I didn't think there was a connection."

"There probably isn't. Still . . ."

Liss saw the problem. "I'm sorry if you were embarrassed."

"I'll get over it. And it did give Childs a good laugh."

A short silence fell before Liss murmured, "A *messy* search?"

"What?"

"You said Mr. Bailey's office was tossed. Someone made a mess of it."

"Right," Sherri said. "Childs said it was obvious that it had been searched."

Liss frowned. She remembered peeking into that room when they were looking for the archivist and finding it unoccupied. She hadn't noticed anything drastically out of place, but then she hadn't known what it was supposed to look like. Besides, the lights had been off, leaving the entire room in deep shadows.

"And our motel room in Antigonish was searched," she said aloud. "And Benny's room at The Spruces was a mess too. Don't you see? We may have had things backward. What if Benny's room was searched because the killer thinks *she* found what he's been looking for? Maybe she went into hiding for a good reason."

"It's a theory," Sherri conceded. "Not a very sound one, but I'm trying to keep an open mind."

Liss came back to the bookcase that formed one side of the cozy corner. Resting her elbows on its top and her chin on her fisted hands, she gave her friend a hard look. "I know you think I was crazy to call what I found a treasure map, but that theory made sense to begin with. What if Benny still thinks it leads to something left behind by the Chadwicks?"

"Why would she? Didn't you tell her that Lester Widdowson was the one who hid it?"

"She may not have believed me."

"But she knew Widdowson." Sherri shook her head. "No, I don't buy that theory."

"What if someone else thinks the map is older than it really is?"

Sherri set down her go-cup. "What are you getting at?"

"Maybe there's another person involved in this, an individual we know nothing about. Someone who searched *Benny's* room."

"X?" Sherri didn't bother to hide her skepticism.

Liss narrowed her eyes. "Why not? If Benny started out thinking that the map led to a Chadwick treasure, maybe someone else is laboring under the same misconception." She tried to put together a logical sequence of events. "What if whoever killed Bailey was after the file he made for Margaret? Once he . . . or she . . . had it, that person would still want the map, leading to the burglary in Antigonish. That failed because I had the map with me, in my tote, and later I put it in our safe-deposit box at the bank, out of reach."

"By then there were plenty of copies around," Sherri reminded her.

"Yes. I even gave one of them to Benny, so maybe . . ." She broke off, shaking her head. "No, that can't be right. As Lucas pointed out, they only show one side of the map. X would be after the original."

Sherri looked confused. No surprise there, Liss thought. She was confusing herself trying to work this out.

"Who else knows there's something written on the back?" Sherri asked. "Does Benny?"

Liss let her head drop to the top of the bookcase with a thump. Her voice was muffled. "I can't remember if I told her about the squiggles or not. I don't think I did. If someone else is treasure hunting, it may not matter."

"Fine. I'll give you the possibility of a Mr. X, and if he even suspects there's more information to be found on the original map, I agree that he's going to want to get hold of it." Exasperation laced Sherri's voice. "But *if* he exists, then he's dangerous. For goodness' sake, be careful. No more playing Nancy Drew."

Liss glared at her. "I'm not in any danger. You said yourself that Benny couldn't have killed Orson Bailey. And forget what I just theorized about X. I can see for myself that's a pretty unlikely scenario. What can I say? I'm starting to grasp at straws."

Sherri gathered up the bakery bag, her go-cup, and Liss's mug and carried them toward the stockroom. "You've really got to stop watching crime dramas on television. Even the writers on *Castle* wouldn't have pitched that Mr. X plotline."

"I thought you were keeping an open mind."

"Oh, I am. And right now, I'm going back to the office to call Sergeant Childs and find out, one way or the other, about that folder Bailey put together for you."

Liss followed her friend into the back room and took charge of putting away the leftover doughnuts while Sherri tossed the go-cup in the trash and rinsed out Liss's mug. All the while she wondered if her newest theory was all that far-fetched. There *could* be an X, and if there was, then chances were good that Benny knew who he was. He almost had to be another Chadwick descendant.

That brought her back to where she'd started—she needed to find Benny, and the sooner the better.

As soon as Sherri left, Liss called Beth to ask her to work that day at the Emporium. On the short walk from the shop to her house, she rehearsed what she would say to Dan. He wasn't going to be thrilled about her decision, but she hoped he'd feel better about it when she asked him to go with her. It wasn't as if she meant to do anything dangerous.

She opened the workshop door and walked into a haze of sawdust and the sound of wood being milled. From anyone but his wife, goggles, ear protectors, and a Red Sox ball cap would have hidden the identity of the man bent over the machine. Dan was so intent on what he was doing—producing legs that would go with the jigsaw-puzzle tables that were his specialty as a custom woodworker—that it was a good five minutes before he noticed he had company.

"Hey there," he said into the sudden silence that ensued when he flicked a switch. "What brings you home in the middle of the morning?"

"I've got a favor to ask you."

His smile faded a bit. He took a good look at her face, enough to reassure him that nothing serious was wrong. "Coffee break?" he suggested.

Liss was already afloat, but she agreed. While he ate the last of Patsy's doughnuts and inhaled an additional twelve ounces of caffeine, she filled him in on Sherri's reasons for eliminating Benny from suspicion in the Canadian homicide. Then she laid out her proposal.

"We'll take Benny's photo to the front desk of all the lodgings in the vicinity and ask if the woman shown in it is a current guest. Easy peasy. No mess, no fuss. And no chance of Benny twigging to what we're up to unless she happens to be right there in the lobby when you and I show up."

"I don't know, Liss."

"She's not an ax murderer!"

That got a smile out of him. "Probably not." He polished off the last drop of coffee and stood to take his mug and plate to the sink. When he finished rinsing them off, he turned to her. "Just let me get the sawdust off me and we can get started."

While Dan cleaned up and changed clothes, Liss plotted their route. Besides The Spruces, Moosetookalook didn't offer much in the way of accommodations for guests. They could walk to Marcy's Bed and Breakfast, since it was just around the corner on High Street, right across from Graziano's Pizza. They'd start there, but they'd drive. They'd need transportation to get to the rest of the places on her list.

Marcy was full up, but Benny was not one of her guests.

"Good thing we brought the truck," Dan said as they climbed back into the cab.

"You're awfully cheerful about this." His attitude made her suspicious. "You don't think we're going to find her, do you?"

"Nope. Not if she doesn't want to be found. And if she is at one of the places we check, that probably means she wasn't hiding at all. Ergo, she's innocent."

"Ergo?"

He sent her a cocky grin and turned the key in the ignition.

Their second stop was the Day Lily Inn, a mile or so out along Upper Lime Street. It had eight units and no restaurant. The complimentary breakfast consisted of day-old pastries and bad coffee served in the lobby. The proprietor claimed to have gotten a good look at all his current guests and swore Benny wasn't one of them.

"I'd remember a looker like her," he said, giving Liss a friendly leer.

Having known him all her life, and well aware that he didn't have a lecherous bone in his skinny body, Liss responded by giving him a peck on the cheek. "Thanks, Wally. See you at the next Small Business Association meeting?"

"Maybe. Depends."

That was what he always said. Like many in the community, he found it hard to get away from what was essentially a one-man business to do much of anything else. The only help he had was a part-time housekeeper who came in daily to clean the units.

Back in the truck, Liss consulted her trusty *Maine Atlas and Gazetteer*, the only reliable guide to roads in an area where GPS regularly directed cars down dead-end dirt tracks or substituted the local post office for a street address. She had a pretty good idea where most of the hotels and motels in the surrounding area were located. What she was looking for was confirmation that she'd picked the most logical route to take her where she needed to go.

"Our targets are in two clumps. One in Fallstown to the south. One in the opposite direction, taking in the ski areas. I think we can rule out the Sinclair House over in Waycross Springs. It's a good hour by car and just as expensive as The Spruces."

"Agreed. So—north or south?"

"South. Fallstown is closer."

Twenty minutes later, they pulled into the parking lot at the Fallstown Motor Lodge. It boasted fifteen rooms and low rates and had the added advantage of being walking distance from downtown shops, the county courthouse, the Fallstown branch of the University of Maine, and the local brew pub, a place called the Meandering Moose. It was not, however, the current location of Benny Beamer.

They left the truck in the motel parking lot and walked around the corner to the Lonesome Stranger B&B. Its four rooms, all done up in cluttered high Victorian décor, were rented out to a wedding party.

Before continuing the search, they had lunch at the Moose, taking a table in the restaurant half instead of the lounge. Food always cheered Liss up. She was brimming with optimism as they set off for the newly built Comfort Inn on the outskirts of Fallstown.

The desk clerk studied Benny's picture for a long time, but in the end he shook his head. "Doesn't look familiar," he said.

"Is there anyone else we can ask? This is a pretty big place. Maybe you weren't on duty when she checked in."

Another head shake answered her. "Might be big and new and all that, but we aren't exactly turning folks away. Get a week when there's nothing going on in town and we're close to empty from Sunday night till Friday. There's only a handful of people staying here right now and she's not one of them."

"Guess we head north," Dan said in a resigned voice when they were back in the truck.

"Not yet." Liss refused to be discouraged. "We need to visit Lakeside Cabins first."

"Their rates are outrageous at this time of year."

"I know. But maybe Benny's less interested in saving money than she is in hiding out. It's worth a look."

Located a couple of miles outside of Fallstown on the shores of Loon Lake, the housekeeping cabins were scattered through a wooded area to ensure privacy. Liss had

228 Kaitlyn Dunnett

known the owner, Geraldine Robin, for years. Gerri had bright beads for eyes, well suited to her surname, but in personality she more closely resembled a bird of prey. She was always ready to pounce on the least infraction. She took a hard look at Benny's photo and then, like the clerk at the Comfort Inn, shook her head.

"Nope. Haven't seen her. Friend of yours?"

"Not exactly."

"Run out on a bill at The Spruces?" This was directed at Dan and accompanied by a smirk.

"Yeah, that's it. Give us a call if she shows up here, will you?"

"She shows up here, I'll boot her out so fast it'll make her head spin. I hate deadbeats."

Hiding a grin, Liss thanked her and left. On the way back to the truck, she punched Dan in the shoulder. "Wretch! You lied to the nice lady."

"Nice lady my aunt Fanny. That woman has always rubbed me the wrong way."

"Good thing Lakeside Cabins is one of the most un-likely places for Benny to go to ground. I suppose we should try Orlin next."

That small town was located a half hour's drive north of Moosetookalook. It would take them almost an hour to get there. Five Mountains Ski Resort was Orlin's premier hostelry. The place was huge, offering every level of accom-modation from simple single rooms to a luxury condo. If Benny was staying there, she could easily slip through the radar, but Liss was determined to take a stab at finding her. She knew a few people who worked there and sought them out after they struck out with the desk clerk. None of them remembered seeing anyone who looked like Benny. Describing her small stature didn't ring any bells, either.

"There are other ski areas, other motels, and other B&Bs," Liss said.

Dan just gave her a look.

"Yeah. I'm ready to quit for the day, too."

Halfway home, Dan cleared his throat. "Tomorrow's Friday. If Beth can't work and you need to keep the shop open, I can continue the search on my own. I was planning to take next week off anyway."

Liss started to ask why, then remembered that Tuesday was their anniversary. Not only that, but sometime in the next few days, her parents were going to turn up in Moosetookalook. She didn't even want to think about that!

"What do you say?" Dan asked, reminding her of his offer.

"I'm not sure it's worth your time, or mine, either. We've already hit the most likely possibilities, and now that I think about it, she could have rented a camp for a week or two. They're all over the place, and not as obvious as hotels and motels and B&Bs."

"True enough. Patsy was saying just the other day that the neighbors on both sides of her place on Ledge Lake are renting out their camps this year. Short and long term." Dan sent her a sideways glance. "I thought at the time that spending a week at one of them might make a nice vacation for us. Still close to home, but far enough away to give us a break."

"That's a really sweet idea."

"But?"

"But I think we'll have to get a lot farther away from Moosetookalook before it turns into a romantic getaway for two."

"I'll look into that," he promised as he pulled into their driveway. "Meanwhile, how about a single evening for just the two of us? No mention of crime. No speculation about treasure. No worries about the future. Turn off both the cell phones and the landline."

"No Red Sox game tonight?"

"Travel day. We could even watch a romantic movie. Your choice."

That, she could agree to.

# Chapter Sixteen

On Friday morning, even though Liss hadn't called to ask her to work, Beth showed up at the Emporium shortly after it opened. With her was her steady boyfriend, Liss's cousin, formerly known as Boxer. She reminded herself to make sure to call him Ed.

Ed spotted Liss's copy of the portrait of the Clan Grant piper as soon as he walked in. After a moment's study, he shook his head. "That is one ugly dude. I hope you didn't pay much for him."

"Everybody's a critic."

"The original wasn't even good for the time. Seventeen hundreds, right?" At her nod, he started to rattle off names of famous portrait painters of that era.

"Let me guess—you took a class in art appreciation this past year?" Her cousin would start his junior year in college in the fall.

"Nope. Part of something called cultural heritage that we have to take for four long semesters no matter what our major is." He shrugged. "It's actually pretty interesting. Mostly. Anyway, the Grant piper was not included in the examples of great portraits."

"Why am I not surprised. It came out of the Chadwick mansion."

"I remember. It was in the dining room. I also heard somebody hid a treasure map inside the frame."

Liss stopped straightening inventory. "Beth told you, I suppose."

"Nope. It was Aunt Rhonda." He settled sideways into one of the easy chairs in the cozy corner, his long legs dangling over the arm.

"Rhonda Snipes? But how—? Never mind. I can guess. The Moosetookalook grapevine is alive and well."

"Wrong again. It's her job as a housekeeper at The Spruces that gives her an inside track."

Liss hadn't thought about it before, but now she saw that Ed's aunt was in an ideal position to snoop on guests. "I don't suppose Rhonda knows where Benny Beamer has gone?"

"I can ask. It'll cost you, though." At Liss's lifted eyebrows, he grinned. "Aunt Rhonda only knew bits and pieces and Beth is in the dark about a lot of it too. I want to hear the *whole* story."

"And you think I know it?"

"Most of it, yeah. The rest you'll probably figure out before too much longer."

"Thanks for the vote of confidence."

It couldn't hurt, Liss supposed, to go over it all again for her cousin's benefit. The exercise might give her some new ideas.

Since the shop was, not unusually for this hour of the day, free of customers, she used the computer that also served as a cash register to call up the scans she'd made. She had everything in there now—the material from Nova Scotia, the contents of Dolores's file folder, and both sides of the map. Once Ed and Beth joined her behind the sales counter, Liss began her show-and-tell.

They already knew all about Blackie O'Hare's legacy.

Her cousin had been very familiar with both the Chadwick mansion and the tunnel the Chadwicks had built from their basement to Ten Mile Stream. Not surprisingly, he was fascinated by the map.

"So this Lester Widdowson guy hid it behind the portrait?"

Liss nodded.

"That old place sure saw a lot of action before they tore it down."

"More than its share," Liss agreed, and finished filling him in.

Ed considered that in silence for a few minutes and then surprised Liss with a question. "Did you know that my great-grandfather Harry Snipes was a bootlegger too? To hear Uncle Cracker tell it, he was thick as thieves with the Chadwicks. Makes sense. This town wouldn't have been big enough back then to support two smuggling operations. My guess is that he worked for them. He probably wasn't smart enough to go it alone."

"He'd have had animal cunning," Liss mused aloud. "Present company excepted, there are no intellectual giants in the Snipes family, but the entire clan has definitely been blessed with street smarts."

"Yeah," her cousin agreed with a hint of sarcasm, "only occasionally do they get caught and sent to jail. Anyway, some of the old man's stuff is still in the attic over at Rhonda and Cracker's house. He's real proud of having a grandfather who outsmarted the revenuers."

Beth had said little during the last hour, but she had been paying close attention. "It's not so smart to keep evidence of illegal activities," she remarked, making it obvious that she didn't share her boyfriend's enthusiasm for exploring Cracker Snipes's attic.

"I'm not sure anything to do with Prohibition is relevant," Liss said, "although if it turns out that Benny really is writing an article, I expect she'd be interested in whatever you find."

"First you have to find *her*," Beth said.

"Ask Aunt Rhonda. She's at work," Ed added helpfully.

"You really think she knows?"

"Fifty-fifty chance of it. You should hear the stories she tells about guests at The Spruces. Most of the time they ignore the housekeeping staff. It's like they're invisible. So she overhears all kinds of things."

"Most of the time?"

"The ones who do notice her are apt to be looking for something the hotel doesn't offer." He glanced at the clock on the wall behind the sales counter and beat feet for the door, leaving her to make what she would of that statement. "If I'm going to look for old Harry's stuff, I'd better go over there while everyone's at work."

"Cracker and the boys have jobs?" Liss asked Beth after he'd gone.

"Amazing, isn't it? They're directing traffic for a road crew."

"He's not going to break in, is he?"

"Are you kidding? They never lock the doors. They haven't got anything worth stealing." But she still looked worried.

"Something bothering you, Beth?" Liss wasn't sure she wanted to know, but she felt compelled to ask.

"I just wish he'd stay away from them altogether." She sighed. "I wish his last name wasn't Snipes. They have such a terrible reputation and if Ed and I ever get married, I'll be a Snipes too."

"There's a way around that."

"Don't marry him?"

Liss shook her head. "Keep your maiden name."

That got a smile out of Beth, but before they could continue their conversation, the phone rang.

As soon as Liss picked up, Sherri rushed into speech. "I just got a report on what was on the back of the map."

"That was fast."

"My expert never had a treasure map to play with before. Do you want to know what he found?" She didn't wait for an answer. "It's a continuation of the directions, telling you how far from X you need to go to find the real treasure."

Liss held the receiver away from her face and stared at it before putting it back against her ear. "You mean like in—"

"Yeah. Just like in *Indiana Jones and the Raiders of the Lost Ark*. Turns out it was Lester Widdowson's favorite movie."

Morning was just giving way to afternoon when Liss drove into the staff parking lot at The Spruces. She'd hoped to spend the afternoon at the Chadwick place, following the new set of directions on the map, but Sherri insisted they get permission from Brad Jardine first. So far, she'd been unable to reach him.

She felt a trifle guilty as she left the car and headed inside. Once again, she'd left Beth on her own in the shop. She told herself that things wouldn't get busy until after one, and that Beth could handle it, and that Margaret was at home, right upstairs, available to ride to the rescue if Beth felt overwhelmed. None of that made her feel any better, but she didn't turn around and drive back to town, either.

Rhonda was just coming out of a room on the third floor. She sent Liss a wary look as she tucked something into the pocket of her uniform. "Help you?"

"I hope so. I'm looking for Benny Beamer."

"She checked out." Rhonda chewed steadily, cow-like, on a wad of gum. Neither the sight nor the sounds it made were appealing.

"I was hoping you'd know where she went."

Rhonda said nothing. Liss had the feeling she was expecting her to say more, but she couldn't figure out what it was. Finally, looking exasperated, Rhonda took her hand out of her pocket and rubbed her thumb and fingers together in the universal sign for "give me money."

"Oh." Embarrassed, Liss realized she only had a few dollars on her. "I don't suppose you'd take a check?"

Rhonda's lips twitched. A moment later, she was laughing so hard that tears ran down her cheeks. She patted at them with a dust rag as she struggled to get herself under control. "You crack me up," she sputtered. "This time—one time only—I'll answer your question for free."

"Thank you," Liss said.

"Might not be worth much anyway. Curly-top asked me about hotels over to Waycross Springs. 'Nice accommodations' is how she put it." Rhonda pushed her cart along the hallway, moving past Liss to get to the next room. "I told her to try the Sinclair House."

Waycross Springs took an hour to reach by car, but once Liss told Sherri what she'd learned, it took only a phone call to confirm that Benny was indeed registered there. They set out a short time later.

Like The Spruces, the Sinclair House dated from the end of the nineteenth century and still reflected the spirit of the Gilded Age. It had been upgraded to the twenty-first century with similar subtlety and style. Free Internet access existed side by side with gracious and elegant dining in a room that reeked of palatial splendor.

Liss had a nodding acquaintance with the owner's wife,

Corrie Sinclair, but it was Sherri's badge that got them the information they needed. Although Benedicta Beamer was a guest at the hotel, she was not in her room.

"Do you know where she went?" Sherri asked the desk clerk.

"Pine Woods."

Liss had never heard of it and said so.

"It's a nursing home located just on the other side of Waycross Springs. Ms. Beamer said she was going to visit someone there."

Armed with driving directions, Liss and Sherri headed for Pine Woods. Liss felt more and more tense the closer they came to their destination. She had been trying to avoid thinking about nursing homes, senior citizen housing, and assisted living facilities. To actually pay a visit to one took her way out of her comfort zone.

To Liss's surprise, the front door of the facility was locked. To get in, Sherri had to press a button and identify herself over a speaker system. When a security camera swiveled to look right at them, Liss managed a sickly smile.

"Is this a nursing home or a prison?" she whispered.

"I expect they have patients with Alzheimer's, so they're wise to take precautions to keep them from wandering off. Do you have any idea how many calls rural police get every year because an elderly person has gone missing? If we have to search for them in the woods or near bodies of water, the results are rarely good."

Liss's spirits drooped even lower. Envisioning a future in which she'd be responsible for her parents' safety depressed her. With all the advances in modern medicine, it seemed absurd to think that no one had found a way to stop memory loss, let alone some of the degenerative ailments that made it difficult for older people to get around.

"Move fast," Sherri said when a loud buzz and the click

of the door unlocking signaled that they'd been approved for entry. "I've had experience with this kind of system. Hesitate and the door automatically locks itself again."

Once they were inside, Liss expected someone to appear to greet them, perhaps even ask them to sign in, but apparently vetting them at the door was sufficient. The entrance hall opened into a large room comfortably furnished with armchairs, sofas, and card tables. A large, flat-screen TV was mounted on one wall but no one was watching it. In fact, there were only a handful of residents visible. Several casually dressed women gathered around one of the card tables were engaged in a cutthroat game of Nurtz—four-handed solitaire—and didn't look up when Liss and Sherri appeared.

Liss blinked and adjusted her thinking. She wasn't certain what she'd expected a nursing home's residents to look like. There were no housecoat-wearing old grannies here. Neither were there any stylishly dressed matriarchs. Blue jeans or yoga pants paired with tunic tops seemed to be the uniform of the day, at least for the women. The two men in the room wore jeans and T-shirts. One was hooked up to an oxygen tank. The other was sound asleep in his chair, bald, liver-spotted head flung back and mouth open to show teeth so perfect that they had to be dentures.

"Directory." Sherri pointed to a floorplan prominently displayed on a bulletin board. Next to it a list of names and room numbers had been posted.

"Great. Except that we don't know who it was Benny came here to visit."

"No Chadwicks or Beamers," Sherri reported after a quick scan of the residents' names. "I guess we'll have to hunt up someone on staff. You'd think there'd be a nurse around."

A cry of triumph came from the card players. "I win

again!" crowed a scrawny woman with pumpkin-colored hair.

The three who'd gone down to defeat shifted their attention to Liss and Sherri.

"Can we help you girls?" The woman's face was deeply lined but her eyes were bright and inquisitive as a baby bird's.

"Did you happen to notice another visitor arriving here earlier today?" Sherri asked. "A small woman a little younger than we are. Very light, curly blond hair."

"What about her?" A raspy, smoker's voice emanated from a wizened little woman who had to be eighty if she was a day.

Liss warned herself not to stereotype. Neither the woman's age nor her prominent widow's hump had stopped her from slamming cards down on the table at top speed.

Sherri sauntered over, all smiles and charm. She'd changed from her uniform into civvies before they left Moosetookalook, since Waycross Springs was well out of her jurisdiction, and Liss knew she did not intend to reveal her profession unless she had to.

"We'd like to talk to her," Sherri said. "Do you know who she came to visit?"

"Old lady Drucker," croaked the smoker.

"She's having a good day," bird's-eyes chimed in.

"Left-hand corridor, second door on the right," the winner of the game contributed. She looked younger than the others, but not by much, and she was what Liss had heard old-timers call a BMW—a big Maine woman.

Following the directions they were given, Liss and Sherri found a door that stood open. Inside, an aged woman sat in a wheelchair. Benny Beamer was seated facing her, a notepad on her lap and a pen in her hand.

Sherri put out a hand to stop Liss from entering. She

was right, Liss realized. Benny had not yet noticed them and there might be some advantage to eavesdropping until she did.

"He meant well," Mrs. Drucker said.

"I'm sure he did." Benny's eagerness was palpable and she spoke in a way designed to encourage confidences.

"Nineteen thirty-three, it was. Just before they repealed the law. And my what a handsome lad!"

"Walter Chadwick?" Benny asked.

The old lady hooted with laughter at that. "Not that tightfisted old bastard. I mean Harry Snipes. A real charmer, he was. Brought me a gift of silk stockings once. These legs don't look so good now, but in my time I had real nice gams."

*Good grief,* Liss thought. *How old is this woman?* To have been wearing stockings in 1933, she'd have to have been born close to a hundred years ago.

It was then that she caught sight of the object resting across the old lady's knees. It was, unmistakably, a *Boston Post* cane. Decades ago, that now-defunct newspaper had given one of those canes to just about every town in New England. They were presented to the oldest living resident. Upon the holder's death, each one was supposed to be passed along to the new oldest living person in town. After all these years, there weren't many of them still in existence, let alone in the keeping of a person entitled to have possession.

"They must have made a lot of money," Benny said.

"Made it and spent it." Mrs. Drucker smacked toothless gums together. "Easy come, easy go. That Effie, she liked nice clothes, and if they cost a bundle, she liked them even more."

Figuring that Effie had to be a nickname for Euphemia,

Liss leaned closer, reluctant to miss hearing a single word that related to the Chadwicks. That tiny movement was her undoing. Benny looked up and saw them.

Her pale face flashed pink, but she was quick to get herself under control. She turned back to Mrs. Drucker. "What else did she spend money on? Jewelry? Art?"

"Who?" Blank-faced, the old woman stared at Benny as if she'd never seen her before.

"Euphemia Chadwick."

"Do I know you?" Mrs. Drucker asked in a voice that quavered. All of a sudden, she looked afraid. Her eyes darted from Benny to Liss and Sherri, standing in her doorway. "I don't know any of you. Go away." Sounding petulant, she added, "I want Susan."

"*Who's Susan?*" Liss mouthed at Sherri.

Her friend shrugged.

Demands for the unknown Susan escalated in volume, accompanied by an unnerving wail that eventually caught the attention of someone on the nursing home's staff. A trim, efficient-looking, middle-aged woman in white pants and running shoes and a flowered nurse's top skidded to a stop at the door.

Her words to the three visitors were curt.

"You're upsetting her. Leave now."

Then she was kneeling beside Mrs. Drucker's wheelchair, her voice gentle and her manner as comforting as that of a loving mother calming a small child.

Back in the common room, Benny turned on Liss and Sherri, sputtering in indignation. "It has taken me four visits to get something out of that woman. This was the first time she's been anywhere near coherent. You two ruined everything!"

"What, exactly, were you trying to get out of her?" Sherri

steered Benny to a grouping of easy chairs well away from the other occupants of the room.

The four Nurtz players, engaged in another cutthroat round of the game, didn't seem to notice their return. The bald guy was still asleep. The other man had disappeared.

"Who the hell are you and why should I tell you anything?" Benny demanded.

Liss blinked at her in surprise. Benny had seen Sherri, in uniform, at the auction and she'd seen her again at the hotel. She'd run away from her. Hadn't she?

"This is Chief of Police Campbell from Moosetookalook, Benny. She has good reason to want to ask you some questions."

Still seething, Benny flung herself into a chair. "Fine. Ask."

Sherri took a seat directly across from her. "Let's start with you telling me the reason for your interest in the Chadwicks."

"I told her." She jerked a finger at Liss. "I'm an independent scholar. I'm writing an article so I can get a regular gig at some college."

Sherri fixed her with a steely gaze and waited.

Sherri was a small woman, but Benny was even smaller. Liss felt like a giant standing there looming over both of them. She hastily settled into the third chair.

"We know you're a Chadwick descendant," Sherri said.

Benny slumped in her seat. Bowing her head, she stared at her hands. After a few moments, she looked up. After sending an enigmatic glance Liss's way, she focused on Sherri.

"I don't suppose you'll believe me, but the family connection is irrelevant. I only discovered the link after I started my research. I admit that having a personal interest added to my enthusiasm for the project, but that's not why I started it."

"Why did you leave The Spruces?"

"I needed to be closer to Mrs. Drucker. I figured it was going to take some time to get her to remember what she knows. In case you didn't notice, she has Alzheimer's."

"Can the sarcasm, Benny. You left Moosetookalook in a big hurry, almost as if you were trying to avoid being questioned."

Benny glared at her but said nothing.

"What did you have hidden under your mattress?" Sherri asked.

"How—?"

"We saw the mess you left."

Benny shrugged and once again kept mum.

"We wondered if someone else had searched your room after you left," Liss said.

"Who would do that?"

"Oh, I don't know," Sherri cut in before Liss could say more. "Do you have any other relatives who may think they have a claim to the mythical Chadwick treasure?"

The look on Benny's face suggested that she thought Sherri had lost her mind.

"Seriously, Benny," Liss said. "Could there be someone else in your family who thinks X marks the spot where a Chadwick hid something of value? A cousin? An uncle?"

"I'm an only child of an only child," Benny said. "My parents died years ago. As far as I know, I don't have any living relatives."

"No one who might have heard the same family stories you did growing up?"

"What stories?"

"There must have been stories. Someone had to have given you the idea there was a buried Chadwick treasure. Don't bother to deny it. I know you were out there digging in the middle of the night."

"Oh, not this again!"

"If you weren't, then where's the flower? The lady's slipper. Do you have it in your room at the Sinclair House?" Liss had given Rhonda every penny of her spare cash in exchange for answering a second question, but all her cousin's aunt had been able to tell her was that she hadn't noticed any flower in Benny's room when she cleaned it. She couldn't swear that there hadn't been one.

"I tossed it." Benny's tone was glib and she emphasized her lack of concern with a careless wave of one hand. "I didn't want to take the chance of getting arrested."

"Ladies, please," Sherri interrupted. "Can we get back to my question? What did you hide under your mattress, Ms. Beamer?"

"Look, I'm a little paranoid, that's all. There are people, other scholars, who wouldn't hesitate to steal my research and rush their own articles into print before mine is published."

"So you put your *notes* under the mattress?" Sherri sounded incredulous.

Benny nodded. "And sometimes I hide my laptop, too. And I keep the flash drive I use for backup with me at all times."

"All right," Sherri said. "I guess that might make sense. But what about your address?"

"What about it?"

"Don't get smart with me. So far I've found three different addresses for you and you no longer live at any of them."

"My current residence is the Sinclair House."

Sherri drummed her fingers on the arm of her chair, clearly waiting for an explanation. Benny shifted uncomfortably. Liss had to press her lips together to keep from breaking the tense silence that ensued.

"I never have a permanent address," Benny said. "Didn't Liss tell you? I work as a house sitter. Right now, I'm between jobs, so I don't have a street address to give you."

"An independent scholar, sometime adjunct faculty, *and* a house sitter?"

"I've walked dogs and worked as a waitress, too. Not everyone can be lucky enough to find a full-time job with benefits. Look, are we done here? I'm tired of answering stupid questions."

She hopped to her feet, and Sherri rose, too, one hand out to detain her. By now the residents had taken notice of the charged atmosphere. All four card players were staring at them, but the sleeping man continued to slumber, unaware of his surroundings. His uneven snores were the only sound in the room.

"Just one more question," Sherri said. "Where were you between the time you attended the auction and the day you showed up Moosetookalook Scottish Emporium a few weeks later? You didn't, by chance, leave the country?"

Benny looked surprised. "I've been staying at The Spruces. I told her that. I took a room there right before the auction and I didn't give it up until I came here."

"How could you afford their rates?" Sherri asked. "You being between jobs and all? And the Sinclair House is even pricier."

"I had some money saved up. It's worth spending every cent to be on the spot. You don't seem to realize how important on-site research is."

Sherri glanced at Liss. "Anything else you'd like to ask her?"

Liss shook her head. Since her theory about a villainous Chadwick cousin hadn't panned out, she was at a loss. She had to consider the possibility that Benny might have been telling the truth all along, that she might be exactly what she claimed to be. She had an admittedly odd lifestyle, and Liss still didn't quite buy her story about digging up an endangered species of flower and then throwing it away, but what she'd observed of Benny's interview with Mrs. Drucker did seem to verify her claim to be an independent scholar doing historical research for an article.

She watched in silence as Sherri handed Benny one of her official cards with the number of the police department printed on it.

"If you move again, let me know."

"Why should I?" Unspoken, Liss could almost hear the childish taunt of *You can't make me!*

Sherri smiled sweetly at her. "I don't advise that you disappear again. I'd hate to have to send the entire law enforcement community out looking for you."

Head high, looking as indignant as a tiny woman could, Benny stalked out of the nursing home. Liss and Sherri followed at a slower pace. By the time they reached the parking lot, Benny's white van was long gone.

# Chapter Seventeen

Saturday morning dawned chilly and damp, although the temperatures were supposed to soar into the low eighties by afternoon. Still half asleep, Liss climbed into the passenger seat of the truck and let Dan do the driving. It only took a few minutes to reach the old Chadwick property. Two vehicles were already parked in the drive. One was Sherri's cruiser. Liss assumed the other belonged to Brad Jardine and was not surprised to find the developer waiting for them at the wall marked by the X on the map. He huddled in a gray hoodie, a steaming cup of take-out coffee held tightly in both hands.

"Ridiculous waste of time," he grumbled.

"You didn't have to come." Sherri was short with him as she pulled a sheet of paper out of her pocket and handed it to Liss. "Here's what my expert came up with. You want to do the honors?"

Liss read what was written on it and started to laugh. She passed it on to Dan.

"And then go forty paces due west of X," he read. "Unbelievable."

Liss squinted at the sun, slowly rising in the east, before turning her back on it. The direction she was facing was heavily wooded. That figured!

"I have a compass," Sherri said, producing it.

"How long is a pace?" Liss asked.

"Your guess is as good as mine, but you have to figure that Widdowson counted it off himself. He was a tall, skinny, geeky-looking guy, so he probably took long strides."

Liss glanced first at Dan, then at Jardine. Dan was taller. She gestured for him to lead the way, but before he could take the first "pace" the sound of voices reached them from the direction of the driveway.

"I thought this was a private party," Jardine complained.

"I didn't invite anyone," Sherri said.

Liss shook her head in denial, but she wasn't surprised that word had leaked out. Not only was this a small town, but at least two interested parties—Dolores and Rhonda—had been keeping an eye on what the local chief of police and her friend the amateur snoop got up to. Dolores had her bird's-eye view of the town square. Rhonda knew more of what went on at The Spruces, but she also had a conveniently placed nephew to pump for information.

There were three uninvited spectators. Aaron Lucas and Maurice Kelsey arrived together. The conveniently placed nephew in question trailed along after them. There was no mystery about how he'd learned what was going on. Liss had told Beth when she'd asked her to mind the store that morning. Of course Beth would share that information with her boyfriend. No one had told her not to.

Liss nodded to her cousin. He'd hadn't reported finding any interesting records left behind by Harry Snipes, so she assumed he'd struck out in Cracker and Rhonda's attic. She supposed she couldn't blame him for being curious about today's expedition.

She was about to suggest they get started when yet an-other figure emerged from the surrounding underbrush.

Sean Widdowson's appearance did surprise Liss, although she knew Sherri had contacted him to ask about the Indiana Jones connection. Greetings and introductions had barely been exchanged before a rustling in the bushes alerted them to someone else's none-too-silent approach. A moment later, Benny Beamer stumbled into the clearing.

"More research?" There was only a hint of sarcasm in Sherri's voice.

"Did Rhonda tell you, too?" Liss asked.

The question had Kelsey and Lucas exchanging a startled glance. Benny stayed mum.

"Is this everyone?" Jardine tossed away his empty Styrofoam cup with a fine disregard for the environment and directed his next question to Sherri. "Can we get on with this nonsense now?"

Obligingly, Dan turned to face west and set out, counting under his breath. Liss had to suppress a laugh. His idea of "paces" had him looking like John Cleese as he strode through the high grass toward the tree line. She trotted after him, followed in single file by everyone else.

"Forty!" He stopped walking. They were in another small clearing. Years' worth of dead leaves and pine needles carpeted the ground.

"Did anyone bring a shovel?" Jardine asked.

"Here." Sherri had thought of everything, but she wasn't about to offer to dig. She handed it to Dan.

"This ground is as hard as iron," he complained. They'd had showers now and again, but soaking rains had been rare all summer.

Annoyed that everyone else seemed content to let her husband do all the work, Liss scanned the clearing, hoping for some further proof that they were at least looking in the right place. That whole "forty paces" thing seemed pretty arbitrary. Her gaze passed over an anomaly before it registered.

Leaving the others focused on the digging, Liss picked her way toward the spot. Tall grass and shrubbery almost obscured the top of something that was clearly manmade. She stopped when she reached it, surprised to see that it was a well. She couldn't fathom what it was doing out here. There was another one closer to the house that had supplied the Chadwicks with water before the town extended its line out this far. Had there been an earlier building on this part of the property? She supposed that was possible, but she didn't think this was a relic of the nineteenth century. She had a vague notion that older wells were made of brick or stone and came complete with wooden roofs and buckets on pulleys. Obviously, she'd watched too many episodes of *Little House on the Prairie* when she was growing up!

The well was round, about two feet in diameter, and made of cement—or was it concrete? She never could keep those two straight. Whatever it was made of, it had a square opening cut in the top. The well cover was a solid block of the same material. A rusty grab bar stuck up to aid in removing it. Wishing she had something to protect her hands, Liss attempted to hoist if off, but it was too heavy for her to lift.

A rustling sound was all the warning she had before Benny came up beside her. "What have you found?"

"Probably nothing, but I was thinking those paces could have as easily ended here as where Dan is digging."

"Might as well look."

Benny hopped up onto the rim of the well, took hold of the grab bar with both hands, and with one mighty heave had it up and out. Letting it fall to the ground beside the well, she peered into the depths. After a moment, she knelt so she could run her hands along the inside.

Grimacing, imagining the coating of slime that had undoubtedly accumulated there, Liss turned away. Her attention was caught by the discarded well cover. It had landed at an angle, so that the bottom was partially exposed. She bent closer to examine the underside. A small, flat metal box had been carefully wrapped in heavy plastic to prevent water damage and attached to the well cover with duct tape.

For a long moment, Liss just stared at it. Then she started to laugh. The hokeyness just didn't quit!

Benny tried to shush her, but it was too late. Heads were already turning their way.

Liss's cousin Ed loped over, took in the situation with a single glance, and gave a low whistle. "Hey, Dan. You can stop digging now."

The others made their way to the well.

"Careful," Sherri warned as Kelsey started to circle the rest of the party in an effort to be the first to arrive at the scene. "That's poison ivy you're about to walk through."

He backtracked in even more haste.

With everyone gathered around, including her sweaty, dirt-covered, justifiably irked husband, Liss attempted to detach the box. It was stuck tight. Dan had to produce a knife and slit first the duct tape and then the plastic before Liss could extract the metal box.

It was a long way from being a treasure chest and she could tell by its weight that it did not contain gold or jewels, but it clearly held something of value. Her best guess was a slip of paper with a formula written on it. She wanted to open it then and there to find out, but it was welded shut.

Sean Widdowson pushed himself forward. "I'll take that. It belonged to my father."

"Just a minute!" Kelsey objected. "If that box contains material he stole from Cornwall Pharmaceuticals, then it's the property of the company."

Aaron Lucas stepped between Widdowson and Liss and extended one hand in her direction. "Hand it over."

"Not so fast," Widdowson objected.

The two men looked ready to come to blows. Liss saw Sherri's hand move to rest lightly on her holster, but before she had to step in to break up a fight, Brad Jardine put an end to the dispute.

"Gentlemen," he said, pitching his voice loud enough to drown out their argument, "you seem to have forgotten one thing. This box was found on my property. That means I own it, whatever it is."

Relieved to have the matter settled, Liss handed it over.

"That's theft, plain and simple!" Kelsey bleated.

"Your lawyers can talk to my lawyers if you have any complaints," Jardine shot back.

Muttering something about not putting any more money into some high-priced attorney's pockets, Widdowson bowed out of the competition and walked away. A few minutes later, Liss heard the sounds of a car engine starting up and a vehicle driving away.

The rest of the group started to break up, most of them still grumbling. Jardine was set to leave with the box when Sherri put a hand on his arm.

"I expect to receive a report on what you find when you open that, Mr. Jardine. Whether or not it contains a stolen formula, it has a bearing on matters I'm investigating." At his raised eyebrows, she clarified. "There have been break-ins at a local home and business. They appear to be related to the case."

Benny, shoulders drooping now that the excitement was

over, had already left the clearing, but Sherri's explanation produced a scowl from Kelsey and had Lucas putting on his blankest face.

"A word, Mr. Lucas?" Sherri turned her attention on him before he could get away. "At the police station, I think. I'll give you a lift."

Liss sent Dan a hopeful look.

"Go on," he said, resigned. "Ride in with Sherri. I'll fill in this hole and then go home and clean up."

"You're my hero." She planted a kiss on one dirt-streaked cheek. "Thank you."

"Go," he said again. "Can't have you dying of curiosity."

She went.

Twenty minutes later, Aaron Lucas sat in the visitor's chair across from Sherri's desk. Liss was ensconced behind the second desk in the small, crowded room. By now, she felt certain, Maurice Kelsey had called his bosses for instructions and a lawyer was on his way to represent the company's close-mouthed employee.

She found it hard to keep from fidgeting. She had as many questions for Lucas as Sherri did, but since she had no official reason for being present, she knew she should keep them to herself. There was something else troubling her, too, but it would have to wait until she could speak with Sherri alone.

So far, Lucas had not been overly cooperative. He'd admitted that he'd bribed Rhonda Snipes to feed him local gossip, thus confirming how he and Kelsey had known to show up at the Chadwick property that morning. Beyond that, he'd given one-word answers to Sherri's questions, mostly verifying things he'd told her the last time she interrogated him.

"Can you prove you weren't in Chadwick, Nova Scotia?" she asked.

"Hell with it," he muttered, and reached into his back pocket, took out his wallet, and removed a credit card receipt. He passed it across the desk.

"What's this?" Sherri frowned at the badly crumpled slip of paper.

"You wanted proof. There it is. I was exactly where I said I was. Look at the time and date. And look at the *place* where I bought gas. I couldn't have been in Chadwick when that guy was murdered."

Sherri studied the receipt, then glanced at Liss. "He's right."

"Fine. You're not a killer." Liss hadn't really thought he was. She came out of her chair and approached until she was just out of arm's reach. "That doesn't let you off the hook for everything. You've been involved in this from the beginning. You followed us in Canada intending to steal that map."

"I admit nothing except that I came upon the scene of your burgled hotel room after the fact."

"Settle down, people," Sherri said. "Liss, back off." She smiled, showing lots of teeth. "I believe you, Mr. Lucas. You're a professional. As you told us before, if you had broken into that motel room, you wouldn't have left any trace."

"Damned straight."

"So let's talk about some break-ins that *were* professional. Break-ins that, coincidentally, happened in my jurisdiction. This is a one-time offer, Mr. Lucas. You tell us the truth and I won't pursue the matter. Liss here won't press charges."

Silenced, Liss watched her friend hold Lucas's gaze until her eyes started to water and she was forced to blink.

He laughed. "Points for trying."

"Do you really want to do this the hard way? I didn't find any unidentified fingerprints, but there was a hair. Everywhere we go, we leave DNA evidence behind. Are you sure you want to risk testing the assumption that I can prove you were there?"

He had a good poker face, but a slight tightening of his jaw gave him away. He couldn't be 100 percent certain Sherri was lying about the hair. Liss, on the other hand, was pretty sure she was. Would Lucas call her bluff or take the deal?

Sherri was sweating lightly by the time he spoke. "Why should I trust you?"

"Because I don't want to go to the expense of proving I'm right. This is a small town. We have a limited budget for law enforcement. Oh, don't get me wrong. I'll do it if I have to. But I'd prefer to get my answers here and now. In fact, I'm hoping you did break in. Otherwise, I've got to go looking for someone else."

Liss, wisely, kept silent while Lucas waged a silent debate with himself. It lasted only a few seconds, but those seconds seemed like hours.

"Okay. Deal. I checked out the gift shop. Later I was in her house." He jerked his head toward Liss. "She damned near caught me that time."

"Find anything interesting?"

"No. It was a total waste of time."

"What about Benny Beamer's room at The Spruces?"

He looked blank, and this time Liss didn't think it was deliberate. "What about it?"

"Did you search it?"

"Why would I? She didn't have anything I wanted."

Sherri looked at Liss. "Do you believe him?"

"Oddly enough, I do."

"Okay, then." Sherri made a shooing motion in Lucas's direction. "You can go."

Once he'd left, Liss took his place in the visitor's chair. "Did you really think he searched Benny's room?"

"No, but I thought I'd better ask. I don't think anyone searched it, other than the two of us. I think she left it that way herself."

"Any word from your contact in Canada? Do we have confirmation yet that Benny was there when Margaret and I were?"

Sherri narrowed her eyes. "No word so far. Why? Have you decided that she was the one who burgled your motel room?"

Liss drew in a deep breath. "The messy search part fits, but there's something else, something that happened out at the Chadwick place this morning. I'm beginning to think that we need to reconsider Benny as a suspect in Orson Bailey's murder."

"Has she grown a foot and turned into Wonder Woman since the last time I saw her?"

"She didn't have to. I know we originally thought she couldn't have killed him because she wouldn't be strong enough to stab him and then move the body to another room, but I watched her lift off that well cover as if it weighed nothing at all. Seriously, Sherri, that sucker was heavy. When I tried to move it, it wouldn't budge. Benny Beamer has serious muscles hidden under those long-sleeved shirts she wears."

"I've got good news and bad news," Sherri said when she walked into Moosetookalook Scottish Emporium later that afternoon. "Which do you want to hear first?"

"Hit me with the good," Liss said. "I need cheering up."

She'd been trying to reach her parents for the last two hours. Every call went straight to voice mail.

"Benny was definitely in Canada at the same time you and Margaret were. Not only that, but the RCMP confirms that she tried to book a room at the same motel in Antigonish where you and Margaret stayed. A desk clerk identified her from the photograph I sent to Sergeant Childs. They were full up because of the Highland Games and she kicked up quite a fuss when she was turned away."

"That's the *good* news? I can hardly wait to hear what you consider bad."

"It *is* good," Sherri insisted. "Since she was right on the spot, that means it's entirely possible that she ransacked your room. She probably took your laptop and Margaret's jewelry and burgled those nearby rooms to cover up the fact that she broke in to search for the map."

"Okay." Liss wasn't sure where this was going.

"Since she's now a viable suspect in that crime, our Canadian friends will show her photo in Chadwick, and because the RCMP is interested in her activities, I have grounds to interview her again, maybe even bring her in for questioning."

"*That's* the good part?"

"Yes."

"But you don't have proof of anything. That means you can't arrest her, not for the burglary, and certainly not for Orson Bailey's murder."

"And that's the bad news." Sherri took a closer look at Liss's face. "What's wrong?"

"Nothing. I hope. I haven't been able to connect with my folks. I don't know where they are." Her concern for her parents put every other issue in the shade.

"They're somewhere between Arizona and Maine." Sherri's voice was dry.

"Oh, that's a big help!"

"If you're really worried, I can—"

"No! I'd never live it down if Mother found out there was a BOLO issued for their car."

"You know they're grown-ups, right? Checking in with you is probably the last thing on their minds."

Liss blew out a breath. "You're right. And in a way I'd just as soon put off the big reunion. On the other hand, the sooner they get here, the sooner I'll know what's really behind this move to Maine. The suspense is killing me!"

She tried to make light of her fears, but they continued to prey on her. She hated knowing that her parents were approaching the point when they would no longer be able to function on their own. She dreaded the moment when she'd have to be the one to take away her father's car keys because it was no longer safe for him to be behind a wheel. She couldn't imagine dealing with a mother who no longer had a fast, if annoying, comeback to every innocent remark her daughter might make.

"Focus, Liss." Sherri's sharp-voiced command snapped her out of her funk. "Do you want to come with me to talk to Benny?"

Liss glanced at her watch. It was a little early to close the shop, but at the moment she had no customers. For a Saturday, business had been excruciatingly slow. "I'm coming."

She stepped around Sherri to lock the front door and flip the OPEN sign to CLOSED. "Is she still at the Sinclair House?"

Sherri had her phone out. "Checking now, but she was supposed to tell me if she moved and she didn't say anything this morning at the dig site."

If Benny had been lying all along, Liss had serious doubts that she would abide by that promise. She busied herself tallying up the day's receipts and shutting down the cash register, listening with only half an ear to Sherri's low-voiced conversation with the desk clerk in Waycross Springs. She looked up, startled, when her friend ended the call with a muttered oath.

"What?"

"Gone."

"Checked out?"

Sherri nodded. "Late last night she got a call herself, apparently from Rhonda Snipes. The woman at the Sinclair House knows Rhonda. She recognized her voice. It looks like I'm going to have to have a little chat with Boxer's aunt."

"Ed. He goes by Ed now."

"Whatever! I've been putting off dealing with Rhonda for too long already. Word is that she's established a nice sideline soliciting tips in exchange for information. Not just at The Spruces, either."

"Is that illegal?" It sounded more like entrepreneurship to Liss. She didn't like Rhonda, but she had to admire her ingenuity.

"That depends on the information." Sherri waved off more questions. "I'll deal with her later. Right now my priority is locating Benny."

"Maybe she's back at The Spruces."

"I wouldn't bet money on it."

Several phone calls and a great deal more muttering later, Sherri's hunch was confirmed. Once again, Benny had disappeared. Liss and Sherri were still at the Emporium, considering their next move, when Sherri's phone buzzed.

Liss watched her friend's face as she listened to the person on the other end of the line. Whatever had happened, it wasn't good.

"Well?" she asked when Sherri disconnected.

"That was Brad Jardine. Someone jumped him from behind, knocked him out, and stole the box we found this morning."

# Chapter Eighteen

It was evening before Liss heard any more about the assault on Brad Jardine. Sherri stopped by Liss and Dan's house on her way home from work. Liss took one look at her friend's haggard expression and slumped shoulders and all but shoved her into a kitchen chair.

"Have you had anything to eat? You look like you're about to drop from exhaustion."

"I'm fine," Sherri insisted, but she didn't object when Liss hastily unwrapped the leftovers she'd been about to put in the refrigerator and made up a plate for her. "Thanks."

"Would you like coffee or lemonade?"

"I'd like a stiff drink, but it better be coffee. I have a feeling I may not be done for the day."

"Dig in." Having refueled her friend, Liss went back to a sink already full of soapsuds. "Talk to me while I do the dishes."

Liss was certain that at Sherri's house, Pete and the kids had already finished their meal. There were few families that dined fashionably late in this part of Maine. Unless shift work interfered with a regular schedule, most people had the food on the table as soon as everyone was home from work for the day. She and Dan often set up TV tables and ate while watching the local news at five-thirty. They were almost always through with supper by the time the national news came on an hour later.

"Jardine has a nasty bump on his head but otherwise he's fine. Mad as a wet hornet, but fine." Sherri paused to eat another few bites of the chicken stir-fry Liss had put together when she got home from work.

"Did he see who hit him?" Liss asked.

Dan, temporarily abandoning the Red Sox pregame show he'd turned on in the living room, appeared in the doorway. He, too, listened attentively for Sherri's answer.

"He says he didn't see or hear a thing. He felt a moment's pain and when he came to, the box was gone. That said, I don't think there's any doubt about who stole it. I've spent the last five hours digging into Benny Beamer's past."

That caught Liss's full attention. Leaving the rest of the dishes to finish later, she joined Sherri at the table. Dan stayed where he was, propping up the door frame.

"Tell."

Sherri took another sip of her coffee. "She's a total fraud, for one thing."

"Not a college instructor?" Liss guessed.

"Oh, she held a couple of adjunct positions, just like she said. Part-time instructors work cheap and apparently their credentials aren't always checked as thoroughly as they should be. Benny was involved for a while with a guy who makes a legitimate living as an adjunct professor of English. That's how she figured out how to impersonate someone like him, but it turns out that Benny never even graduated from college. She won an athletic scholarship to cover her tuition, but then she was expelled. No one's saying why, but it had to be something fairly serious."

"Back up," Liss interrupted. "Athletic scholarship? What sport?"

"Gymnastics."

The cats, hoping for something, preferably chicken, to drop into their mouths, sat on either side of Sherri's chair, trying to look as if they hadn't eaten in the last decade. Sherri ignored them.

"Gymnastics," Liss repeated. "That explains a lot. Gymnasts are tiny, but they're strong. The loose clothing Benny always wears fooled me into thinking she was too weak to haul a dead body around."

"It's the next part of her story that really gets interesting." Sherri ate a few more mouthfuls of the stir-fry before she explained. "Her first job after she was expelled was as a receptionist at Cornwall Pharmaceuticals. She was there for six months . . . at right about the time Lester Widdowson was getting ready to leave the company."

"And around the same time he bought the Chadwick house?"

"Give the girl a medal." Sherri pushed her plate away, having polished off every morsel.

"That means it's likely that Widdowson heard about the place from Benny," Liss mused.

Lumpkin put his front paws on Sherri's thigh and checked to make sure there was nothing left. Sherri glared at him until he got down again. Liss was too lost in her own thoughts to notice.

College degree or not, Benny knew how to do research, and Liss was willing to bet she'd grown up hearing plenty of stories about the Chadwicks and how they'd made their fortune. It was easy to imagine her talking Lester Widdowson into buying the property. If he'd mentioned that he was looking for a private place to run his own experiments and if Benny already knew about the land once owned by the Maine branch of her family, she might well have believed that there was something to be gained by visiting the mansion in person. Of course she'd have jumped at the chance to put the property into friendly hands. Since she could play the part of "sweet young thing" to a T, it would have been a piece of cake for her to charm an older man like Widdowson. As if to confirm her theory, Liss remembered something else.

"Dolores told me that Lester Widdowson had a woman with him the day he came to the library. That was right before he bought the place. I wonder if that was Benny?"

"Didn't Dolores recognize her when she came back to town? I know Benny used the library at least once in the last few weeks."

Liss shook her head. "The woman with Widdowson waited for him outside, by the car. Dolores only saw the top of her head."

Sherri's brow furrowed. "I don't get it. If she was here with him then, wouldn't she have searched the mansion and the grounds at the time?"

"Maybe she did." Liss's agile brain scrambled to realign the known facts with logical speculation. "What if she's known since then that there's no Chadwick treasure? What if it's the formula she's been looking for?"

Sherri slid her chair away from the table and stood. "At the moment I don't care what she's after. I just want to find her. But first I'm going to go home and give my kids a hug before they go to bed."

Dan was blocking the way out. "Hold up for just a second. You didn't tell us what else you found out about Benny. Where did she go after she left her job as a receptionist?"

"That's even more suspicious," Sherri said. "She did a

complete disappearing act for nearly a year. Then she turned up under arrest for trying to trick an old woman out of her savings. She was using a different name, which is why her shady past didn't pop up the first time I did a background check."

"If she knew Widdowson stole from the company they both worked for, it makes sense that she wouldn't hang around. If he'd been arrested, she could have been accused of being his accomplice."

"Maybe. Apparently, she took up with a con man and was using his last name, even though they weren't married."

"Was any of what she told us true?" Liss asked.

"Oh, sure. The house-sitting gigs were real. Funny thing, though. After the owners got home, they noticed there were things missing. Not the obvious objects like jewelry or computers, but items they'd stored in attics or cellars and had no reason to look for right away." Sherri edged past Dan, working her way along the hall toward the front door.

Liss trailed after her with another question. "Why come back now? Why would she think Widdowson left something valuable behind?"

"Your guess is as good as mine. Maybe he told her what he had planned." Sherri glanced at her watch. "I've really go to go. Amber and Christina will already be in bed."

Her hand was on the knob, but before she could turn it, Liss heard the sound of running footsteps. They were followed by a frantic pounding on the outside of the door.

Aaron Lucas stood on Liss and Dan's front porch, his fist raised to knock again. He looked surprised to find Sherri there, but his gaze touched only briefly on Moosetookalook's chief of police before fixing on Liss.

"We need your help, Ms. Ruskin."

"You'd better come in." Liss stepped back and gestured toward the living room that opened off the hallway.

"Do you want me to stay?" Sherri's reluctance was palpable.

Lucas didn't look thrilled by the idea, either. His tone was grudging. "I suppose you'll have to find out about it sooner or later."

"Find out about what?" Although Dan glowered at their unexpected visitor, he didn't try to prevent him from entering the living room. He even went so far as to mute the television, although he did sneak a peek at the score of the Red Sox game that had started while he was in the kitchen.

Lucas raked his fingers through his dark hair. He didn't sit, and he couldn't quite meet Liss's eyes. "Kelsey received a phone call about an hour ago. A woman offered to sell him the formula Widdowson hid in that metal box."

"How do you—?"

Lucas almost cracked a smile at Sherri's expression of disbelief. "How do I know the box was stolen? It didn't take long for that story to spread."

"This woman," Liss said. "Did you recognize her voice?"

"I pinned it down when she called a second time to arrange the exchange."

"Benny Beamer?" Sherri asked.

He nodded. "Benny Beamer."

"Did you know she worked for Cornwall Pharmaceuticals at the same time Lester Widdowson did?"

When Lucas looked even more grim and didn't answer, Liss guessed he had not.

"She wants money in exchange for the formula," he said after a moment, "and before you ask, Kelsey brought a large amount of cash with him. He anticipated having to pay bribes. We're covered there."

"So what's the problem?" Sherri sneaked another peek at her watch.

"And why," Dan asked, taking a threatening step toward the other man, "did you come here?"

"I think you've already guessed," Lucas said, taking a prudent step away from Liss's husband. "The Beamer woman set conditions. She wants Ms. Ruskin to act as courier."

Just after dark, despite vehement objections from her husband, Liss drove away from the house with the bag of cash Kelsey had provided sitting on the seat beside her. She was nervous, but not scared. In spite of her suspicion that Benny had killed Orson Bailey, she could think of no reason for the other woman to harm her. Benny would take the money and run.

The drop site was in a remote area of town, accessible only by a poorly maintained dirt road. Liss had slowed to a crawl the moment she turned onto it. She had almost reached the spot where she'd been told to leave the bag, a location Sherri and her officers would have staked out by now, ready to arrest Benny the moment she showed up, when the cell phone in Liss's jeans pocket began to vibrate. She tried to ignore it, but it stopped and started again. She was tempted to haul it out and shut it off without even looking at the screen, but the faint possibility that her parents were finally returning one of her calls changed her mind. Since the end of someone's driveway conveniently appeared off to her right, she pulled in next to the mailbox and answered.

"Such a Goodie Two-shoes," Benny Beamer said. "I knew you'd be one of those people who have to keep both hands on the wheel."

Liss was too startled to say anything. She peered into the darkness around her. Was Benny out there, or was this just a ruse to keep the courier off balance? Either way, getting this phone call was not good. Clearly, the other woman had no intention of showing up at the location she'd given Aaron Lucas.

"Drive a little farther," the voice in Liss's ear instructed. "Around the curve so your car can't be seen from the road. Then get out and walk into the woods on your left. Don't forget to bring the money."

Resigned to doing as she was told, Liss followed orders. She shivered a little as she turned off the engine and the headlights. It would be hard for Sherri to spot the car and she couldn't track Liss's phone with GPS because Moosetookalook didn't run to fancy, expensive tracking equipment. It didn't matter, Liss told herself. Benny was a city girl. She wasn't likely to be too far away. Besides, she had no reason to do anything worse to the person doing her bidding than tie her up and leave her in the woods.

Somehow, that thought was not as reassuring as it should have been.

"I need three hands," she muttered, trying to figure out how to hold a flashlight in one, keep the phone pressed to her ear with the other, and still carry the bag containing the payoff. Her solution was to open the trunk and haul out one of the totes she used for groceries. Since it had long straps and could be slung cross-body, she appropriated it to carry the payoff.

"What's the holdup?" Benny demanded.

"On my way," Liss said. "How far?"

"I'll tell you when to stop." She sounded testy.

When Liss heard rustling in the woods and saw a faint

beam of light off to her left, she assumed it was Benny shadowing her. She kept walking, but beads of sweat broke out on her forehead. She didn't like the sensation of being stalked.

Liss had never been any good at judging distance and there was no path to speak of, so when Benny finally barked out an order to stand still, she had no idea whether she was a hundred yards or a quarter of a mile from where she'd left the car.

"Hands over your head," Benny ordered. "Don't turn around."

Liss complied and braced herself in case she was about to be bashed over the head. Instead, Benny came up behind her and relieved her of her cell phone. Uncertain whether the other woman was armed, Liss didn't move a muscle. From the sound of it, Benny was disabling Liss's only link to the outside world.

"Are you wired?" she asked.

"You've been watching too many cop shows." Sophisticated listening devices were another thing the Moosetookalook Police Department couldn't afford.

She jumped when Benny touched her again, this time to take away her flashlight. Liss didn't risk looking behind her, but if the twin beams were anything to go by, Benny had placed it on the ground next to her own light. Next she patted Liss down using both hands. Did that mean she didn't have a weapon? Should she try to overpower her? The memory of Benny lifting that heavy well cover without breaking a sweat dissuaded her. Hand-to-hand combat was a very bad idea.

"So, what's the plan?" she asked, pleased to hear that her voice didn't betray how nervous she was. "Do you intend to return the box?"

Benny laughed. "Sure, but it won't have anything in it. Now, moving very slowly, place the tote on the ground."

Liss did as she was told.

"Put your hands behind you."

"So," Liss said as she felt a cord wrap around her wrists. "You're going to keep both the formula and the money and leave me behind, tied up." That was pretty much what she'd expected, but she still felt uneasy. "You realize I might not be found for days. I could die of exposure."

"Not likely."

Liss wasn't so sure about that. The temperatures had been in the eighties all week. Thirst and heat prostration would be serious problems if she was left exposed to the elements for too long. She refused to think about the possibility of wild animals finding her while she was helpless to defend herself. Bears weren't unheard of in the area.

"You could tie me loosely. You'd still be long gone before I worked myself free."

A derisive snort answered this ploy, along with a shove that had Liss sitting down, rather abruptly, on a large fallen log. When Benny knelt in front of her to bind her ankles, Liss thought about kicking her in the head, but before she could put that plan into action, she was distracted by the unexpected discovery that she *did* have wiggle room in the cord around her wrists.

Whatever Benny's other talents, she wasn't any good at tying knots. Liss felt the cord loosen enough that she could slip first one hand and then the other free. Elated, she struggled to keep her expression neutral and her hands out of sight while she considered what to do.

Finishing her task, Benny rose and picked up both flashlights and the tote.

Liss sat very still. If the cord around her ankles was as poorly secured as her hands had been, it would fall right off the moment she stood up. Why on earth hadn't Benny used duct tape? Not that she was complaining. She'd bide her time, then escape. There was no sense in giving Benny a chance to do something more permanent.

But she *was* curious. As Benny started to turn away, Liss blurted, "Will you answer a couple of questions before you go?"

"Why should I?"

"If I'm going to have to spend several uncomfortable hours, if not days, alone in the woods, the least you can do is leave me with something to think about. Don't you want to impress me with how clever you are?"

In fiction, Liss had heard this last-minute confession called "the ritual spilling of the beans." There were times when this made for pretty unbelievable reading, especially when the villain stopped on the brink of killing the hero to tie up all the loose ends in the story. She wasn't really expecting Benny to oblige her. It was hardly in the other woman's best interests to linger.

Benny, however, was confident that she'd outsmarted the opposition and just conceited enough to think that she had plenty of time to make her getaway. She turned back on the brink of leaving to ask a question of her own: "How much do you know?"

"Sherri found out that you worked for Cornwell Pharmaceuticals at the same time Lester Widdowson did, and Dolores Mayfield, the librarian, knew that Lester had a woman with him when he visited Moosetookalook."

"Not bad."

"I think you knew about the stolen formulas back then, and that you had a pretty good idea of how much one of them might be worth to a rival company."

"Of course I did. Why do you think I befriended the old geezer? He was stupid about it, though. The company found out what he'd done and came after him."

"So you split. Smart."

She shrugged. "Even smarter, I kept track of him. I knew about it when he died. When I saw the notice for the auction, I figured it would be worth my while to pay another visit to this backwater."

"You suspected Widdowson was paranoid enough to have hidden at least one of the formulas somewhere in the house?"

"I thought there was a good chance of it." She leaned toward Liss, her corkscrew curls grotesque in the eerie light provided by the flashlights. "But here's something you can't know, Miss Amateur Detective. I broke into the Chadwick house before the auction and checked all the hiding places I discovered when Widdowson bought the place."

"You didn't know about the one in the brick wall. And there was nothing in the hidey-holes in the house, was there? Too bad you didn't think to check inside that trunk while you were at it. You could have saved yourself a lot of trouble."

Benny's scowl looked positively demonic. Liss bit back the next smart remark hovering on the tip of her tongue. Taunting the other woman was not the smartest thing to do under the circumstances.

"I lied to you." Benny made it sound like she was boasting.

"Big surprise. About what?"

"I was still around after that trunk was loaded into my van. I saw you drop the portrait and find a paper. I thought it might be the formula. That's one of the reasons I stuck around."

Now that Benny had gotten started, she didn't seem to

be able to shut up. Liss was glad to let her talk. The hard part was keeping her own mouth shut. She had so many questions she wanted to ask.

"I really am doing research, you know. I like those teaching gigs, and I figure a legitimate publication will get me more of them."

The woman was a bundle of contradictions, Liss thought. No wonder it had taken so long to figure out that she was up to no good.

"Remember that day we ran into each other in the bookstore? You told your friend the whole story of finding the map while I was right there listening." Benny laughed again. "You were the one who thought it would lead to Chadwick treasure, not me. I'm not that stupid!"

Liss kept her opinion about that to herself, knowing that if Benny had identified herself as a Chadwick descendant right after the auction, she'd have been happy to show her the map. Heck, she'd probably have given it to her.

"You really should be more circumspect," Benny said. "The woman at the coffee shop knew all about your plans to visit Nova Scotia, including the stops you intended to make. I didn't have to follow you. I went ahead."

Liss's heart sank. Benny's words seemed to confirm her worst suspicion, that it was her fault that Orson Bailey had been murdered. If Benny hadn't been after the map, he might still be alive. Of its own volition, the damning accusation slipped out. "You murdered an innocent man."

"Not so innocent! And it wasn't murder."

"He ended up dead." Liss started to stand, only remembering at the last moment that it would not be a good idea to let Benny know how easily she could get free.

"That wasn't my plan." Now she sounded like a sulky little girl again. "My plan was to get to Bailey first and con him into getting a copy of the map for me. I've had plenty of experience manipulating older men, especially the ones who devote themselves to research and haven't a clue how to deal with women. Bailey was a different kettle of fish. He figured out I was up to something and he lost his temper. He had the nerve to grab hold of me and try to throw me out of his office. I don't put up with that kind of treatment. I shoved him away."

Liss felt sick to her stomach at the vivid image that sprang into her mind. Benny must have pushed him hard enough to cause him to fall backward, impaling himself on his desk spike. She had to swallow several times before she managed to speak. "If it was an accident, why did you move the body?"

"I wasn't about to stay there and be arrested." Benny spoke as if this should have been obvious to even the most dull-witted person. "I hid him to give myself more time to get away."

"You ransacked his office."

She shrugged. "Since I was there, I figured I might as well find out what he'd dug up for you and your aunt. It was my family's history, after all."

"Did you take his wallet, too?"

That produced a grin. "Money is always helpful. It wasn't cheap to stay at The Spruces. Good thing I had plenty of cash stashed away from a con I ran in Cleveland. But what I really wanted wasn't there. You still had the map."

"So you went on to another place on our itinerary—Antigonish."

"Stupid name."

Benny didn't have to admit that she'd trashed the motel room looking for the map, or that she'd taken items and broken into other rooms to make the ransacking look like a simple burglary. Lucas had been telling the truth when he'd said he came upon the scene later. When he searched someplace, like the Emporium and Liss's house, he was neat about it. Along with her other despicable qualities, Benny Beamer was a slob.

"So now what?" Liss asked.

"Now I go on my merry way. Maybe they'll find you and maybe they won't. I don't really care."

"Nice."

"You're a loser—no great loss to anyone, stuck in this hick town in the back of beyond." Benny sneered as she turned away. "I'll bet you'd never even been out of the state of Maine before that trip to Canada."

*Wrong,* Liss thought. *So wrong.* She didn't bother to argue, or to tell Benny about the years she'd spent on the road as a professional dancer.

Liss had planned to let Benny get a head start before discarding the cords and making her way back to her car. Risking her own neck was just plain foolish. But it went against the grain to give someone like Benny a chance to escape justice. Before she could think better of it, Liss slipped free of her bonds and started after the other woman at a dead run.

"Hey, Benny," she called.

The sound of her name was all the warning Benny got. The moment she swung around, Liss's kick struck her hard in the solar plexus. The former gymnast had no opportunity to use her greater upper body strength against a long, well-aimed dancer's leg. She bent double, grunting in pain, and lost her footing when Liss gave her a shove. Flipping her over, Liss knelt on the small of her back, twisted her arms behind her, and bound her wrists, using the same cords Benny had brought to the party.

Her ankles followed . . . and Liss *did* know how to tie knots.

The next day, Liss slept late. It was Sunday and the Emporium was supposed to be open, but she didn't care. Only later, when she finally rolled out of bed and was inhaling her first cup of coffee, did Dan tell her that he'd called Beth to mind the store.

"You may as well take her on as full-time help for the rest of the summer," he added. "She's worked more hours than you have this month."

It was only a slight exaggeration.

"Sherri called," he said.

"What news?"

"The RCMP will be extraditing Benny Beamer. Meanwhile she's down to Fallstown in the county jail."

"Good."

"And Aaron Lucas contacted Sherri to give her an update on the formula Benny tried to sell them." His grin warned her that things hadn't turned out quite as Cornwall Pharmaceuticals had hoped.

"Let me guess. Jardine's fancy lawyer got his paws on it before they could escape to Connecticut?"

"Nope. Better. After she took it off Benny, Sherri let Kelsey have a look at it. It wasn't what he was hoping for."

"Don't tell me it was an explosive?"

He shook his head. "Turns out it *was* the potential wonder drug Widdowson had been working on, but in the years since he walked off with it, a rival company independently developed the same drug and it turned out to have so many dangerous side effects that now nobody wants anything to do with it. The formula is worthless."

"Serves them right that they won't profit." Liss got up

to refill her mug. "After all, the company was willing to turn a blind eye when Aaron Lucas broke the law. He may not have ended up stealing anything, and Sherri can't charge him with breaking into the Emporium and our house, but he admitted that he did."

"Sounds to me as if it's a case of poetic justice as far as they're concerned. I'm just glad we've seen the last of both Lucas and Kelsey. They're on their way back to Connecticut. So," Dan added, sliding into the chair next to his wife and trailing his fingers up the length of her arm, "since you've got the rest of the day off, how should we spend it? I was thinking—"

Liss never got to hear what he had in mind for the two of them. They were interrupted by a vigorous knocking at the front door and the sound of her mother's voice.

Bracing herself, Liss went to let her parents in. She expected to find suitcases piled on the porch, but only Vi and Don MacCrimmon stood there, grinning at her like a pair of naughty children. She glanced at the car parked at the curb, but could see no sign of boxes, bags, or other luggage inside.

Liss's father engulfed his daughter in a hug while her mother gave Dan a kiss on the cheek. Then the two men shook hands and the two women embraced.

"Have you come far this morning?" was all Liss could think to ask. They both looked fresh as the proverbial daisies.

"Not at all." Vi's smile was a sunburst. "We got here yesterday afternoon and thought we'd settle in before we came to see you."

"You . . . settled in? You mean you're not staying with us?" Liss didn't know whether to panic or cheer.

"Of course not. While we look for a permanent place in the area, we're renting Patsy's neighbor's year-round camp."

"So you never even considered moving in here?" Dan sounded as if he needed to be certain he'd heard correctly.

"Good God, no!" Violet MacCrimmon laughed, eyes twinkling. "That would never work. I love my daughter, but she's simply too difficult to get along with. If we were forced to live at close quarters for more than a week, I'd probably end up strangling her."

# A Note from the Author

As usual in one of my Liss MacCrimmon Mysteries, I use a mixture of real and fictional places and events. Moosetookalook, Fallstown, and Orlin, Maine, and Chadwick, Nova Scotia, do not exist, but Antigonish and its annual Highland Games are real and so is the Gaelic College on Cape Breton. Harpswell, Maine, is also a real place, located right next to Bailey Island, where I began writing this book back in June of 2016 on a writers' retreat with three of my fellow Maine Crime Writers. I owe more than I can say to the encouragement and support of Kate Flora, Barb Ross, and Lea Wait, and this book is dedicated to them with my heartfelt thanks.